Praise for *Swords of the Six*

"This book is the best book I have ever read. I can't wait to read the next one."

—**Josh Minter** (age 13)

"I just finished reading the *Swords Of The Six* this evening. Scott Appleton has done a fantastic job with his first fantasy novel. I am looking forward to seeing the characters develop and evolve. I can't wait for *Offspring* to hit on the shelves!"

—**Janice** (Indiana)

"*Swords of the Six* is a wonderful story with swords, battles, dragons, and a little romance, making for a book that you won't want to put down. I can't wait to read the next book!"

—**Ellen Seta** (Cincinnati, OH)

"Appleton has written a brave introduction to the series and filled it with characters both imaginitive and inspiring. . . . A fun read!"

—**Robert Treskillard**, author *Merlin's Blade*

"What a wonderful story of love and forgiveness, filled with action, romance, and heartache. I can't wait to read the second one!"

—**Connie Wolters** (age 27)

"*Swords of the Six* was exciting and adventurous with never a dull moment. Right away I was pulled in and I couldn't wait to find out what would happen next."

—**Kelley Salveggio** (age 18)

"Scott writes with a passionate desire to communicate truth . . . timeless truth that many have forgotten. In his words you will find valor, self-sacrifice, and above all, love. If you want a life-changing story and heart-moving themes, open a book by Scott Appleton."

—**Bryan Davis,** author of the bestselling **Dragons in Our Midst**® series

"Scott Appleton has a big story to tell and just the kind of outside-of-the-box imagination to pull it off. Swords of the Six is a tale replete with heroism, betrayal, despair, and hope. If you like stories that take you to the edge and make you think, Scott Appleton has a tale for you."

—**Wayne Thomas Batson,** author of
The Door Within and *Sword in the Stars*

"If you are a reader who enjoys a good adventure, a bit of romance, and a wonderful cast of characters, *Swords of the Six* is the book for you to read. As you read the book, you feel like you are right there with the characters. Five Stars!"

—**M. York**

"This is a stunning story that looks into the very essence of time and humanity and the burdens of wisdom and sacrifice. A book about honor and forgiveness and time and sacrifice. Can't wait for the sequel!"

—**Paul E. May** (Massachusetts)

"I saw this on a shelf in a bookstore in Connecticut. I read a lot of fantasy and thought I'd try it out; I'm glad I did, it was an enjoyable read with some new ideas. Will be getting the rest of the series!"

—**Heather G.** (Virginia)

"What a great book! This book brings the reader in and all you can do is turn the page. Great story with out the bad language and smut. I cannot wait for Book Two, *Offspring.*"

—**Donna Cripe** (Connecticut)

"Rusted swords, a righteous dragon, a fiery blade, a fallen dragon, an orphaned boy, and six sisters bound by prophecy. This is the tale of Swords of the Six, and it is only the doorstep of an epic series."

—**Nathan Petrie** (Kentucky)

THE SWORD OF THE DRAGON SERIES · BOOK ONE

1

SWORDS OF THE SIX

LIVING
INK
BOOKS
Writing Worth Reading™

SCOTT APPLETON

Swords of the Six
Volume 1 in **The Sword of the Dragon**® series

Copyright © 2011 by Scott Appleton
Published by Living Ink Books, an imprint of
AMG Publishers, Inc.
6815 Shallowford Rd.
Chattanooga, Tennessee 37421

ISBN 13: 978-0-89957-860-6
First Printing—February 2011

THE SWORD OF THE DRAGON is a trademark of
AMG Publishers.

Cover illustration by Jennifer Miller

Cover layout and design by Daryle Beam at BrightBoy Design, Inc.,
Chattanooga, TN
Interior design and typesetting by Kristin Goble at PerfecType,
Nashville, TN
Edited by Rebecca L. Miller, Bonnie Appleton, Jennifer Salveggio,
and Rick Steele

Look for *Offspring*—the next book in **The Sword of the Dragon** series,
releasing spring 2011

Printed in Canada
16 15 14 13 12 11 –T– 7 6 5 4 3

This book is for my brother, Brian.

Without your encouragement I wouldn't have pressed forward with *The Sword of the Dragon*. You were my first reader and loyal fan.

CONTENTS

PRONUNCIATION GUIDE

Albino: al—buy—no

Al'un Dai: al—oon die

Auron: or—on

Barlin: bar—lin

Caritha: cuh—rih—thuh

Clavius: clav—ee—us

Corbaius: kor—bay—us

Dantress: dan—tress

Drusa: droo—suh

Elsie: el—see

Eva: eh—vuh

Evela: eh—veh—luh

Ganning: gan—ning

Glandstine: gland—stine

Gwen: gwen

Hasselpatch: has—ell—patch

Helen: hel—en

Hermeneudis:
   her—men—ooh—dis

Hestor: hest—ore

Honer: hone—er

Ilfedo: ill—fed—oh

Kesla: kess—luh

Laura: lore—uh

Letrias: let—ree—us

Levena: leh—vee—nuh

Melvin: mel—vin

Miverē: mih—veer—ee

Oganna: oh—gahn—nuh

Ombre: ahm—bray

Ramul: ruh—mool

Rose'el: roh—zell

Seivar: sigh—var

Specter: spec—ter

Turser: ter—ser

Valorian: vuh—lore—ee—an

Venom-fier: ven—um fee—air

Xavion: ex—zave—ee—uhn

AUTHOR'S PREFACE

Whereas I have undertaken the task of telling the whole tale of *The Sword of the Dragon*, I found it necessary to write a part of the story I had not intended to. The story of Ilfedo and the sword of Living Fire is epic, both in length and in scope, but after much consideration I determined to tell the story which led in to the main story line, first.

Thus was born *Swords of the Six*. For my intents and purposes, it is the novel that foreshadows and sets the stage for the larger story to come. A prelude novel, if you will, that opens approximately one thousand years before the main story begins.

Though not as large in scope as the novels which will follow, *Swords of the Six* holds a special place in my heart. It gave me the opportunity to tell how the six sisters first obtained their swords and the web of evil in which the world of Subterran was being bound. The Eiderveis River, with its troubled history, carried me along the sisters' path and left me to follow their footsteps through the forests to the ruins of the wizard's temple once haunted by the witch, that mistress of darkness.

Take nothing for granted, in the tale before you. There are foreshadowings of things to come. Things evil and things good. Victory is not obtained without sacrificed. Neither is heroism a word with which every warrior may be labeled. And sometimes the price of doing the right thing is higher than we are prepared to pay. It may cost a hero or heroine their blood. Or, it may cost them their very *life*.

Let the adventure begin,
—Scott Appleton

PRELUDE:
BLOOD OF THE
RIGHTEOUS

H is black scales shimmering with the blood of a thousand warriors, the dragon Valorian spread his wings and drew back his long neck. Smoke rose from his nostrils, veiling the glint of sunlight in his dark eyes, and a swath of flames issued from his maw. Mauled men lay wounded and dying all around him.

Line upon line of grim-faced men knelt behind their shields, facing the creature, whispering silent prayers as the dragon's attack melted the shields of those closest to him and roasted them inside of their armor. The screams of the dying birthed anger in those closest to the victims. With fierce determination the lines of men rose with cries of revenge and charged the dragon.

But he looked upon them with disdain and stabbed his serpentine head into the ground, burrowing into the soil. Within moments his sleek body and ashen tail followed his head, disappearing into the inordinately small hole.

The warriors froze in their tracks. Beyond their ranks they could hear the march of thousands more of their allies. They heard shouts of victory and could only hope it did not originate with the enemy.

The ground collapsed under a dozen of the warriors. Valorian rose through the soil, his mighty claws raked the warriors near at hand, spilling their blood into the pools forming around their companions. The warriors raised their swords and some sought to impale the monster on spikes, but Valorian growled with delight and burrowed into the ground.

The warriors fell back, fearful of his next assault. But they did not retreat far enough. The black dragon burst into their midst and slew a hundred more by the might of his claws.

Stumbling over one another, the warriors sought to escape. Valorian burrowed into the ground yet again and a rout ensued. Men panicked, dropped their weapons and fled.

"Weak and futile!" The dragon growled as a small line of braver souls formed in his path. "Are all of Albino's warriors as children in comparison to me? Are they mere fodder?" He swung around and the scales along his tail rose like barbs. "Treat me not as any other foe," the dragon uttered darkly. His tail whipped into the warriors' midst and the scales along it cut through their armor, snagging like hooks in their flesh.

Valorian drew out his tail, half-a-dozen warriors impaled upon it. He smashed their bodies against the ground.

"Weak fools! Ye are blind; powerless!" The dragon spat thick black ooze from his maw. He reached out with his claws, grabbed one of the dead men caught on his tail, and tore off the stained armor. "Weak," the creature repeated. As the weary warriors watched, Valorian swallowed his victim whole.

Leaving their courage in the dust, the men ran hastily after their fellows. And the dragon rent the air with a roar of victory.

But those who fled came to a sudden halt and parted like the sea as another warrior rose in their path and commanded them to rally. He briskly strode forward and the trembling warriors obediently turned to face the dragon again. Advancing alone against the dragon, the wind whipping his white cape around his ankles, the captain silently raised his arm and closed his fist.

Fresh troops slipped through the ranks of the weary and wounded, buffering them from the struggle to come. A unified force. They aligned behind their captain. Spearmen stood steady, the shafts of their lances a line two hundred strong. From behind them marched the shield bearers and a mixture of archers and swordsmen, taking up defensive posture between them and the monster. The sunlight glinted on their gold helms and the silver emblem of a dragon engraved upon each.

They waited in silence as a second warrior, a prince, emerged from their ranks and drew a scimitar from his scabbard.

❧ ❧ ❧

Brian's boots ground into the compacted dirt as he made his way through the ranks to join his mentor and captain. Stepping between two spearmen he glanced down that line of tall men bedecked in their mail coats, their fists gripping the wooden shafts of their spears. The spearheads glinted in the afternoon sunlight, pointed at the heavens.

He hurried forward. The shield bearers and the archers side-stepped before him, clearing a path through their midst. And he walked fifty paces.

But the white-caped figure that stood between him and the dragon raised a commanding hand. The warrior captain looked over his shoulder at Brian. "Come no closer." And his blue eyes held Brian's gaze.

"With respect, Xavion," the prince objected, drawing his cream-bladed scimitar from its scabbard and frowning.

Xavion slowly shook his head down at him. "Leave this creature to me."

Hiding his trepidation with two backward steps the prince adjusted the gold helm on his head, made a slight bow, and smote the flat of his blade against his breastplate. Behind him the distant shouts of allies and enemies and the ringing of metal blades against shields marked the battle's continuation. He could only hope the enemy would not gain the upper hand.

The young prince watched his captain.

Xavion stood out in stark contrast to the creature he faced. His white cape and graying beard gave him the appearance of a righteous prophet framed by the dragon's pitch black form. And from his side the aged captain drew his sword. The sunlight played through its blade as if it were cut from diamond, casting rainbows of color on the dark ground.

Valorian roared delight and stabbed his head into the ground, slithering out of sight only to emerge moments later. The ground beneath Xavion rose and the dirt fell away to reveal the dragon's serpentine head. The captain fell aside but grabbed hold of the dragon's scales and stabbed his blade through one of the leathery wings.

"And now this duel bores me," the dragon hissed. It turned as if to flee and Xavion leapt after it. The scales along Valorian's tail rose and he coiled it around the man's torso, pinning his arms to his sides with painful ease. "And so I end this, Xavion! Thou should've stayed in the bounds of Emperia; for all that is here will be mine until Yimshi's light fails in the heavens."

A scream of agony from the captain rolled over the ground, reached Brian's ears and those of the warriors standing near at hand. He raised his scimitar. Anger burned in his heart as he saw blood flow unhindered down the captain's breastplate. "*Charge!*"

The prince ran. With all his strength he sped toward the dragon, closing the distance and hearing the sound of several hundred men charging behind and around him. Their cries thundered around him as they threw their spears at the dragon and shot their arrows.

Dropping Xavion, Valorian opened his mouth and crouched low to the ground with wings flexing. His dark eyes scorned the rescuers and fire roiled from his mouth, engulfing the assailants nearest the prince.

Brian did not wait for the dragon to attack again. He ran to where Xavion had fallen and, with one hand still clenching his weapon and the other arm hooked around the larger man's chest, dragged him from the fray.

The dragon slaughtered the warriors. Brian gritted his teeth as the screams of the wounded and dying mixed with those of their brave comrades covering their wounded captain's escape. Xavion shook his head as if awaking from sleep and immediately stabbed his sword into the ground, bringing Brian to a jarring halt. The prince felt as if he were a ship on high seas and some-one had just dropped an anchor overboard.

Letting the man slip from his grasp, he swallowed hard.

"Brian." The captain did not need to say more. His eyes burned into Brian's, unwavering in their rebuke. With one hand the captain unclasped his punctured breastplate and let it clatter to the ground. There it rested with the gold emblem of a dragon shining from its snow-white face and his blood caking to its surface.

One sweeping glance at the captain's bloody chest told Brian all he needed to know. "But Master . . . you cannot go on like this. The fight is over."

Xavion grunted. The muscles along his sword arm rippled and hardened. Holding on to the sword's handle he stumbled to his feet, staunching the flow of blood from a rip in his chest with his free hand. The crimson fluid pulsed from his chest, leaking between his fingers.

All around them the warriors, on whom this battle depended, fled to the rear. Valorian launched himself into the fleeing men, landing with enough force to knock those nearest him to their knees. Without hesitation he lashed out with tooth and claw, then followed through with swaths of flame.

"My Master," Brian said as he saw tears flow down Xavion's cheeks. They were standing only a hundred feet from the slaughter. Any delay and they too could end up as these other warriors. "Master, the battle is lost! You *must* order the men to withdraw."

But the captain swung around and landed a punch to Brian's jaw. The prince fell back, stunned. He could feel tears burning in his own eyes as he returned his mentor's gaze.

"Do not ever dare to speak to me of such a thing again." Xavion rose to his full height and flipped his sword with practiced ease. He pointed its blade at the dragon. "Stay behind if you must. But if you do then you are not the warrior I have trained you to be.

"Flee now and live. Or, stay . . . and fight while the enemy is near."

The captain ran now, ran toward the dragon with death in his eye. And the prince's heart beat stronger and his hand held his blade with greater certainty as he too ran in opposition to the retreating forces. He saw Xavion's white cape fly over the dying and the dead, saw the warrior's crystal blade sparkle once again in the sunlight.

With a glance the dragon recognized Xavion. Its wicked eyes opened wide and it turned to meet the captain's assault. But

Xavion had slipped between the dragon's forelegs and pulled back his sword. And he thrust it upward at an angle so that it slipped between the dragon's scales and sank up to its hilt.

Opening its mouth with a roar of pain the dragon thrashed on the ground. Brian stopped his charge and the dragon threw Xavion into the air. Spreading his arms and clenching his fists, he caught his captain, or, rather, the man's body crashed into his and they fell. The impact forced the air out of his lungs and the captain's body weighed on his chest.

Xavion growled and rolled off of him, stood up. Somehow he had managed to keep his sword. He wrung its handle and leaned down to grasp the prince's shoulder. His eyes conveyed his gratitude and he again faced in the dragon's direction. "Valorian," he yelled as a handful of warriors banded to his side. "*I* still live."

"Ye are fools! Filthy fools!" Valorian raked the ground with his claws and stepped on a wounded man, silencing his cries. "Now," the dragon said, "darkness will fall."

Thunder rumbled in the distance and storm clouds rolled over the rocky landscape that rose and fell in a series of jagged hills to the south. The clouds hid the blue sky and encroached upon the sun before conquering it. What had been a field lit by daylight now faded into all-encompassing darkness.

Silence spread like a plague over the field of battle. Then a point of light appeared before the survivors, pulsing and swelling into a bubble of phosphorescent green light that dimly illuminated the face of its orchestrator. The black dragon rested the bubble in his palm and imprisoned it in his clawed fingers. In its steadying glow his eyes and scales shone with foreboding malevolence.

"Meet the fury of my revenge with courage if thou art able, Xavion." The dragon tasted the air with his forked tongue. "Meet thy doom at my hand if thou canst bear it. For this day ye shall fall."

Xavion did not respond with words but his hand found Brian's shoulder in the darkness. "Spread the word," he whispered between labored breaths. "Tell the men to fall back to northward hills and seek shelter in the caves."

"Fall back? But you have wounded him—"

"Do as I say!"

A bolt of green lightning zipped to the ground and Brian expected some of his allies to cry out, for it struck the very place where their reinforcements stood waiting. But a chill ran up his spine as the momentary brightness revealed not ranks of the living but ranks of the dead. The spearmen and the archers, along with the swordsmen sprawled on the ground, chilled in pools of their own blood.

No sign of the assailants could be seen. Then the prince thought his eyes deceived him. For the Grim Reaper congealed out of thin air and stood over the fallen. A scythe blade hovered in the air above the being's head and he leaned over a fallen warrior. The prince felt his heart stop beating for an instant. He had heard stories of such a being, a being of evil walking the world of Subterran and harvesting the dead in order to feed upon death. But it could not be true. It must not be believed. Evil could not gain such strength. Could it?

As he watched, darkness swallowed the specter of death, wrapping him in its impenetrable cloak. He could see nothing until another bolt struck.

This time he glimpsed a few bodies falling from the sky and heard a screech . . . half a human scream and half a bird's cry. Far above his head a thousand wings snapped against the air.

In that moment he saw Xavion's livid countenance. But greater than the look of fury on the man's face was the look of horror in his eyes.

Gone, dead, in the blink of an eye every man standing on that field had fallen.

As grief swept over him and his captain, three bolts of green energy fell from the sky, crisscrossing and weaving together on their journey to the earth. Valorian roared and flew into the air, holding the bubble of light before him. The lightning struck the bubble, fed it, grew it until the dragon let it plummet toward the ground. Brian heard the creature roar again and he saw a host of winged men flock to it.

"Art'en!" Now the manner of his fellow warriors' deaths became apparent to him. The Art'en creatures now circled Valorian, screeching horrifically as more of their species congregated around him. There had to be a thousand of them. Maybe more. In the darkness it was impossible to tell.

The phosphorescent energy bubble plummeted toward the stony ground, radiating green on the ground and even reflecting off the cloud cover. It had swelled until it was large enough to house several men. Brian froze. What should he do? There was nowhere he could hide. Not in time at least.

Just as the bubble struck the ground and exploded with stone-crushing force, Xavion leapt in the explosion's path and wrapped his body around the prince's. "Xavion! No!"

But Brian could not shift the powerful warrior from the path of destruction. Xavion's arms held him with fierce resolve. "I will not lose you, too," he heard the old man say.

Helpless to free himself the prince allowed himself to cry. Trembling, he felt the comfort of Xavion's arms draw him as a son into his father's bosom. A wave of heat screamed past him and his mentor. It built in its intensity. Stones exploded by and bodies lit up like matches all around him.

Xavion's arms squeezed him without mercy until he ventured

a look up at his martyr's face. Blood ran from the captain's lower lip as his teeth bit into it. Sweat beaded on his face and his skin turned beet red and his eyes squinted shut.

The inferno raged around them and, when Xavion's pain reached its human limit, he opened his mouth in a scream more terrible than anything the prince had ever heard. The heat singed the graying hairs on his head and face. His skin blistered. Then, as a final tornado of heat whirled around them, the captain's strength failed. He collapsed in a faint over Brian's shoulder and the storm ceased.

Winged men rained from the sky a couple hundred feet away, their eagle-brown feathers shivering. They landed crouching and then stood and ran barefooted toward Brian. The majority of the Art'en force landed a good distance away. Only a handful ended up close to the fallen captain and the weakened prince.

Desperate and determined to escape the brutal death awaiting him and the captain, Brian grunted, half-dragging half-carrying the unconscious man. The stony ground impeded his progress and his armor weighed him down.

He glanced over his shoulder to see two of the humanoid creatures closing the distance to him. The ground sloped upward ahead of him and he let Xavion's limp form roll off his back in order to catch his breath. A small stone mountain rose out of the slope a hundred yards ahead of him. And in its face the Creator had carved a perfectly spherical orifice not more than a few feet broad. It promised shelter.

Spinning on his heel, Brian frowned. Keeping his eyes trained on the two winged figures bounding toward him, he loosed his breastplate. Casting the breastplate aside he took off his helmet and removed his chain mail shirt. He stretched his aching arms and exulted in his newfound freedom of movement.

Carefully he picked up his helm and fitted it again over his head. A little protection was better than nothing.

A gust of wind slapped his blond hair across his face. He tucked it under his helm. Sheathing his white-bladed scimitar, he unraveled a whip from his belt and wound it loosely around his wrist. Then he stood with legs spread wide and loosened the black, coiled leather, dropping its length on the ground.

The nearest Art'en bounded nearer, dark wings folded on its back and sinewy arms flexing. Brian let it come no closer. With a flip of his arm and a flick of his wrist he sent the leather snaking through the air. It lashed the humanoid creature around its waist and in that moment the whip, through the power with which it had been crafted, rendered the Art'en weightless.

The creature's gray skin paled a sickly green and it screeched like a wounded bird. Brian pulled back his arm, drawing the whip taut around his prisoner, then he spun on his heel and threw the weightless Art'en up the rocky slope. The whip released the creature in midair.

The Art'en flailed, its wings unfolded in an attempt to stop its course toward a sharp boulder. But too little distance remained. It hit the boulder chest-first and crumpled to the ground.

Turning, the prince faced the other creature. It had landed and now bounced toward him, screeching so shrilly that Brian almost dropped his weapons to cover his ears. The creature folded its wings around its body, its human arms slipped between the feathers clawing the air in his direction.

Brian recognized this Art'en strategy. He had seen these beings face armored men, carrying no weapons themselves, and prevail. They would leave their upper bodies vulnerable to attack, luring their opponents into striking. But when their enemy swung their weapon the Art'en would drop to the ground, balancing on their hands, and kick both feet into their enemy's chest.

A strategy such as that, the prince determined, would not work on him. He feinted with his sword as if to cut across the Art'en's chest. The creature's mouth stretched into a maniacal grin and it dropped beneath the oncoming blade's path. But the prince had preceded the creature and he now held the pommel of his sword on the ground . . . blade pointed at the creature's chest.

A startled cry escaped the being's lips as it threw its abdomen onto the blade. The cream-colored metal entered its body and the prince stood up muttering, "Why? Why all this death? Why?" As he watched the winged man twist in death's throes he gritted his teeth. The world should not be this way. Peace should reign; not suffering.

He felt a little sick to his stomach. Should he end this being's suffering or leave it to die? But no, he would not murder. He'd acted in self defense but he would not slaughter even one enemy.

The Art'en cried for mercy, holding its wound with weak desperation.

Brian growled and picked up his captain. Anger gave him the extra strength he needed to carry the larger man up the incline and he laid him deep in the cave where not even Valorian could reach.

From outside the cave came the pained cries of the wounded Art'en. Brian left his captain and stood in the cave's narrow entrance. The clouds thinned overhead, allowing an ethereal glow to cover the landscape. He watched as the remaining Art'en swarmed toward the hill then stopped to screech at him. Their numbers dotted the battlefield for as far as he could see. Their numbers had grown.

The Art'en stopped when they reached their comrade. Brian expected them to stoop down and carry the wounded creature away. Instead the lead creatures jabbed their bare feet into the birdman's side, cackling when he screeched with renewed pain. Spreading their wings the Art'en sprang into the air, carrying themselves laboriously toward the darker southern horizon.

Valorian was nowhere to be seen.

Cautiously, the prince stepped out of the cave and glanced up the bare mountainside. The dragon was not there.

He leaned his scimitar against the cave entrance and set his whip next to it. Then, praying to God he would not regret what he was about to do, he skidded downhill and knocked the wounded Art'en unconscious with his fist and rolled it onto his shoulders. The creature proved awkward to carry. Its wings dragged on the ground and its sinewy form threatened to slip off his shoulders every step he took. But he at last reached the cave entrance and dropped the wounded individual as gently as possible.

Something thudded onto the slope and Brian turned to face a blast of air. The dragon Valorian loomed there, dark eyes furious. He roared deep and long, mouth agape, until sparks flared in its slippery throat. "Puny and weak human . . . tell me what you have done with thy commander's body and I will spare thee a test of fire!"

Brian's heart beat furiously in his chest. He froze, unable to answer and not knowing what to do.

"Tell me!" Valorian balled his claws into a fist and pounded the hillside, crushing the stones into pebbles.

Scooping his weapons with one hand and grasping the wounded creature's shirt with the other, the prince dragged both deeper into the cave and around a bend. He leaned the Art'en against the cave wall a short distance from the wounded captain. They would be safe here for the time being.

Dull thuds echoed into the cavities and tunnels branching from the cave as Valorian drove his wrath into the mountainside.

But the stone rose solid around Brian, concealing him and Xavion.

Time passed and the cave grew quiet. Brian removed his armor and tore his shirt into bandages. Xavion's noble face now bore burns of such severity that his flesh reeked.

Tearfully, the prince stumbled in the dimness until he heard a faint trickling of water. He found an underground stream and soaked his torn shirt in it. Then, returning to his captain, he gently cooled the man's face. Skin peeled away from the man's flesh.

No. No. Oh Xavion, I am so sorry. Brian sobbed. His hands trembled as he withdrew the cloth from Xavion's face and looked upon that of the warrior. The face that he knew and loved had been exchanged for a face of horror, of seared flesh.

And the prince wept.

That night strong winds whistled through the prince's hiding place. Xavion awoke. His blood-shot eyes slowly took in their surroundings and his gaze hesitated on the wounded Art'en. He grasped the prince's shoulder with his mutilated hand and wearily nodded.

"It's good to see you," Brian choked out, resting his hand on the man's shoulder.

"You . . . have you . . ." Xavion spat blood and coughed. "Have you cared for the creature?"

"Yes, Master." Brian followed the man's gaze back to the Art'en. Its chest rose and fell with difficulty. "I could have killed him. But—"

"But then you," the captain coughed, "would be no better than he . . . And—"

Brian allowed himself to smile and he answered the question as his mentor had before instructed him to: "And why would God grant mercy to me, who was His enemy, if *I* do not demonstrate forgiveness to my enemies."

They sat there for a while, neither speaking. Xavion spat more blood and groaned as he rested his head against the cave wall.

"Try to stay still." Brian put a freshly wetted cloth on the man's forehead and another on his raw neck. "You must sleep.

"Reinforcements will come. The white dragon will see to it . . . And Kesla and the rest of the Six are due to arrive any day. Even Valorian would think twice before coming at us again when we are in their company."

Xavion's eyelids shut, squeezing drops of blood between them. Brian dabbed them with a cloth to keep the blood from caking the man's eyes closed. Then he grabbed his weapons, tiptoed through the cave and stood guard in the shadow of its entrance. A crescent moon painted the battlefield misty blue.

For several hours he stood and then his weary body convinced him to lean against the cave wall. A couple hours later he slid into a sitting position and closed his eyes. He only needed a minute . . . maybe not even that long . . . oh how he longed to sleep. The silent moon drew longer shadows outside and a weak wind breathed across the landscape, nudging the stench of death ahead of it.

❦ ❦ ❦

The prince fell asleep and dreamed of Prunesia, the land of his birth. He saw his father sitting upon the pale-yellow throne in Millencourt Hall. The doors at the far side of the long hall lumbered open and blinding white light shot through. The king's courtiers gasped and backed to the walls, bowing their heads.

His father stood and the hunch in his back became painfully apparent as he limped forward.

"Mighty prophet," the king bowed his head. "Welcome to my humble hall."

The king and all in attendance waited.

At last a dragon's roar pierced the quiet. It shook the hall to its foundations, bringing everyone except the king to their knees. The creature roared again and Brian felt the pain wrenching at its noble heart. The dragon emerged then, its pure white scales pulsated with light as it angled its bony head downward. Its pink eyes focused on the king.

"My dear friend and ally." The dragon growled as tears flooded down its face. It opened its maw as if to continue, then ground it shut. Its wings unfolded from its sides, unveiling the body of a youth wrapped in them. The dragon set the body on the stone floor in front of the king and withdrew its wings.

The king's knees shook as he looked at the body. He sank to the floor, burying his face in the corpse's chest. His hunched shoulders shook and his crippled form wept. Then the king turned his face upward as if seeing through the rafters to the heavens . . . and he screamed with rage.

And the dragon looked on and his tears flowed like a flood around the king. Brian's heart broke at the sight and he tried to approach his father to comfort him, but when he looked at the body his father held he fell back. For the body was his own.

The crippled king screamed again with strength born of pain beyond reckoning. And the dragon, that noble white creature, roared with such terrible power that the walls cracked and began to crumble, falling toward the king's courtiers.

❈   ❈   ❈

The prince fought with his nightmare and at last awoke. The light of the moon had waned; perhaps due to moisture accumulation in the atmosphere. Mist roiled over the ground, veiling it.

Whatever the cause he thought he detected movement on the slope. Could it be a trick? Valorian was cunning. Maybe the black dragon intended to slip his agents into Brian's cave by hiding them in the mist.

Not on my watch. The prince closed his fingers around the handle of his sword.

A human figure rose out of the mist not ten feet away. "Brian, is that you?"

"Kesla?" Relief washed over Brian like a warm blanket. The man was like a second father to him. Four other warriors stood in the mist behind the first. "Thank God you have come!" The prince relaxed his hand, let go of his scimitar and stood.

He beckoned them into the cave and led the way to Xavion. "The captain is . . ." He stopped outside the cavern sheltering the wounded warrior. "Well," he said, "you will have to see for yourself."

One of the other men strode faster and looked down at the prince. "*He* is wounded? Where is he? Let me see him *now!*"

Kesla's arm smote the man solidly in the chest. "Speak out of turn again, Letrias, and I will make certain you regret this trip."

Letrias laughed and looked up at Kesla. "Watch your tongue, warrior. The future belongs to me."

"Kesla?" Xavion's weak voice sounded from the dark chamber.

"Yes, my captain. It is me." Kesla drew his sword from its sheath. Its blade glowed, illuminating the cave and the bloodied body of the revered warrior as he lay on the stone floor. To his right the Art'en's eyes glowed like a cat's.

"What is that doing here?" Letrias demanded. He too drew his glowing blade from its sheath and behind him three other blades split the darkness.

Auron, Hestor, and Clavius formed a half-circle behind Kesla, Brian, and Letrias. Brian smiled down at his captain. "They have come, my master."

Xavion's mutilated face slowly wandered over each of his men. Then his eyes closed as if lacking the strength.

The men let out long breaths as Kesla knelt next to Xavion. Then Clavius and Hestor joined arms with Letrias and Auron, forming a human litter. Brian and Kesla hefted the captain into their arms and watched them walk out of the cave.

Brian tried to tell Kesla how relieved he was to see him, but the man averted his eyes. "Kesla, what is wrong?"

"Darkness has fallen, young prince," the warrior said. "And I do not expect to see the return of light." He lifted the Art'en with ease and left the cave. The prince followed.

Dawn's first rays of light glowed in the east, but clouds hung in the sky.

The warriors dropped Xavion on the stony ground. His eyes popped open and he screamed with pain. Brian drew his sword and ran to assist his captain. But Letrias stood in his path and laughed, pointed his blade at the prince's chest. "Do it, Kesla."

Brian heard the Art'en shriek and glanced over his shoulder just as Kesla pulled his blade out of the creature's heart. Kesla gazed back at Brian, his eyes downcast.

"What have you done?" The prince took a step away from Letrias. Auron, Hestor, and Clavius encircled him. Kesla cut off his escape. They drew their crystalline swords.

But a figure rose behind Auron and Letrias. "Traitors!" Xavion's bleeding fists smote the men in their backs, sending them to the ground. The captain stumbled but drew his sword and stabbed Clavius in the leg. His disfigured face could not cry, even as he grabbed Brian with one arm and shielded him with his body.

The warriors attacked and Brian begged Xavion to release him. "You can't face them alone! Not like this! Please, Master, let us fight together!"

Xavion looked down at him, held his gaze. Brian knew that the captain could read rage in his eyes.

As Xavion released him, Brian swung around, letting loose his whip and cracking it in Hestor's face. The warrior's face cracked open and he covered it with both hands, dropping his sword.

Xavion bellowed at Letrias as the man thrust his sword at Brian. He battered back the handsome, thinner man with his sword and punched him in the chest, sending him panting to the ground.

Clavius and Auron converged on Brian. Expertly they thrust and parried, staying ahead of his sword maneuvers. He dropped his whip. It would do him no good in close combat. His already tired body refused to move quickly and his white blade faltered against the crystalline ones wielded by the two warriors.

"This is madness! Why? Why are you doing this?" He saw Xavion stumble under Letrias's fresh attack. "Why?" the old warrior repeated. And blood ran from his eyes instead of tears. "Why?"

"Oh, please." Letrias spat on the ground, stood back to catch his breath, and brushed the dirt from his garb. "Isn't it obvious old man? The time of the white dragon is drawing to a close. A new era is coming and *we* want to be part of it." He smiled sardonically and gestured to Kesla. "And now watch your prize pupil show you what he is learning.

"Kill him, Kesla!" Letrias laughed. "Do this deed or the agreement my master offered you is nullified. Kill the captain!"

Brian dropped to the ground as Clavius and Auron struck at him with their swords. He rolled to the side, picking his whip off the ground and then standing. Without hesitation he loosened it and snaked it around Letrias's legs. The man fell, weightless. Brian pivoted on his foot, snapped the whip. Letrias flew through the air like a rag doll and struck a boulder before sliding down its face, landing on the hard ground with a dazed expression on his face.

He turned, looking for Xavion.

Tears ran down Kesla's face. He had engaged in a duel with Xavion. Their movements were blinding fast and their blades rang against each other again and again. The sun rose in the east. Its first rays glinted off a brass ring on Kesla's finger.

Auron and Clavius rushed into the fray and Hestor, snarling through his bleeding face, struck Xavion from behind. Even as the aged man fought for his own life he pleaded with them to spare the prince's.

"Cowards! What have you become? Why are you doing this?" Soon sobs rocked his shoulders.

Dropping his whip, Brian rushed to Xavion's aid. He slashed his white blade everywhere the traitors' crystal ones appeared. He gazed into the faces of the men, their blades poising to kill. Dark-featured Auron had once fought with him in battle against the wizards. Hestor and Clavius? They'd been brothers and uncles who'd taught and defended him. Now they wanted to kill him and Xavion.

Why? Why? Why? He felt the tears fill his eyes and heard himself repeating the question aloud over and over again. "Why? Why? *Why?*"

"Stop it," Kesla sobbed. "Stop it! I can't stand this anymore!" He swung his blade, Brian parried and his eyes locked for a moment with the traitor's. In that instant Brian saw regret, anger, and confusion in the man's eyes. "I'm sorry," Kesla choked out.

Somehow Brian believed him. Perhaps it was because he needed to, and because he wanted to. During that moment he found the courage to forgive Kesla for the ghastly crime he was committing, even as he fell under the weight of Kesla's swing . . . and felt his back split open, his insides twisted, another crystal sword of the Six impaling him.

He saw Letrias stumble up to Xavion from behind and grasp his charred shoulder. "You've failed, old man!" Letrias drew back his sword arm and thrust his captain through his back. The sword's point protruded through Xavion's chest.

Xavion fell to his knees, sliding off the blade. His blood, on Letrias's sword, spread from the point all the way up to its handle, then drained off, leaving rust in its wake. Hestor and Clavius gasped and dropped their weapons. The swords sank into the crimson pool forming around Xavion. The blood covered their weapons as it had Letrias's, leaving them covered in rust.

Choking on his own blood, Brian fought for air. He could hear Auron laughing, as if this were all a joke, but the sensation of the blade sliding painfully out of his back proved that it was not.

The white-bladed scimitar slipped from Brian's fingers and he fell forward in a kneeling position. He knew now . . . he knew that death was coming, but he smiled to himself in spite of it. What was death but a threshold; the threshold to eternity with his Creator.

"My poor boy, please . . . please forgive me." He heard Kesla's voice plead into his fogging mind. He tried to reply that yes, he was forgiven—but he could not. Blood had flooded his lungs and clogged his throat.

A roar filled his ears. With his last strength he pulled his sword toward himself and broke it, broadside, across his knee. The enemy would never use it.

The ground shook violently and, as his vision darkened, he saw a flash of white dragon scales dispelling the darkness and knew that salvation had come . . . too late.

PART I

SEEDS OF SALVATION

1

SHIZAR PALACE

Albino the dragon took another powerful stride and the marble floor trembled beneath him. Nearly one thousand years had passed since the fall of his famed and beloved Six; the warriors in whom he had placed utmost confidence. But only one had stayed true. He felt a growl build in this throat. "It may have been better if I had killed Letrias, too." He dipped his head beneath one of the white arches supporting the vaulted ceiling and his horns merely grazed it.

The white-bearded man alongside the dragon shook his head. "That would have solved nothing. The roots of wizardry had already spread too far." He tapped his hooked shepherd's staff on the shiny floor and straightened his hooded, white robe. "If Letrias had fallen, another man would have risen to take his place, leaving Subterran no better off than it is now."

The dragon turned and his claws sparked against the palace floor. "You are right, Patient. But ever since that fateful day when the Six fell . . ." He sighed. "I wonder how things would have turned out if I had done things differently."

"Albino, my friend." The shepherd's ocean blue eyes looked up at him with naked honesty. "The past is passed. Let it remain so."

"Yes . . . the past is behind us." Albino's claws scraped the marble. He flared his nostrils. "But the future has not been written. Letrias will pay for his treachery . . . in time."

Gesturing with one clawed hand at an opening in the wall, Albino waited for Patient to precede him through the large doorway. The shepherd's sandals whispered over the floor, his white robe draped comfortably around his shoulders as he took long strides into the spacious room.

The man turned his head ever so slightly to gaze around the room. Patient bore himself with the sureness of a king.

The dragon flexed his white wings. His palace was in no way small to other beings, but for his nearly seventy-foot-length it sometimes felt cramped. He pulled himself through the doorway. He stood to the side of the oval room, curling his bone-hard tail around his legs, leaving the rest of the room's marble floor clear for Patient.

Sunlight filtered through stained glass windows set high in the chamber walls. Rays of light streamed down, warming six eggs against the back wall, surrounded by fresh-cut, golden straw. The smell of the straw was pleasant, clean. It filled the air with a dry, grassy scent reminiscent of a warm spring day.

Casting a silent, questioning glance at the dragon, the shepherd crossed the room and laid his hand on the egg closest to him. The white, reflective shell speckled with blue, stood level with his chest. Slowly he looked back at the dragon. "May I assume that these eggs are the reason you brought up the fall of the Six?"

Albino growled. "War is brewing. Out of distant lands the wizard, Letrias, gathers followers. Corrupt men, and a few women. I have seen the might he will wield and he will soon bring it to bear on the lands of the dragons, the lands of Venom-fier."

"Yes, I too have seen it." Patient pulled his hand away from the egg. He fixed his undeniable gaze on each of the remaining eggs. "Letrias has grown powerful," he said, his eyes pausing on the egg farthest from where he stood. "But you and I cannot intervene. You know the consequences if we do.

"War is harsh, but I would rather its cruel lash strike Venom-fier than that he become less of a dragon than he is." His sandals stirred small clouds of dust as he walked through the straw, approaching the egg farthest from him. He glanced up at the dragon. "We cannot interfere this time, my friend."

Clenching his jaws together, Albino rumbled deep in his throat. "We cannot afford to do nothing."

"I love peace as much as you do," Patient said. "But we must look to our own lands and let a new history be written." The shepherd reached out and touched the last egg, also blue speck-led, but only waist-high. "Dragons and men, and all intelligent creatures of the world must learn that life is a gift to be protected and not taken for granted.

"Let the war come. Let humankind *and* dragonkind learn to love the good and hate the evil."

The dragon relaxed his jaw. For a moment he had thought that the shepherd might oppose his plan. It was a bold one, con-ceived of not long after Letrias's treachery. "Then let us think as one, my friend; for, a hero must rise among humanity in the days to come, or there will be no one to whom they can look for guid-ance. Dragonkind has the war-like Venom-fier and his wisdom to guide them in the days ahead, but humankind has no one."

Leaning over the egg, Patient put his ear to its shell. A smile deepened the wrinkles at the corners of his mouth. "I take it you have a hero in mind?"

Albino gave a stiff nod of his elegant, horned head. "I have not directly chosen who that hero will be. I trust the Creator to show me at the appropriate time. But for the moment I have chosen the tool that will bring him when the time is right."

Stretching his neck, the dragon nuzzled the smallest egg. "I have poured all of my energy into this undertaking," he said softly, turning his pink eyes toward the other five. "Each of these eggs holds one of my offspring. And one of my offspring has the power within her to bring about the wizard's end, though not through war, nor by her own hand. Her role is vital. *She* will be special."

Patient again leaned toward the smallest egg, and Albino pulled away, his gaze locked on that egg.

Closing his eyes, the old shepherd again placed his hand on the shell. "Special—yes, my friend—and she will be beautiful, strong through your blood, though not strong enough to win the war." His eyes startled open, returned Albino's gaze. Holding up his hand with fingers splayed, he closed it into a fist. "Letrias would crush her in a heartbeat."

"As I told you," the dragon said. "She does not have it within herself to win the war, nor will the deed be executed by her own hand." He focused on the smaller egg. "She is not the one to bring down the wizard. She is a *means* of bringing about his end."

"How?" The shepherd held up his hand as soon as the question left his lips. He faced the egg and closed his eyes while replacing his hand on its surface. After a long moment, his countenance brightened. "There are subtle differences between this child and her siblings. Playful, vivacious even. A lover?"

Dipping his head in a slight bow, Albino rumbled satisfaction. "Among the six offspring I have created, she alone has the ability to bring about the salvation of humankind."

Withdrawing his hand, the shepherd looked up at the dragon. "I see no savior, no man able to turn the tide."

"That is because he is beyond your sight. The Creator will provide him when the time is right and I will know him. But he will come, nevertheless, and I will guide him into Subterran at a time I deem appropriate."

"Ah!" The shepherd smiled. "You plan to use the sword."

"Yes. It also is a tool to bring about Letrias's end."

A shadow passed through Patient's eyes. They half-closed. He seemed to listen to an inaudible voice, his head inclined toward his chest. Then he again stared at the egg. His voice dropped to almost a whisper. "Have you seen this, my friend? Have you seen the future?"

"Of what do you speak?"

"Death; I see death. There is a dark path down which she must walk. One out of which I see no light—Wait! I was mistaken."

The dragon pointed at the egg with his claw. "You see, don't you? You see with greater clarity?"

"She will be born of both races," the shepherd said in hushed tones. "And she will be gifted with physical beauty and fierce strength."

"A tool," the dragon interposed. And he was pleased to see his friend frown in puzzlement.

"Another tool? But what of the savior you mentioned?"

"You will see, my friend." The dragon set his foot back on the hard floor. "You will see."

Albino led the shepherd down the hall for a little distance, then faced the wall. He turned right and then to his left, searching. But not a soul was in sight.

"Inner sanctum, open to me!" Immediately the wall turned to ice, the stones changed composition until they appeared semi-transparent and crystalline. Inclining his head, he indicated that

Patient should proceed first. The shepherd stepped through the wall and it swallowed him out of sight, crackling behind him like a thawing cube of ice.

And Albino followed. The wall felt cool on his scales, but not frigid as one might have expected. His snout broke through the wall first, then his head slid free and he pulled his body into moist, warm air.

His muscles relaxed as he strode forward. The room he had entered was enormous, larger than any other in Shizar Palace . . . and more magnificent.

Beneath his feet spread a floor made from a sheet of glass thick enough to bear his weight without cracking. A gentle river of water flowed under the glass. It reached only a couple feet deep and a bed of innumerable sapphire jewels glowed with radiant, rich blue light through the water and into the room.

A gold altar rose from the center of the room on a pillar of gray stone. Encircling it stood a line of white dogwood trees. Engraved forms of children and women and men kneeling in prayer, graced the walls of the altar. The image of a winged dragon with head bowed in obeisance was etched into each of the four corners of the altar. Delicate white petals wafted down through the still air from the tree branches, covering the smooth floor.

Albino delicately moved forward.

Patient knelt before the altar and slid the hood off his head. And he remained silent for a time.

The familiar high, black walls surrounded them. A stairway of stones, nearly twenty feet broad, curved up from the floor, ascending to the palace roof.

Above him the ceiling was transparent. The clear blue sky could be seen through it, and a white cloud fled the wind.

"Albino," the shepherd said, rising to his feet and turning to look up at him, "my stay with you will be short. The flocks and herds of my mountains require my attention. In this season most of all."

Returning the man's gaze, Albino let a flame escape his nostril. "The birth of my children is paramount, Patient. Your flocks and herds can do without your attention for a short while. I want you to witness this event."

"And I do not want to miss it." Patient stepped away from the altar as a ray of sunlight angled through the ceiling and glared off the gold.

"But you wish to leave?" Albino narrowed his eyes. "Why, my friend?"

Stepping closer, Patient looked across the glass floor, his eyes seeming to follow the flow of the glowing water to the various plants growing along the walls.

"It is nothing problematic," the shepherd assured the dragon. "But I had to leave Corbaius and Melvin in charge during my absence. And . . . they have been at odds lately."

With a gentle shake of his head, Albino moved toward the altar. "Corbaius, I trust completely. His heart is pure.

"But sometimes Melvin's spirit feels"—he clutched for the right word—"elusive."

"He is a restless one, but harmless," Patient said, following the dragon back to the altar.

"I hope you are right." Albino looked down at the altar, feeling the sunlight warm his bony crest. Upon the altar's flat lid had been engraved: 'To the one and only God and Creator.'

"It is not always easy to discern the will of God, my friend. The powers I have been given must be used to further His will."

"And do you believe that your decision to create offspring, with the powers He's given you, falls within His will?"

"Yes." Albino growled. A wisp of smoke curled from between his razor teeth. "I will raise them in the fear and love of Creator

God. They will walk in His commands." He let a long silence endure. "And evil will fear them as it fears me!"

The dragon's thoughts turned inward. He remembered the desecration Hermenuedis wrought upon a holy altar. A sacrifice of human blood made where a sacrifice of prayer had once been offered. Evil spirits spread their roots in that wizard's soul and made their dwelling in the temple he'd erected for his mistress.

"Let us pray that what you say *will* come to pass," the shepherd said.

"Come, my friend," the dragon said, his claws clicking on the glass floor as his four legs ate the distance to the room's wall. "I sense my children are preparing to arrive."

The black wall crystallized before him as he approached. He forced his head through the cool surface, buried his body in it, and emerged into Shizar Palace's main hallway.

A popping, cracking sound preceded Patient's staff into the hallway. Then he stepped out, materializing beside the dragon and smiled up at him. "Of this I have no doubt, my friend: that your children will walk in the light."

⁂ ⁂ ⁂

The tiniest cracks appeared in five of the dragon's eggs . . . all except for the smallest one. Albino coiled his bony tail around his body and backed against the wall. Cracks spidered across the eggs' shells and a red-haired maid hurried into the room with two blonds towering after her. The time had indeed come.

Standing next to the redhead, Patient leaned with both hands on his staff.

"Gwen, Helen!" The redhead combed her shoulder-length tresses away from her forehead and her green eyes darted up at the other maids. She jabbed her finger toward one of the eggs and hustled to it, a towel thrown over her arm. "This one is coming first. Be ready with the swaddling blankets."

"Yes, Mum!" the women answered in unison. Their bright blue eyes seemed to intently follow the redhead. They had long, gold hair that fell straight down their backs to their narrow waists.

"Elsie," Albino said to the redhead.

"Yes, my lord?" The middle-aged woman glanced over her shoulder at him. Her green eyes started to wander back to the eggs, drawn like magnets to the sounds of additional cracks forming.

The dragon pointed with his claw at the egg in front of her. "Pry away the shell so that the child may come forth."

Elsie tossed the towel over Helen's arm, and faced the egg. Gingerly, she pushed the fingers of both hands into one of the cracks and pulled.

Suddenly, the shell collapsed outward. Elsie, some of her weight resting on the shell, slipped on the floor. She fell on her back with a startled cry as blood and multicolored fluids rushed from the egg and covered her from her neck to her feet.

Helen and Gwen stood like statues. But Albino spotted a sac flow out of the broken eggshell and drop toward the marble floor. Helen and Gwen did not appear to notice. They gawked at Elsie as she lay on the floor.

Albino growled, thrust his mighty arm past them, and caught the sac in the palm of his clawed fist. It wobbled in his palm; wet, fragile, threatening to burst open. If it had been allowed to hit the marble—

Standing to her feet, dripping red and green-gray liquid, Elsie swallowed her embarrassment. "My lord, I am so sorry . . . I just . . . did not expect—"

"There is no need to apologize," he said, but he flared his nostrils at Helen and Gwen. They apologized profusely and bowed, backing away.

Albino reached out with his free foreleg, held one of his claws in front of his mouth and heated it with his breath until it glowed like an iron poker plucked from a furnace. Using this claw, he broke the sac, freeing the child inside.

"My lord!" Elsie's mouth opened wide. Her green eyes stared in disbelief.

Beside the dragon, the shepherd chuckled. "I dare say you have surprised your staff."

Elsie shook her head and reached out as the dragon cut the child's umbilical cord with the heated claw. "She . . . she is human! How is this possible?"

"Yes, they all are." Albino allowed Helen to take the child and swaddle it.

"A baby girl," Elsie said as soon as she recovered her senses. "Have you chosen a name for her, my lord?"

"This one?" The dragon looked down at the softly crying baby. "She is the eldest. I will name her Caritha, for she will lead her sisters in the days that follow their sorrow."

"The days of their sorrow?" Elsie might have asked more, but the dragon shook his head and looked at the other eggs.

"Ask for no explanations," he rumbled. "Bring her to the nursery, Helen. And return quickly. My children will not wait."

Helen rushed to carry out her master's bidding, all the while humming to baby Caritha and shushing her to sleep.

As soon as Helen's footsteps faded down the hallway, four more eggs started to hatch. The spidery cracks that had formed on their shells, now spread like webs, weakening the casing that had kept the dragon's offspring in darkness.

Elsie hurried to each egg and pulled the shell apart. Having learned from her first efforts, she kept her footing. Soon she and Gwen had their hands full, lifting the four new arrivals into the world.

The straw soaked up much of the liquids that burst from the eggs, but the hem of Elsie's skirt and her slippers were drenched.

Patient stepped forward as Gwen gathered up a second baby. He took the next one, wrapping it in a corner of his white robe.

After cutting each of the infants' from their sacs, and severing their umbilical cords, Albino held the last of the four arrivals in his palm.

"My goodness, they are all girls!" Elsie said.

"Yes," he rumbled softly. And he laughed as the child squirmed in his palm and screamed beyond reason. "You, my dear child, are alike in beauty to your sisters, yet you have an indomitable spirit . . . You will be called Rose'el."

Gazing at each of the other three infants in turn, he chose their names. One he called Laura. "You, my daughter," he said, "will achieve victory by supporting your sisters."

"And you, my littlest one." He nuzzled his next daughter. "You will be called Evela. For, you must nurture a tender heart and sound mind to fulfill the meaning of that name."

The other maid returned and took Rose'el from him and the unnamed child from Patient. As the red little face passed under his scrutiny, Albino called her Levena. "For I do not know what else to call you. This name carries with it all my love, for it means 'one whose destiny is uncertain, yet whose path is blessed by Creator God.'"

Thanking the maids for all their help, Albino bid them bring the four new arrivals to the nursery and summon the wet nurses.

"We will return quickly, my lord." Elsie trudged toward the doorway.

With a gentle touch of his claw, the dragon held her back for a moment. "No. You, Helen, and Gwen have done enough for now . . . It is my desire to bring this last child into the world with only Patient as witness.

"See to the needs of my first five children." He pulled back his hand, releasing her. He shifted his gaze toward the last egg. It budged ever so slightly in the hay. This child was ready to leave the confines of her shell. "Go now, Elsie . . . I want to bring this one into the world, myself."

Elsie shuffled out of the room. Helen and Gwen, arms occupied by his crying offspring, made awkward half curtsies, and then followed.

Together the dragon and the shepherd approached the final egg . . . the smallest egg.

The dragon touched it with the tips of his claws. His body glowed with white light. Brighter and brighter he glowed, until rays of light radiated from between his scales.

Raising his hand, Patient shielded his eyes.

With his body throwing blinding, pure light, Albino felt the power in his blood boil. It surged through him. Electrical bolts of energy crackled on his hand and latched onto the egg. They entwined, meshed, knit their way around the shell until they covered it.

His claws penetrated the shell without cracking or breaking it. They passed inside and gently clasped the sac. In that instant, Albino let the energy building in his hand, explode outward from his claws. The egg crumbled into dust, the liquids evaporated, but he lifted the sac from the midst unharmed.

Drawing the sac closer to him, he cut it open and severed the infant's cord. Patient reached over and dried her body with his robe. Albino picked up a clean cloth lying near the straw and wrapped his child in it.

As her first cry sounded like a note of music in the quiet room, he said in a low, gentle voice, "Welcome, my youngest daughter. Welcome into the world, my little Dantress."

⋈ ⋈ ⋈

Albino sliced through the thunderhead cloud. His powerful wings reached forward and pulled back with methodic rhythm, propelling him ever faster to the far reaching fields of green and the palace built thereon. He dipped under the waving banners to land in one of his flower gardens, and strode past the tall bright spires.

Warm, midday air blew steadily across his bony face. Songbirds of varying colors and sizes landed on his back. He strolled down a broad, stone path until he came to a bench on which sat a little dark haired girl. "Hello, my child." He stretched out his neck and smiled down at her.

Dantress closed a leather bound book she'd been reading and set it on the bench beside her. The spine spelled out *Fairies: Blessings or Pests?*

"Father, when can I fly with you again?" Dantress turned her pleading dark eyes to him. "Please, I promise to be good!"

He chuckled at that. When was *she* ever bad? He looked around the garden for his other daughters. Two heads bounced into view behind a long, high hedge.

"Come on, Laura," he heard Evela say. "When do I get a turn?"

"Humph!" Rose'el responded. "Her turn ended an hour ago."

"Be quiet you two," Laura said. "You'll get your turns soon enough. Levena and I aren't ready yet."

Albino shook his head. Fatherhood, he never would've guessed how complicated it could be. He took a step toward the squabbling sisters. "I'll be right back, my child," he caressed Dantress's cheek with the broad side of his claw.

"Yes, Father." She picked up *Fairies, Blessings or Pests?* and continued to read from a quarter way through the thick volume.

From behind the hedge Rose'el and Laura exchanged heated retorts. He sighed; Dantress was an angel, truly, beside the others. Though Evela, also, rarely offered complaints or argument.

Caritha's voice interrupted the argument behind the hedge. "All of you, be silent!"

The sisters quieted as if a spell had been cast upon them and Albino craned his neck, glimpsing his oldest daughter striding stern-faced toward Evela, Laura, Levena, and Rose'el, who all stood as if soldiers rebuked by a commander warrior.

"Shame on you, Laura and Rose'el. What a ruckus! I could hear you from the other side of the garden!" She raised her hand and pointed at Laura. "Trade places with Evela. Let her take a turn jumping the rope. Levena, did you get a turn?"

Levena shook her head.

"Very well then! Rose'el, give your end to Levena. . . ."

Chuckling deep in his throat, Albino stepped back to Dantress's side. "No jumping rope today?"

"Jump rope?" She puckered her face in disgust. "I'd much rather go with you to the forest." She set aside the book, slipped a leaf between its pages and stood on the bench, hands folded. "Please, can't you take me?"

Feigning resignation he sighed, picked her up, and set her on his head. "Hold on tight." As her little fists grasped his horns, he raced down the path, spread his wings, and jumped into the air. He could hear her yelling with glee and begging him to go faster.

He climbed higher into the sky and swerved east. The land sped beneath him. The fields gave way to trees and then to thick forests. Justice Hill, a high plateau richly dressed in flowers and green grass with a lake at its center, rose above the lush forests of his domain. Here his ancestors had laid the foundation of law upon which he had established his kingdom.

The ground raced toward him as he approached. He leaned back, angled his wings, landed on the soft earth, digging in his claws for an easy halt by the lake. Into his ear Dantress sighed. He chuckled; she always liked it when he landed, but she preferred it to be more dramatic with the dirt flying and his claws slicing deep into the ground.

"We are here, my little one," he said. He knelt and she slid off his back, catching her hand on one of his scales in the process. "Ouch!" She sucked on the cut and looked sheepish; he'd warned her about doing that.

He strode several paces and motioned with an inclination of his head for her to follow. "The trails into the forest are well hidden to most eyes," he said. "Stay close to me and do not wander off."

The plateau's edge sloped at a rather steep angle to the wall of trees at its base, some sixty feet down. The smell of pine filled his nostrils as he descended to the needle-strewn forest floor and squeezed between two of the sappy tree trunks. Before him now lay a sunlit, straight, narrow path. Narrow, that is, for a dragon. Yellow and purple flowers lined the way, each blossom releasing its own perfume into the gentle breezes that stole around his feet.

Dantress danced ahead of him into a woodland clearing, startling a flock of gold finches and robins feeding in the grass. She started after them, but he held her back. "Stand still, my child. Let them come to you." She stopped, stood still, fixed her gaze on the trees.

The moments seemed to drag by as the birds deliberated with one another. Albino smiled at a large, red-gold cardinal that landed on a nearby branch. "Good day to you, Flame! May I introduce the youngest of my daughters?"

"This is your youngest, Sire? This is Dantress?"

"She is indeed."

Flame stretched out his wing and preened a feather, then turned one black, shiny, accusing eye at the child. "Since you are the offspring of the great dragon I am compelled to welcome you to our Sanctuary, though your behavior thus far gives me reason to doubt that the noble blood truly runs through your veins."

"There now, Flame, she meant no harm." Albino put his clawed hand reassuringly around Dantress's shoulders. "She was merely playing."

Flame hung his head in shame. "Forgive me, Sire! I did not mean . . . I only thought . . . I've acted like an unhatched chick . . . but she is with you, of course." He flew to Dantress's shoulder and balanced himself there. "Welcome to our Sanctuary, Dantress, and please forgive me for any insult I dealt you."

She stroked Flame's fluffed chest feathers and his eyes fluttered shut.

"Ah! Such a fine massage."

Flame remained on her shoulder and others soon joined him. Before long she had managed to befriend the majority of the flock; some she caressed and others she engaged in conversation. They boasted of their nests and of their offspring, they told her how pretty and sweet they thought she was. When Albino said it was time to go the birds sang her off. Even Flame waved his red-gold wing as they left the clearing and continued walking down the trail.

Not far down the trail they came to a broad river. Albino stretched over it and anchored his forefeet in the mud. His rear legs splashed into the cool, fast-flowing water. "Climb over my back," he instructed.

First grabbing onto his tail, Dantress pulled herself up and walked across, arms spread wide for balance. Though his scales were hard as iron he felt her feet cautiously stepping on his spine.

She walked onto his head and down his snout then stepped onto the trail on the other side of the river.

"Where are we going?"

"To meet some more friends of mine," he said as he pulled himself up and shook the river water off his underside. Leaving the river behind, he led her deeper into the forest. No pines stood along this path, only white birch and oaks. Clover, green as in new spring, covered the ground on either side of the crushed stones covering the path.

An ancient tree, its trunk as thick as Albino's body, had fallen across the way. "Up you go." Albino picked her up and set her on top of the log. He leapt to the other side before helping her down.

He knew, further up the path, the trees gave way to a wide, open meadow. He forced his powerful legs to slow to Dantress's pace. When they arrived at the meadow—filled with all manner of colorful flowers set upon by butterflies—he closed his eyes and breathed deeply. Ah, it was wonderful to be alive!

When he opened his eyes deer and antelope, a bear, a lion, and a gazelle pushed their way into view. They carried themselves proudly, yet each, in turn, lowered their head in respectful recognition of his presence. He dipped his head back at them and rumbled deep in his throat, proudly drawing their attention to the fair child accompanying him.

Dantress pushed a long, dark tress out of her eyes. Wolves trotted forward now, too, bowing to her, then vanished back into the forest. A moose followed, his killer antlers perched magnificently over his soft face. His lips twisted at the corners into a smile.

"Blood offspring of the dragon, may you live long!" He winked at her, then strolled into the trees.

One rabbit, its gray fur glossy from too much grooming, walked to the dragon on its hind legs. Its nose twitched and its ears shivered. "G-great and m-mighty one." Perhaps it meant to say more, but it hopped away before anything else came out.

Albino watched as the bear approached Dantress. Its burly black, fur-covered body dwarfed her. Yet she showed no timidity and, indeed, he saw her smile at the animal and speak to it.

In this way they passed the time until Yimshi's rays turned from gold to a shade of orange. "Dantress? It's time to go."

"Already?"

She reluctantly followed him out of the forest and back to the plateau. The western horizon's clouds dipped into deeper shades of red and purple.

He sniffed the air. "Mm hmm! Smell those hazelnuts!"

She lifted her chin to test the air and closed her eyes to enjoy the sensation. The day of her birth came briefly to mind and he thought, with a twinge of regret, that he favored her over his other daughters. Not that he loved her more than he loved them; but he felt that she was of the same spirit as he—in tune with nature, in love with the things he loved.

"Come," he said, nuzzling her affectionately with his elegant head, "daylight is fading. I promised your sisters last night that I will read another story by the fireplace before Elsie tucks you all into bed." He helped her onto his neck and stood, facing the wind.

"Promise me, Father," she begged into his ear. "Promise to bring me back?"

"Of course, my child. I'd love to."

Tensing every leg muscle he threw himself into the wind with wings spread. The air caught him and he flapped his wings and drew his legs tight against his body. The plateau shrank out of sight behind him as the crimson solar disc settled below the horizon.

RUSTED SWORDS

Rules are rules!" Elsie pushed Dantress back to her pillow and proceeded to tuck in the bed sheets so tightly that Dantress nearly gasped. As soon as she'd finished, Elsie stood straight and yanked the cord tighter around her dark red night gown.

Dantress, her arms wedged under the sheets, let the woman kiss her on the forehead. "But what if the fairy's story is true, Aunt Elsie? It sounded so . . . intriguing."

"You listen to me, young lady: I've no intention of letting you wander the palace at night and *you* shouldn't even consider it. Your father gave me clear instructions that no one is to wander the palace after bedtime . . . and I'd think that is especially pertinent at your age." She reached out with her right hand and stroked the girl's dark red-brown hair.

"Fairies tell tales that would make the ugliest troll sit and listen to them. But don't waste your brain wondering about their stories, my dear, for even the wisest cannot say when a fairy tells lie or truth.

"This fairy you talked to . . ." she snapped her fingers, "What was his name? Miverē?"

Dantress nodded.

"Right! Don't believe a word of what he said, child. He's a member of the Bladegrass family and they have developed a—err—reputation for telling tales." She yawned, long and loud, covering her mouth with her left hand. "The hour is late, Dantress. Your sisters have fallen asleep, and it is time you do the same." She smiled, yawned again, and walked out of the chamber, closing the heavy oak door behind her.

The room settled into darkness and Dantress rolled onto her side. She knew that the Bladegrass fairies often misrepresented facts, but in her heart she trusted Miverē. And he would certainly never lead her in harm's way. If he really had discovered a secret chamber . . . what she wouldn't do to see it! It would surely be a welcome break from her daily routine.

She tossed and turned under her sheets. The room held her in its deep silence. At last the tinkle of a tiny bell in the bedroom wall warned her of a fairy's approach.

She frowned. Should she stay in bed or risk meeting her little friend?

A flame appeared in the darkness; a tiny flickering flame like that of a match but housed in glass. It hovered toward her and Miverē's impish face peered from behind its silver housing. The lantern swung from the fairy's minute fists.

"Time wastes away, the hour draws late. Are you coming, fairest of the dragon's daughters?"

Fluttering from the wall, gold light glowing from his silver lantern, the fairy landed on her chest. Miverē's transparent oval wings beat slowly to keep his delicate frame balanced on the soft covers. He flipped his shoulder-length red hair over his back. His green eyes shone like jewels in the dimness, matching his green shirt and leggings flecked with gold.

Reaching behind one of his large pointed ears, Miverē fiddled with the tiny feather tucked there. It seemed only yesterday that she and the fairy fashioned that feather into a quill. It had proved quite useful, for Miverē employed it often to write her little notes and remained forever in her debt.

He tapped one bare foot impatiently on her chest and buzzed his wings. "Well? Well, are you coming, fairest of the dragon's daughters?"

"Shush!" she whispered. "Do you want to wake the others?"

"No, no. We must race time, for the light appears at midnight. Come, fairest of the dragon's daughters." He hovered above the sheets, legs swinging in the air, and beckoned her to follow as he retreated toward the bedroom door.

Taking great care not to ruin the neatly tucked sheets, Dantress slid her body from under them and swung her feet over the side of the bed before slipping them into a pair of fluffy white slippers.

"Hurry," the fairy urged, pulling a little glowing wand from his shirt and pointing it at the bedroom door to make it open as if of its own accord. "You will miss the light of the secret chamber."

She pulled her robe around her shoulders and slipped as quietly as possible from the room. With a wave of the wand, Miverē closed the door behind her without a sound. She followed his bobbing lantern down the dark, marble-floored hallway to a broad stairs leading to the first floor. The hard and smooth wood of the stair railing felt cool under her fingers. She straddled it with her legs and slid down. When she landed Miverē hovered just ahead of her, looking back from moment to moment to see that she still followed him.

They touched ground level in the palace. Through one tremendous hall after another she followed the fairy, always keeping her eye on the light streaming in moderate beams from his lantern. It seemed forever until they reached the palace's main hall. They followed it past the chamber in which she'd hatched, past the doors to the kitchens and dining hall on her right, past the mahogany grating on the left-hand wall—it prevented entry to one of her favorite rooms, the library. At last the hallway bent to the right.

Gold and silver tiles patterned the floor here in front of the Fairy Tree. Its bark glowed soft blue and shifted into white the farther it grew up the high, sprawling branches. The leafless tips of the branches glowed like hot pokers pulled from a blacksmith's forge.

She stopped for a moment to stare at it, thinking of the fairy families that inhabited it. Miverē lived here too.

"Come, come, fairest daughter of the dragon." Miverē hung his lantern on a narrow twig extending from the fairy tree, then beckoned with his wand, moving into an adjoining hallway branching off to the right.

"Where are we?" she asked.

"A little used servants' corridor," Miverē said. "This leads to the far end of the palace, but we will not go that far . . . Here, here it is!" He waved his wand. Flakes of light flew from it, outlining a brass latch cleverly hidden in the midst of an antiquated painting: six figures robed in white, wielding what looked to be swords made of transparent crystal.

Dantress tilted her head back for a better view. How beautiful. But what lay beyond? She reached out and pulled on the latch but it creaked in protest, and she released her hold.

The fairy laughed, a tinkling laugh, and flitted to her shoulder where he stood chuckling until she looked at him. "Are you afraid of being discovered, fairest of the dragon's daughters?"

"I shouldn't be here at this hour, Miverē. I'll be in trouble if Elsie discovers me . . . You know how she is."

"Unfortunately," the fairy replied, rolling his eyes. Then he leaned forward, grinning, and tapped her cheek with his wand. "I like you, fairest of the dragon's daughters, you are fun to adventure with.

"Come! See? The light of the chamber is revealed, for it is midnight. Is it not as I have said?"

Blinding white light flashed from the latch. Dantress raised her arm, shielding her eyes. An instant later the light diminished. She lowered her arm, gazing in wonder at the lighted outline of a very broad and very high door. Large enough, she reasoned, for the great white dragon himself to enter.

"Well, well? What do you think, fairest of—"

"Miverē, how did you find it? Where does it lead?"

His wings humming, the fairy flew off and spun in the air. "How did I find it, you ask? It was two years ago. I'd taken a nap one night on one of the lantern's housings when I was startled to hear the great dragon burst past me.

"Being curious I followed him. It was around midnight. The door blazed with light, and he pushed it open. He entered and it closed behind him . . . I slipped in just before it shut. Do you want to see what is inside the chamber, fairest of the dragon's daughters?"

"Even if I did, Miverē"—she put her hand on the cool wall, the hidden door now clearly visible—"I could never open it. It must weigh as much as an elephant and there are hand devices on the doors around the rest of the palace, but this door has no such device."

"Push on it," the fairy said, gesturing encouragement. "You will be surprised how easily it moves. And don't worry; there is nothing evil hidden within."

Dantress raised her eyebrows skeptically and gave the door a gentle push. It creaked inward on unseen hinges, swinging away from her like a lumbering giant. It touched a wall in the dark passageway behind it with a muffled knock and she swallowed uncomfortably. The passageway smelled slightly musty and the fairy's wand did not cast enough light to reveal what lay inside.

But she took a brave step forward and Miverē flew ahead of her. He threw more dust from his wand, dropping glowing specks on the floor.

She followed him slowly down the passage. It was good that she did; rough stones composed the floor and it sloped downward. Moist dirt clung to the stones as evidence that Elsie's broom and mop had never found this corner of the palace. Something about the air grabbed at her insides, as if she'd intruded on old secrets that did not wish to be disturbed. And she quickened her steps in order that she might stay close to Miverē's friendly glow.

"And here we are," the fairy whispered, zooming up and away into the darkness. He sparked a flame into an enormous lantern hung from the ceiling over thirty feet above her head, and then he dropped back down, landing with impressive grace on her shoulder, where he sat pompously. "See, fairest of the dragon's daughters? What did I promise you?"

Flames spread in the lantern and the light reflected in several mirrors set in the ceiling, revealing an oval chamber about a hundred feet long and almost as wide. Red liquid filled a tarnished silver basin set on an iron pedestal at the room's end. Six short swords, held in place by rusted clips, hung behind and above the basin.

She tiptoed toward the weapons. Something drew her to them; whether simple curiosity or some other unexplainable desire she could not tell. The lantern light flickered on the grimy stone walls of the chamber, a few cobwebs swaying from the ceiling. Miverē, surprisingly, said nothing.

Dantress stopped a few feet in front of the basin. Rust covered the swords' pommels and the interweaving vines etched into them. But leather wrapped the swords' handles so that one could hold them without fear of getting cut. However, grime covered the leather, making the handholds most uninviting. Moisture droplets speckled the sword blades with red and leaked from their tips, running into a tray draining into the basin. The crimson liquid filled the basin to the half-way point.

"Disgusting," the fairy said. "Creepy, too."

Tilting her head, Dantress peeked from the corner of her eye at the little figure still sitting there on her shoulder. She arched her eyebrows. "It's only rust, Miverē."

"Rust, fairest of the dragon's daughters? Rust you say?" He raised his tiny fist, bent a narrow finger, and pointed. "Look again . . . 'tis blood in that basin."

"Blood?" She reached out, determined to touch the substance in question. But the fairy jumped up and flew to her hand, swatting it with his wand before she could do so.

"What are you doing?" He shook his head and frowned. "Don't you realize what this is?"

"Miverē! That hurt!"

"I hope so, fairest daughter of the dragon! This basin is filled with the blood of the innocent slain by these swords. I heard the dragon say so himself, the night that I followed him inside this chamber."

"And *what* does that have to do with me?" She rubbed the burned spot of flesh upon her hand and narrowed her eyes.

He sighed, shook his little head and crossed his arms, nodding toward the basin. "Did you read the curse?"

Dantress looked at the basin's outer edge, to the letters etched in it.

Cursed be the one who disturbs the blood of the innocent, And blessed is she that restores the sword of the captain to its former purity

Horror filled her. She turned from the sight, struggling not to let her nausea overcome her. Blood! A whole basin of it.

Racing from the chamber, Dantress wheeled around and pulled on the edge of the massive door. It swung toward her and the fairy flitted through just as it closed. She leaned against the hidden door, unanswered questions crisscrossing each other in her mind.

⊘   ⊘   ⊘

"Miverē," a voice rumbled from the pitch black hall as soon as the massive door thudded shut "return to the Fairy Tree; I will speak with you in the morning."

The fairy froze. He must have recognized the voice of the great white dragon. "Yes, of course, your Majesty. But, please understand . . . I meant no harm—"

"This is not up for discussion, Miverē. Return to the tree. I will speak with you in the morning." The white dragon's head penetrated the small circle of light created by the fairy's lantern. The dragon's words were smooth, patient, yet they were decisive.

Miverē flew off as he was bidden, casting Dantress a cautious glance.

Darkness fell upon Dantress as soon as the fairy left. She couldn't see her hand if she held it in front of her face.

Four streams of white-hot flame shot from the dragon's toothy mouth, penetrating the darkness and lighting up Albino's

pink eyes so that they appeared to glow. The streams of fire—
two from his lower jaw, two from his upper—coalesced into his
upheld hand. When a ball of bright fire accumulated between his
fingers, Albino stopped breathing flames. "Come with me, my
daughter," he ambled down the hall, the ball of flames lighting
his way. "We have much to discuss."

❈ ❈ ❈

The dragon approached the mahogany grating and it slid up
without him so much as touching it. The doors also, behind the
grating, opened as if of their own accord. He extinguished the
ball of fire in his hand. Dantress groped her way into the dark
room and the dragon closed the doors behind them. She could
see nothing.

But Albino's claws clicked on the smooth marble floor as
he strode around her and forged through the darkness. A few
moments later a tongue of white and yellow fire pierced the darkness. It arced from his open maw and struck the oil-soaked wicks
of an ornate, gold chandelier swinging from the ceiling far above.

The chandelier lit the room with a steady light, not too bright
not too dim, just right for reading. Rising in sculpted majesty,
his white membranous wings folded to his scaled sides, was her
dragon father.

Books and scrolls rose all around him, on shelves and in
bookcases that rose at least eighty feet to the ceiling. Albino spat
flames into the mammoth fireplace on the back wall, igniting
the logs therein. They soon crackled pleasantly.

"Come, my daughter, sit and talk with me."

She swallowed. She'd been wrong to follow the fairy; she knew
that. But, somehow, acknowledging that fact did not appease her
conscience. Albino had every right to be angry with her.

"So," the dragon began, his voice a gentle rumble, "Miverē found the chamber containing the Swords of the Six and he told you about it. I presume you went willingly." His pink eyes twinkled at her as she sat uneasily in a red chair by the fire. He grabbed a wooden pole and playfully jabbed it in his best imitation of a fairy. "Or did he force you at wand point?"

He laughed and Dantress laughed with him. She breathed a sigh of relief; he did not seem angry or disappointed. "No, Father." She shook her head. "He did not force me; I went of my own accord."

"I suspected as much." He leaned the pole against a bookcase and turned to face her. "Thank you for being honest with me." He pulled a scroll down from one of the shelves and rolled it in his claws. "I'm not angry with you, my daughter, but your action was not wise . . . Show me your hands."

Obediently, she showed them to him. He sniffed them once and looked them over. "Good, you did not touch the blood. I was afraid you might have."

"Miverē stopped me. I was going to touch it," she admitted, lowering her head. "But I didn't know any better."

"I'll have to thank that mischievous little fairy for that; he might have saved your life." The dragon snaked across the room, glancing at the giant clock. The hour hand dipped below one o'clock. The library doors opened. Twisting his massive head, he gazed down at her. "I did not realize the time. Come now; it is way past your bedtime, my dear. I'll see you back to your room. Tomorrow we will talk about the swords, when your sisters are awake, for this matter involves them as well."

Dantress yawned and followed him out of the library. He brought her back to her bedroom door and opened it with one claw. "Goodnight, little one. Go to sleep this time."

⚭   ⚭   ⚭

Dressed in identical dresses of royal purple bound at the waist with white sashes, the six daughters of the great white dragon stood in a half-circle, uncomfortably facing him in the moist chamber and taking turns glancing at the basin of blood and the rusted swords on the back wall. How close Dantress and her sisters resembled one another, Albino mused.

All of them had long dark brown hair, tinged with red. Their black eyes looked around intelligently. But Rose'el rose a few inches taller than the rest and Dantress bore a superior beauty. Perhaps it was her smile, bright and playful. Or maybe the grace of her neck and the way her eyes seemed to gaze into your soul. Albino put those thoughts aside and focused instead on their similarities; in that lay their strength; their great potential. In order for his plan to succeed he would need them to work as one unit.

He reached for one of the swords, the sword of Xavion. Slowly he growled and, keeping his pink eyes trained on the rusted weapon, held it forth for his daughters to see.

"Keep your ears attentive, my children, for what I am about to reveal has serious consequences for you all. It is the reason I brought you into the world. It is the reason these swords now rest in solemnity.

"A very, very long time ago . . ."

⚭   ⚭   ⚭

Albino hurtled toward the rocky slope. His maw opened with a roar of agony and anger so profound that the stones shattered and the five traitorous warriors dropped their swords to cover their ears. Xavion, his noble face mutilated beyond recognition, sprawled on the ground. His blood pooled around him and Letrias cowered next to him.

The young prince of Prunesia was gasping for air and Kesla's face streaked with tears as he lifted his head to see the dragon.

"My poor boy . . . forgive me," Albino heard the man say. But the deed was done; Brian pulled his white-bladed scimitar to him and broke its blade broadside across his knee.

Albino's heart flared inside his chest. The pain of loss exploded from his innermost being in a roar that knocked Auron, Hestor, and Clavius to their knees.

And at that moment he perceived the light of Brian's soul depart his body. The Grim Reaper congealed beside the sinful scene and wafted like a dark mist toward the body of the innocent victim. It raised the dreaded scythe and swept its blade downward. Once that serrated metal touched Brian's skin it would . . .

Albino crashed into the Grim Reaper and the ground split beneath him, forming a rift a dozen feet deep. His claws slipped through the wispy being as it tried to elude him. But his mind netted it with invisible bands that forced it to take physical form. Grasping the dark being, he missiled it into the mountainside. An avalanche buried the villain under tons of rock and dirt, but not before its hands and head reverted to smoky vapor.

Hestor and Clavius scrambled away from him. He snarled and pinned their legs to the ground with his claws. The warriors screamed and cried for mercy as their blood painted his claws.

He released them but as Hestor struggled to his feet, Albino turned him about so that he could look into his eyes. "What you have sown by this treachery you shall now reap!" He raked his razor claws down Hestor's front and dropped the man's limp body.

Dragging himself away from Albino, Clavius trembled. His fingers dug into the ground and he sobbed. "Dark spirits, why have you not come to my rescue?"

"Truly you have fallen from the heights of glory to the depths of darkness." Albino roared, drew back his long neck, opened his powerful jaws and snared the man. Grinding his teeth together, he broke Clavius in half. The warrior's soul faded into darkness.

Albino wheeled on Letrias, blood and guts leaking between his teeth as he parted his lips. He grasped a nearby boulder and crushed it in his scaled hand. As the fragments of stone rained on the ground, flames roiled in his half-open mouth.

Eyes wide with fear, Letrias spread forth his hands. Energy sizzled along his palms and his lips trembled. "You are not all-powerful, Albino. Hermenuedis is more than a match for you . . . and he has taught me how to wield"—his eyes radiated the bluish light amassing between his fists—"to wield mighty *power*!"

The energy shot from his hands, bolts as thick as his wrists sped toward Albino's chest. But they passed through his body as if he wasn't really there; as if he were only composed of air.

Storm clouds gathered. The sunlight faded.

"I will waste no more breath on you," Albino said. He drew back his head and threw a steady stream of yellow fire at Letrias.

But Letrias was spared incineration.

The clouds spiraled toward the ground and a giant winged man dropped to the dirt, crouching between Letrias and Albino. Then it loomed above the traitor and held out a black orb that absorbed the flames and grew in size until it became the size of a large boulder.

Albino's flames burned white-hot and a portion of sandy ground beside the Art'en wizard turned to glass.

"Be gone, cursed artifact!" Albino let another roar issue from his mouth as he stretched out his claws. He clenched his fist and the wizard's orb burst into a billion fragments.

"Hermenuedis," he rumbled "you have carried your wickedness to its final day!"

"No, Albino, thisss day isss mine!" The wizard screeched.

Suddenly, Valorian dove from the heavens. A ray of sunlight penetrated the clouds and glinted off the dragon's black scales.

Albino found himself roaring with delight; now two of his vilest enemies were within his reach. Long had he awaited this day.

Valorian folded his wings to his sides, forming himself into a living arrow. He shot toward Albino. But he passed through the white scaled body as if it weren't there.

Hooking the creature with his claws, Albino flung him down the slope. The black dragon's body furrowed another rift in the hard earth.

❧ ❧ ❧

All six of his daughters had listened with rapt attention as he recounted the treachery enacted that day. Now he sighed and said, "The rest of the tale does not merit telling. And it is not a wound I want to open."

The sisters exchanged horrified glances. Rose'el and Caritha said they thought the atrocity merited retribution of the worst kind. The other sisters voiced revulsion; how could best friends turn so readily upon one another? And why did Kesla weep?

But he swept his hand toward the swords arrayed over the basin. "Behold the weapons of my trusted Six. Each of these swords was once a magnificent weapon of crystal, the blades were long," he said. "Now they are diminished. The power I infused in them at the time of their creation is lesser now and the blood of the innocent caused the blades to shrink to what you see here now."

To one side, Dantress raised her hand. "You have a question, child?" he asked.

She nodded. "Father, what happened to the rest of the Six? Were they killed?"

He regarded her in silence. This was the question he'd been dreading and the one that he had expected to hear.

Caritha, standing off to the right, frowned at Dantress. "Father will tell us what he wants us to know—"

"She's right, you know," Rose'el added. "Why do you always ask so many questions?"

"Because he said I could—"

Rose'el scowled, but Albino rebuked her with his eyes and turned to the curious one . . . *the special one.* "Some of the Six survived my attack. Letrias fled with Auron. And Kesla? Well, *he* escaped alone."

He looked at the sword in his hand. Xavion had been a valiant man, a man bound by honor, and loyal. Letrias had robbed Albino of a dear friend on that horrible day and Albino would not forget that.

"It is of the Accursed Three who escaped that I wish to speak to you, for they followed the path of evil and Letrias did so with eagerness. He became strong in dark magic, almost as powerful as his former master, and Auron became his apprentice.

"Lesser in power is the other man, Kesla. But he is growing in strength and has been seen wandering the ruins of the wizard Temple of Al'un Dai." He growled again. "In the ruins of that vast fortress built by Hermenuedis in his own honor, Kesla may yet discover the path to ultimate power and raise up enemies against me.

"You I have created, my beautiful daughters, so that you may stand against this tide of evil. This is your purpose, this is your calling."

They looked at each other then back at him. "Us?"

Evela timidly offered "We're not even of age."

Dantress's eyes blazed for an instant, he thought, with fire. She stepped forward and stretched out her hands, looking down at her palms. They glowed for a brief moment and she glanced up at him. "I can feel it, Father. I can feel something inside of me growing and spreading, strengthening me."

It was the call of their blood; Albino knew it to be so. His blood flowed through their veins, giving them that other sense. It was a dragon trait. The other girls fell into silence, observing their sister.

"Can you not feel it as well?" Dantress demanded of them. "Don't you feel something powerful rising within you?" She reached out her hand and held Evela's.

Evela's eyes opened wide, "I *can* feel it!" She grasped Levena's hand and Levena grabbed Rose'el's. Rose'el nodded her head reluctantly and reached with her left hand, taking Laura's, who responded immediately by completing the chain to Caritha.

Albino watched them, amazed. They were only twelve years old, rather young to recognize the powers he'd passed on to them. Yet here they were uniting their hearts with Dantress, an ability that many gifted creatures never gained.

The girls let go of each other's hands. Rose'el's mouth froze in a slight frown; Caritha looked somber. "Father, what do you want us to do?"

Their sudden willingness took him aback. He felt an urge to keep them forever at home in the palace, forever safe from harm beneath his wings. Could he really send them out into Subterran knowing what would happen? The end would be joy, but the path to that end was littered with suffering and sorrow.

Dantress walked up to him and rested her hand on his leg, looking up at him so that he had to twist his long neck to meet her gaze. "Father, what will happen to us?"

He felt tears burning in his eyes. How could he send her when he knew? But then, how could he not? Dragonkind and humankind—both their futures depended on her. But she was so young, innocent, and beautiful.

"There is much pain in your future, my daughter," he whispered. "You will win and lose, both in great measure. But remember, *always* remember"—he passed his gaze over all his daughters, knowing that his next words would be their only comfort in the future—"I will be with you through everything, even when you cannot see me. I will never leave you alone! Do you understand?"

The sisters smiled, even Rose'el, and approached the blood-filled basin, eyeing the swords with new interest.

Handle first, he held out the rusted sword of Xavion. "To each of you I will give a sword of the Six. They will be yours to use in the cause of the innocent and helpless. With them you will fight as one, think as one; they will allow you to join strength as one. I will train you in their use and instruct you in the ways of warfare. Wield these weapons with love, and they will serve you well."

In unison the five sisters standing near the wall reached up and pulled down the swords, their dark eyes gleaming.

"Be careful with those," he said. "Their edges may be rusted, but the blades can still sever your finger.

"Dantress." He rested a claw on her shoulder and pressed Xavion's rusted sword into her hand. "This sword I have saved for you. It belonged to Xavion, captain of the Six." Her mouth dropped open. Her fingers wrapped around the handle and then she grasped it with both hands and held it before her.

The blade glowed softly, a rusted red color. "This sword is special among its brethren," Albino said. "It is the only weapon whose master was not a traitor and for that reason it may one day be returned to its former glory, transparent and beautiful. Watch over it with care, for it belonged to a very dear friend."

"Look, Father! See what we can do?" Caritha, Laura, Rose'el, Evela and Levena raised their swords, touching the points together. He cried out for them to stop, but it was too late. Blue energy sizzled along the swords' blades and joined between them, then dispersed harmlessly throughout the chamber.

The sisters exclaimed with delight, but then they gazed up at him.

"It is finished," Albino said. He shook his head.

Caritha's countenance fell and her smile faded into a frown. "Did we do something wrong?"

"It's all right," he sighed. "The five swords have now bonded as they did with the Six, only this time the sword of Xavion was not among them. I would have preferred that you join all six of the swords and then you might have functioned more perfectly as a single unit."

They looked at the floor and shuffled their feet, but he waved his hand as if it was unimportant. "You will still be able to fight side by side with Dantress; do not worry! Come." He headed out of the chamber. "I will show you how to properly use these things."

A WEAPON
OF LIVING FIRE

Well, well, fairest of the dragon's daughters, practicing *again*?"

Dantress ignored Miverē and evaluated her opponent. Standing in the center of the armory floor she stepped back and pulled aside the outer purple skirt that hid her scabbard. Her fingers felt their way around the familiar leather grip, and she drew out the sword, spraying flakes of rust into the air as she swung it upright in front of her eyes. With both hands she held it there, looking past it to her opponent.

A healthy rivalry had developed between her and her first-born sister. Caritha had excelled with weaponry, as had she.

Caritha stood with dignity and grace, much as a queen. But her eyes roved the room, betraying a busy mind. She ran her hand down the side of her purple skirt and opened the fold to reveal her own scabbard. With lightning speed she slipped the rusted sword from its scabbard and dashed toward Dantress, blade poised level with her shoulder.

They met halfway on the yellow sand covering the armory floor. Dantress struck first, feinting to the left but slashing on the right. Caritha's blade clashed with hers, sending reluctant sparks into the air.

Thunder rattled the glass dome above Dantress's head. Out of the corner of her eye she saw a storm passing over the palace. Jagged electric bolts split thick, dark clouds. But she focused her attention on her sister.

Seemingly unperturbed by her silence and the clashing metal blades, Miverē appeared, flitted onto her shoulder and perched there, though she noted that he kept a firm grip on her neck collar. "It has been four and a half years since I showed you the secret chamber," he said as she parried Caritha's thrust. "I am wishing I never showed you that place; then you would be playing with me."

She whirled, ducking as she did so, and slid behind Caritha. As she brought her sword toward her sister's throat to end the swordplay Caritha spun around and they crossed blades.

The red-haired fairy pulled his wand out and toyed with it, sending random colors from its tip in the form of smoke. "I liked you better, fairest of the dragon's daughters, before you grew up. Don't you ever—" he squealed with startled delight as Caritha's blade sliced through the air above his head. "Don't you ever want to play with me again?"

"Miverē," she said between parries, "I'm a little busy at the moment."

He sighed aloud and drooped his head.

Focusing on the contest, Dantress felt the power of her dragon blood surge. She directed her will into driving her sister back. Her blade glowed momentarily and a wave of blue energy struck Caritha. But her sister closed her eyes, and Dantress's assault evaporated against her blade. A bolt of energy shot from Caritha's sword and smote Dantress in the chest. She fell to the ground. Miverē rolled into the sand. Caritha held the tip of her blade gently against Dantress's throat.

Withdrawing the blade, Caritha held out her hand to assist her to her feet. "Give up!"

"All right, you win." Dantress accepted the other's assistance and then brushed the sand off her dress. "I guess that makes us even."

"If you count last night's challenges? Yes." The corners of Caritha's mouth betrayed a faint smile. "Dinner will be ready shortly. Gwen told me to remind you of that."

"I'll be along in a moment, I need to talk to Miverē."

Caritha sauntered through an exit door and left it open behind her.

"Miverē?" Dantress scanned the sand floor, but found nothing. She looked at one of the massive exit doors in time to see it close behind the green-clad little creature. Poor thing, he was so easily slighted.

She shouted after Caritha, "I'll be late for dinner. Tell Elsie, will you?"

"Of course." The eldest sister returned and closed the door.

Brushing sand from her skirt, Dantress set off after her little winged friend. It took a little while to locate him. He'd gone to the library and wedged himself between a book *Astronomy: Impractical Applications* and a large scroll yellowed with age. As she approached he stood and leaned against the book. His green eyes were bleary and red. Twin tears threatened to overflow his eyes.

"Miverē, what's wrong? Are you crying?" She reached up and held out her hand so that he could climb onto it. Both tears rolled down his face as he plopped into her palm. He folded his wings down his back, wiping a fresh tear from his eye.

She dropped into the plush cushions of an easy chair next to the warm blaze in the fireplace. Fall had arrived and the weather had been cool of late.

"There now"—she held the fairy to her bosom and stroked his bony back—"tell me. What has made you cry? I wasn't trying to ignore you in the armory, but if my silence hurt your feelings then I'm sorry . . . I really am."

"Oh, it is not that, fairest of the dragon's daughters! I do not cry because you were unkind for you are never unkind, but fair and gentle. For this I love you as my best and trusted friend."

"Then what is wrong? Something must be, or else you would not be crying."

The fairy accepted her handkerchief, drying his eyes and blowing his nose with a corner of it. "I was in the throne room this afternoon, cleaning the drapes, when the shepherd and the dragon entered." He drew in his breath. "Is it true that you are going away?"

"Yes, I suppose so. Father wants us to be ready first; he wants us to understand the swords intimately before we do anything *and* he wants us to be able to work as a team. So we will not be leaving soon."

Blowing his nose again, Miverē shook his head. "The great white dragon told the shepherd you are ready, that you are *all* ready. But, but he said that your first mission will be difficult, a lot more difficult than he had planned on assigning you to."

"Well, Miverē, I am not afraid to go. I am a daughter of the dragon, and he will watch out for us—"

"But he said things, terrible things, things that sounded like prophecy. You must not go! I beg you, stay in Shizar Palace where you will be safe. I don't want to lose my best friend!" After this the little fellow started to cry again.

She stayed with him for the next half hour, telling him not to worry but to have faith. "Do you really believe my father would send me if he didn't think it was for the best?"

"N-no, I guess not."

"Well, there you are then! Don't worry, I'll be careful. Besides"—she smiled—"the Creator watches over all His creatures. He will be with me wherever I am."

The fairy stood and flew to her neck where he embraced her. "Be safe, fairest of the dragon's daughters."

Kissing the fairy's forehead she rose from the chair. "Come on. Let's go exploring . . . in the basement. You've always said the rumors of sublevels in the palace are true."

"But isn't the basement forbidden to us? Besides, I have no proof; no evidence that such secret chambers were built—"

"Ah," she interrupted him. "But you were right about the chamber with the swords. Besides, Father never forbade me to go down there. I've heard him tell the maids not to clean down there, but he's never said anything to me or my sisters."

Miverē's face broke into a gleeful, extra-broad smile. "Then let's go. Oh, but first, I left my lantern at home."

⧲ ⧲ ⧲

The Fairy Tree's branches spread above Dantress, and the glass dome far above in the palace roof allowed her to see the lightning zipping through the storm clouds. This storm had lasted all day, an unusual occurrence . . . as was the absence of rain. With all the fuss that the storm put up a deluge should hit the palace at any moment. But none did.

Dantress touched one of the Fairy Tree's butter-soft branches.

Fairies, sitting in their family groups, covered the glowing branches. Every time lightning flashed they exclaimed in unison, "Ooh!" Then thunder clapped, and they cried, "Aah!" until it died away.

Four fairy families lived in Shizar Palace and all of them dwelled inside the Fairy Tree. Miverē's family, the Bladegrasses, boasted the most members. A healthy rivalry existed between them and the next largest group, the Leaflets. Then there were the Clovers and the Stems.

The Clovers stood on a high branch, the men with their arms crossed and the women with their hands folded behind their backs. They were known to be a bit on the strict side, the males dominating more than a little. But they were faithful servants of the dragon and Dantress had seen them shoot recklessly down the halls on more than one occasion to answer his bidding.

Partiers by nature, the Stems came next. A merry group of about twenty of them sat on a branch halfway up the tree, their long gangly legs and distinctive green hair swaying with the movement of their bodies as they toasted each other's health and drank wine from tiny glasses.

On a lower branch sitting primp and proper were a dozen Leaflets, all female. To this family had fallen the blessing and the curse of short stature. Blessing because the male fairies of the other families found the petite females quite attractive, and a curse for the Leaflet males because they often found it difficult to woo females. Dantress stifled a giggle upon seeing one of them casting furtive glances at one of the Bladegrasses on a nearby branch. The lady fairy glanced back at the male from time to time, feigning disinterest and flipping her wavy hair behind her back.

According to the fairies their tree had once grown along the banks of a river called Eiderveis but the wizard Hermenuedis had built his temple of Al'un Dai very near that river and when his war on Subterran had begun the Fairy Tree stood in the midst of it. The great white dragon had pulled the tree—roots, fairies and all—and flown it out of harm's way, planting it in Shizar Palace.

Miverē popped out of a knot in the tree's trunk with his lantern, a happy smile on his face. She smiled back. It felt good to act like a kid again. She looked forward to exploring the palace basement. The great white dragon disappeared down there a couple times per year and, she hoped, she'd discover why.

⛑   ⛑   ⛑

Dank air clung to Dantress as she descended into the darkness. A shiver ran up her spine. Never before had she ventured into this place. True, it constituted a part of the palace, but what purpose it served besides supporting the main structure . . . no one had ever told her.

Miverē stood on her shoulder, the tiny silver lantern held in his outstretched hand. For her part, she held Xavion's sword and its blade glowed enough to reveal a few yards in all directions.

Every step she took, disturbed layers of dust on the stone floor. Visibility outside her circle of light equaled zero. She glanced over her shoulder, and noticed the fairy followed her lead. "We should make sure that we can find our way out of here," she said.

The fairy laughed. "I hope we get lost! This is fun."

"Rose'el would say that this is foolhardy." She looked into his glimmering green eyes, and laughed with him. "But you are right. This is fun."

He pulled out his glowing wand and pointed it behind them. A tendril of white light stretched from its tip, broke off, and wafted down to the floor, painting a glowing line in the direction they had come. Twice more he did this and, when the three strands lay together, they formed a distinct arrow. "There, now we won't get lost."

Slowly, Dantress walked forward. The floor appeared bare for a dozen feet or more, then the light exposed an old trunk. She saw a large chest beside it, and then another, and another. Rusted locks hung from each and every one of them, as if whoever had locked them had done so long ago and had never returned to examine their contents.

She ventured close to one of the smaller ones and tried to lift it, but it didn't even budge. The trunk had been made with wood but its boards were reinforced by bands of hammered iron. They wrapped over its lid and around its base. What could be hidden inside? Or, was it empty? Curiosity prevailed upon her and she pried at it with her blade. But the lid remained immovable.

Reacquiring her position via Miverē's last arrow, she faced in the opposite direction. She walked deeper into the basement. Spiders and other critters skittered out of her path. Cobwebs proliferated in the area. Miverē faithfully twisted on her shoulder, from time to time, to drop glowing arrows in her wake.

The chests and trunks continued to unveil themselves in the darkness. Only they appeared progressively more ancient. Certainly they grew larger. One of them she could have stood in.

Rounding a bend in the path between stacks of chests, Dantress came face to face with a bat hanging from one of the trunks. She screamed. The small creature opened its eyes and snapped at her with its fangs. It fluttered its leathern wings, dropped from its resting place, and flew off.

She slowed her breathing and nervously laughed. Miverē emerged from behind her neck. He cleared his throat and shivered his wings.

"Fairest daughter of the dragon, do not do that again."

Patting her hammering chest, Dantress breathed deeply and exhaled. "Have you had enough for today? Should we go back? Dinner will be ready—"

"But we have only begun," he said. "What about the sublevels?"

"Do you think there really are sublevels?" She didn't expect a definitive answer. The fact that the dragon came down here from time to time had to mean something of interest brought him. But what could it be; the old chests? Or, maybe what was inside them?

Miverē hadn't answered her question. Out of the corner of her eye she saw him scanning the dust and rust-covered chests with his eyes.

"You know"—she stepped over a small metal box lying on the floor—"I overheard Elsie telling Helen and Gwen that there are deadly creatures hidden in the sublevels. She thought that was why Father forbade her to clean this place. The creatures, according to her, guard something; something they've been watching over for *hundreds* of years." She shook her head. "It sounded like fiction, but what if it is true?"

She stubbed her foot on a broken band of twisted steel that had escaped her notice. She kicked it aside. "You are too quiet, Miverē." Then she lowered her voice and glanced about. "Everything is quiet."

After several moments, Miverē nodded. Barely above a whisper, he said, "Everything is *too* quiet. I haven't seen any insects for the last half-hour, nor have I seen any more bats. I don't like

bats, fairest of the dragon's daughters, but they should be here . . .
Maybe we should go back."

He shivered and leaned forward, holding out his tiny lantern
toward the darkness ahead.

Dantress stopped. "All right, we'll go back. If sublevels exist
then they have been well hid. This place is a little too fascinating
for my nerves."

The fairy offered no objection, so she pivoted on her foot,
intending to retrace her steps. But her foot shifted over a portion of the floor that felt like wood and that sloped down. She
slipped, cried out, and fell backward. She somersaulted down
the ramp and hit her head. A headache split her vision for a few
seconds. Letting go of the sword, she held her face in her hands.
The sword's light dimmed, and went out.

By some miracle, Miverē had managed to stay on her shoulder. The silver lantern glowed beneath his fist. It was their only
light and an inadequate one at that. "Are you hurt?"

She shook her head and groped for her sword. "Where are
we, Miverē?"

"It cannot be the basement." He shook his head. "That is
above us now."

"Then this must be . . . a sublevel? Miverē, we are *below* the
basement! The rumors are true." Suddenly realizing how loud
she'd spoken, Dantress hushed her voice. "I don't want to find
out if there are creatures, too." Her fingers touched the cool metal
of her sword's guard. She found the handle and drew it toward
her. As the blade glowed in the darkness, she stood shakily and
faced the direction they'd come. "Let's get out of here."

A rasping voice spoke from behind. "Leaving so soon? I
think not!"

Three long, clawed fingers dug into her shoulder. She
screamed and another three-fingered hand reached out and

snatched at Miverē. He fluttered out of reach and pricked one of the fingers with his wand. It drew back. He landed on her shoulder, holding his wand like a sword, and pinned his lantern to her collar.

The first hand still held her with undeniable strength.

"Release me!" Dantress rolled forward, almost throwing Miverē off. But he held on. She spun to face her unseen assailant. The sword brightened as she gripped it with both hands, and begged it for more light.

Someone chuckled; that same raspy voice. "What is this: a rusted sword, in the hands of a young female human, and a fairy to fight by her side?" The unseen creature laughed. "What do you intend to do? Kill us perhaps?"

"Not if you intend us no harm."

The creature laughed again. Its feet patted the floor, moving away from her.

"If you harm me you will answer to my father," she warned.

Two lithe, lizardian forms towered out of the darkness and rushed her from either side. They moved so fast that she did not catch a glimpse of their heads, but two clubs swung at her. She ducked. The clubs cracked against each other. Splintered wood rained on her hair. "Miverē"—she clenched her jaw—"hold on to me."

Dantress swung her sword at her assailant's soft-scaled underbelly. It pulled into the darkness before her blade struck. She thrust the blade uselessly. A bony black tail swept toward her. She ducked to the floor. The tail cut the air where her body had been and she stabbed upward. The glowing blade loped off two feet of tail, and one of the creatures rasped out a scream. The tail fell to the floor and twitched ineffectually. How glad she was for the hours upon hours of sword practice Albino had insisted upon.

"How dare you," a voice rasped from the darkness ahead. "You will pay for that, human!"

A broad, scaled chest penetrated her circle of light. Four clawed hands swept across the side of her head and two smote her in the stomach.

She doubled over, falling to her knees, and gasped for breath. Her sword clattered to the floor. Darkness crept in.

Miverē screamed and shot off her shoulder. Threads of energy bolted into the darkness. He furiously sprayed the bolts in all directions.

A leathery foot slammed into Dantress's chest. It pressed her against the floor. Sharp nails or claws dug into her chest. Warm blood ran from her cheek where one of the creatures' fists had rubbed it raw. Fear filled her heart and she prayed to God for strength. "It's going to be all right, Miverē." She forced the fear out of her tone, hoping to calm him. He alone, being small, had a chance to escape.

Miverē grew frantic. His toothpick wand waved wildly. In blind rage he charged the foot pressing down on her. But a claw hooked his wing in mid-flight. He cried out as if flames burned his very soul.

"You should not have interfered, little fairy." It was difficult to see by the light of the fairy's wand, but one of the creature's fingers appeared to wrap around Miverē's torso. Purple blood oozed from his fragile shoulders.

The blood within Dantress's veins began to boil. A volcano of rage built, demanding to be released. "No!" Her arm found new strength. She reached for her sword and took it. "You will harm him no further!"

New sensations raced through her body. And, as if out of a dream, she heard a voice in her mind say, "The day has come to see what you were made to be: a chosen seed of an ancient race."

Her arm glowed with white light. She followed an instinct she had not found before. She obeyed its pull and shoved the foot off her chest, pain spiked her ribs, and her consciousness retreated into her mind.

The creature tumbled back into the darkness.

Dantress stood and the light of her sword revealed the long, sinewy arm of Miverē's captor. She did not physically strike out. Instead she focused her thoughts on making the arm release him. A thin beam of energy burst from her sword hand. Her sword clattered back to the floor. She did not retrieve it.

The flow of energy from her hand sizzled against the creature's arm. Tentacles of energy entwined around the arm and spread up it.

"What? Im-impossible!" The creature dropped the fairy.

Dantress darted forward and scooped up Miverē with both hands. He lay limp. His legs and arms dangled between her fingers.

For a moment, Dantress thought she would faint. She stumbled and picked up her sword. Tears stung her eyes. "Hold on, Miverē. I'm going to get you out of here."

❃ ❃ ❃

Dantress never knew how she managed to haul herself and the fairy out of the palace's basement. She slammed the door shut behind her and leaned against it. Some of her energy returned, but she felt strange, different. Instead of sensing only what her physical body felt, she sensed everything around her. Inanimate objects felt connected to her somehow and her spirit felt more than refreshed; it felt as if it had been resurrected to a new plane of existence.

Concentrating on a jar standing against the wall, she touched it with her mind. Its molecules seemed so pliable, so easy to manipulate. She separated them, closing her eyes to better focus. When she opened them, all that remained of the jar was a pile of broken clay.

If she could repair it . . . She closed her eyes and again reached out with her mind, picturing the jar whole. When she opened them, it stood again as it had been; against the wall, and unbroken.

If she could use her mind to fix it . . . things, maybe, just maybe—

Miverē was dying. She reached into his body with her mind and touched his life force, and sensed it ebbing away. The creature had damaged most of his internal organs and he was bleeding internally. His bright green eyes dimmed, his eyelids gradually closing in the sleep of death.

Should she try her new ability on him, on a living subject? What if she failed? She would not be able to forgive herself if she caused his death. But she knew that was nonsense. If she did nothing then he was going to die.

She tore her dress and hurriedly made a bed, laying him in it on the marble floor. His chest heaved a final time and she reached her hand toward him. His life force slipped farther away . . . If she could just grasp hold of it, take it, feed it with her own life before his left him, perhaps he'd have a chance.

Through the darkness that shrouded the little creature she searched for that final shred of life and found it, like a spark in the night. She connected with it, drawing on the love that she had for the creature and infusing it into him. She could see the damaged organs now, oozing purple blood. The life residing in the blood, flowing from his body.

She reached out with her hand and half-opened her eyes. Her hand glowed and a beam of white-blue light fed from it into the fairy's chest. One by one she healed his organs and stopped the bleeding, while still maintaining her hold on his life force. As the process progressed, she felt faint, her vision blurred, and she knew that she had done all she could.

Sleep took her and a dream wrapped her in its hazy fabric.

A man stood on the opposite side of a pool of water surrounded by forest near a small clearing. A waterfall cascaded down the face of a rock into the pool. She tried to see the man's face. There was something about him, something that made her want to know who he was and why he stood there. But the dream faded, and she heard the voice of Patient, the shepherd.

"She of both races, gifted with heavenly beauty and fierce in strength."

In place of the pool and the man, Dantress found herself standing in a large, smooth-walled room, reverberating with a myriad of colors. A scroll nestled in the center of the room, and upon it had been written her full name. Not the name by which her sisters and those around her knew her, but another name given to her by her father, the great white dragon. Beneath her name was the name of another, the name of a child. "Oganna." As soon as she said it, she fell back as if stunned by an invisible opponent.

"It is given to humanity to bear children after their kind," a melodic masculine voice said. "Yet to the daughters of the great white dragon will be given the choice of joining with the race they resemble, the race of humanity. Their lives they must willingly give if they are to bring a life into the world. This curse is laid upon them, but it is a blessing in disguise. For in ultimate sacrifice is proven the ultimate love and a child born out of ultimate sacrifice will bring joy and not sorrow to the one that bears her."

Was this a dream? It felt too real to her. She stood and watched the walls around her, and the scroll in the center of the room, vanish. A black void imprisoned her and a stone chamber, filled with raging flames, burst forth. A two-handed sword rose through the flames. The sword's guard appeared to be semi-transparent, like a crystal, and a thin gold vine wrapped it then passed below to the handle, reinforcing the leather gripping underneath.

It was a magnificent weapon, unlike any she had ever seen or heard of. Flames writhed beneath the shiny steel blade's surface. They fought against the steel and pierced it, twisting out of the blade to wrap around it. This sword seemed to be in command of fire, rather than an agent of it.

"I am the weapon of the ancient and wise One. I came from the ends of the world, and I will arise a weapon of living fire to vanquish the wicked. I speak to you, daughter of the dragon, for you are the child of promise, and it is to you that my prophecy is addressed. Understand what I have said and consider the wisdom that I give you.

"This life you have been given and a path to humanity you will follow. But the day will come when you will desire more and you will have to decide whether or not you are willing to pay the price of ultimate love. Your sacrifice will seed a new race, humanity born of dragon and human blood. Or your life will follow a vastly different course and, eventually, lead to the end of the world and all that is dear to you.

"Remember my instruction, daughter of the dragon. Remember my warning: a life you may bring into the world, but the price of that life is your own."

The weapon receded from her, engulfing itself in flames. Everything vanished and she drifted back onto the plane of normal existence . . . where dreams were part of sleep.

⁜   ⁜   ⁜

"Out! Out! All of you! Gracious me, I've got a sick girl on my hands and the presence of you five is not helping matters. Out, I say!" Dantress, groggily stirring from her strange sleep, heard the patter of her sisters' feet as Elsie closed the door after them.

The woman snapped her fingers, remembering something. She opened the door and called down the hall. "Gwen, bring me more of that herbal cream. Dantress still has a few scratches, and I don't want her skin to scar."

"M'st certainly!" Gwen's muffled voice replied. "I'll get it right away, Mum."

"And bring my apron while you're at it." Elsie closed the door. "Dantress, you're awake? No, no! Don't get up," she pushed Dantress's head back to the pillow. "You've been unconscious for two days, so you had better take it slow."

"Miverē . . . how is he?"

"Fully recovered, my dear. No need to worry. He's been at your bedside almost every hour for the past couple days. Keeps insisting that you saved his life and that he's at fault for what happened to you."

"What?" Dantress sat up.

Elsie pushed her back down with a gentle hand. "We know the fairy isn't to blame, Honey. And the dragon has commended him for his quick actions on your behalf. Miverē came to him very shortly after you collapsed, and he led us to you."

Relieved, Dantress let out a long breath. "Good, I was afraid Father would be angry."

"Angry with the fairy? No. With you, on the other hand . . . Well, that may be an entirely different story."

The door opened, and Gwen hurried in. "Here's the cream, Mum. Oh, and your apron." She smiled at Dantress. "Your

Highness! It is good to see you awake." She grinned and bowed low. "Are you feeling better?"

"Thank you, Gwen. I'm feeling weak, but fine otherwise."

"Well you look wonderful, and the color is coming to your cheeks."

"Out with you, girl." Elsie shooed her toward the door. "You can discuss things with Dantress later. *When* she is back to full strength." She closed the door behind the taller woman and shook her head to get her straying red hair out of her eyes.

"You will have plenty of time to talk later, young lady. For now I want you to try to get more sleep."

Smiling weakly, Dantress closed her eyes. "Thank you, Aunt Elsie. Thank you for everything."

"Go to sleep."

⚞ ⚞ ⚞

It took Dantress a week to fully recover from her ordeal in the basement. Miverē visited her frequently. "Once, fairest of the dragon's daughters, you were only my best friend. Now I owe you my life."

On the first day that she was up and about the palace, Dantress wandered into the library. The dragon lounged there, an enormous scroll set before him on an appropriately sized table. "It's good to see you up, my daughter. Your pallor yesterday concerned me. Last week you gave us quite a scare."

She hung her head. "I'm sorry, Father. It was my idea to explore the basement. I know you forbade others from going there, but—" She searched for an explanation then, finding nothing adequate, shrugged her shoulders. "I have no excuses. I have always wanted to see what is down there, and the rumor of a sublevel to the palace, or more than one, has intrigued me from childhood. With Xavion's sword in hand I thought nothing would happen. I was wrong."

The dragon cocked his head to the side, allowing a curious moment of quiet to endure before he responded. "Very well, I forgive you." He returned to reading the scroll.

Dantress stood still, not wishing to leave but knowing that he expected her to.

"Was there anything else, my child?"

Hesitating for a millisecond, she nodded her head slowly. "What is Living Fire?"

The dragon jerked his head to look at her, amazement showing on his elegant, bony face. He stepped away from the table and focused his penetrating gaze on her. "Living Fire, the power of an ancient and most powerful and wise prophet. You have heard of it . . .? It is a secret not yet revealed to the world. Tell me, what has happened. How do you know of this?"

Leaving out no details, Dantress told him of her dream. As she told him about the sword, his eyes widened and yet a smile almost broke his rigid face.

"Not lightly does the Living Fire speak, my daughter. Listen and believe what it has told you."

"Then it wasn't only a dream?"

"Oh no," he rumbled. "Not a mere dream, but a glimpse of the future." He eyed her up and down. "Something else happened to you that day. Am I not correct?"

"Well, I . . . I struck down a creature in the basement."

He leaned closer. "This much I know, but what is it you wish to tell me?"

"Father, I used no weapons to win that battle. I threw some kind of energy from my body, through my hands. And later, when Miverē was dying, I healed him with the same energy. It was like seeing inside his body and being there to tend to him. I can't explain it."

The dragon drew back his head and laughed a strong, gloating laugh. "The child of promise you truly are, my daughter! This proves it. My blood runs through your veins, as it does through your sisters." He lowered his head to gaze into her eyes. "But in you my blood has taken deeper root. Now you are ready to begin the task for which I made you, the task that you accepted when you took the sword of Xavion.

"Fetch your sisters! The time has come for you all to put your swords to good use."

SPECTER

Dantress fidgeted under the great white dragon's passing gaze. He impatiently tapped his claws on the marble floor. His pink eyes were fixated on the massive double doors behind Dantress. They'd been waiting like this for over an hour, her with her sword in hand—as he'd instructed—while he stood on the dragon throne.

Expectancy filled her heart and mind. What did the dragon have in mind for her and her sisters? He looked eager, almost as much as she felt.

The double doors swung into the room. Caritha and Laura marched inside ahead of Rose'el, Levena and Evela. "Ah, at last, you are all here." The dragon roared with satisfaction. "Come closer, my daughters."

The five sisters joined Dantress. She turned her eyes up the gargantuan steps to Albino's twisted metal perch. A strip of white cloth ran from the top of the steps to their base. Albino's powerful claws scraped the reflective metal, digging deeper into previously formed gouges in his Roost. Light rippled through his white scales.

"A mere three months away are your seventeenth birthdays." The dragon hunched forward, every one of his sharp white teeth showing as he rumbled his satisfaction. "Years ago I told you of the Six and how five of them betrayed me. Their swords are now in your possession and I have observed that you learned how to use them well. And so I have arranged a task for you.

"Here in this palace, in the land of Emperia, I have sheltered you from the cruel world that lies beyond my borders. It is a vast place with beasts and men that will destroy you, my treasures, if you are not prepared for them.

"The Accursed Three walk the world of Subterran as men that have fallen into darkness, and their evil will spread into every dominion if they are not stopped. Therefore I am sending you into the south and to the west, across a sea. On its southern shores flows a river called Eiderveis. When you reach it you may find human settlements . . . but you will not stop—even to rest—because you do not know where their loyalties lie.

"You will search along the river's eastern shore until you find a cottage. Being that the cottage is the only one on that side of the river you will easily find it. There you may stay without fear, for I know the tenant of that place. She is a trusted and old friend. This same individual knows what you must do. Listen to what she says and do as she instructs you."

Dantress looked at the floor. "You will not be coming with us?"

"No, my daughter. You, Caritha, Rose'el, Evela, Levena and Laura must perform this task."

The color drained from Evela's face. "Would it not be better if you came along?"

"Evela, there are things that I am not free to tell you, things that *prevent* me from joining you on this quest. Trust me! It is better that I do not go."

"But, but why?" Evela wrung her hands.

"Do not question things that have already been determined, my child. Stay close to the others and rely on their strengths to outweigh your weaknesses. Together you are capable of more than you realize."

Caritha stepped from the line of her sisters and looked solemnly at the dragon. "We will go as you ask, without question."

A resigned sigh escaped from Rose'el's lips. She shook her head but shrugged her shoulders. "When do we leave?"

"Tomorrow morning. After breakfast," Albino replied.

"We'd better get some sleep then," Rose'el muttered under her breath.

Dantress looked at all her sisters. They did not appear afraid, yet their faces clued her in on their misgivings.

The dragon leapt from his perch and stood over them. Flexing his membranous wings he led them out of the throne room into the main hall. From there he brought them to their bedroom and, bidding them sweet dreams, left them. But they sat awake, wondering what tomorrow would bring.

⊘ ⊘ ⊘

A roar of applause rolled over Dantress and her sisters as the massive doors of Shizar Palace opened inward. They walked out onto the sunlit stone path and their eyes followed its gentle curves as it wended through the masses of creatures standing on the lush, green fields that covered the slopes down to the mountainous region in the west.

She and her sisters curtsied and smiled at their audience. Bears, antelope, deer, lions and birds of confusing variety all mingled in peace. Moose swaggered forward, clearing a path with their antlers. They bowed and then stood at rigid attention in a long line, several hundred strong, their brown chests sticking out pompously. Dantress caught one of the moose's eyes looking at her. It winked.

The ground shook beneath her feet. A seemingly endless procession of brown mammals emerged from the forests to the east, plodding toward the palace. Long, curving tusks shone white in the sunlight, and a steady wind toyed with the long hair covering their bodies. Trunks swayed with the steady movement of their hulking bodies. The moose stepped aside for the mammoths. The largest of the new arrivals dipped his tusks toward Dantress and her sisters.

"Daughters of the great and mighty dragon," a bull mammoth trumpeted, drumming his forefeet on the ground, "upon a journey you now embark, and on foreign soil you will be tested." The mighty creatures continued to gather behind their spokesman, and Dantress could see no end to their number. "Be true to one another, be true to yourselves, daughters of the dragon. Trust no one who is a stranger to the white dragon." He stood still.

The sisters looked up as a shadow covered them. A hush fell upon the creatures. The great white dragon walked through the doors, setting each foot firmly before the other as he strode down the path. He raised his head high, the ridges along the back of his long neck stood stiff, the scales along his body reflecting the sunlight in all directions, making him ghost-like.

"Come, my daughters! This is a day that the creatures of my kingdom will remember forever. Hold your heads high and follow me. The warriors of the past await us!"

The warriors of the past? Dantress suppressed her urge to question. Instead she followed the dragon down the path. She was of royal descent, a princess of Emperia, so she held her head high.

They passed down the green slopes to the west and approached a mountainous region. The masses of creatures followed them to the base of the first mountains, then they stood still and watched the dragon and his daughters depart in silence.

When they had left their audience in the distance, Dantress tried to catch up to her father. But the dragon leapt over boulders that she was forced to climb and soon he had proceeded a good distance ahead of them. A couple hours later he leapt onto a boulder and spread his wings. He reached them into the still air and a gust of wind broke the calm. He lifted into the air, pulling the enormous rock with him as he clutched it with his claws. Speeding up a smooth mountain slope, he angled toward a cave far up its face.

"Is he leaving us?" Evela looked for reassurance from her sisters.

Rose'el harrumphed. "It sure looks that way—"

"Listen to me, both of you," Caritha nearly shouted, pointing a finger at Rose'el. "Father would not leave us alone without good reason. Come on!" She ran after the dragon, who waited at the distant cave.

The sisters followed Caritha up the mountain slope. Everyone except Rose'el refused to complain as their back and leg muscles began to ache from ascending the steep incline. Rose'el muttered unintelligibly under her breath, but even though Dantress could see that she wasn't happy about the situation she noted that Rose'el outdistanced the rest of them and her mouth set in a determined line.

※ ※ ※

The cool mountain air coupled with an encroaching fog that limited visibility to no more than a dozen feet. Dantress looked at her hands, raw from grabbing rough stones and pulling herself upward. But she determined to go on and continued the climb. When she at last grabbed hold of the ledge before the cave entrance, Albino loomed before her and looked down. A grin spread across his bony face.

Her sisters sat on different stones around the entrance. Evela took the opportunity to rub her feet. Rose'el and Laura massaged their hands. Caritha sat quietly with hands folded on her lap. This seemed the moment for the dragon to speak. But when she glanced up at him, his pink eyes blinked.

Then, slowly, the truth dawned on her. This is a test. "Isn't it?" she asked aloud.

Albino merely looked down at her, his pink eyes shining.

"It's a test. It's a test!" She smiled in spite of her pain and turned to her sisters. Closing her eyes she reached out with her mind, probing their aches and pains. Of course! She should have realized. In a moment it all became clear and the power she had discovered that day in the palace basement surged within her.

She opened her eyes. Her hands glowed blue, almost blinding bright. Leaning first over Rose'el, she touched her shoulder. A portion of the energy building within her hands left her body through her fingers and passed into her sister.

Rose'el stood up, almost knocking Dantress over. "How did you do that?" She turned her hands over and displayed them, fully healed, to the rest of the sisters. They gathered to Rose'el and, one by one, allowed Dantress to touch them and heal them.

"Now it is your turn, our sister," Evela said. "Sit down." Dantress sat down, but though Evela tried she could not perform the same miracle for her. "I don't understand," Evela stood back and looked at her hand. "I could feel the power that you imparted. I should be able to—"

"No!" Caritha beamed as understanding dawned on her. "We five are joined through the swords. Don't you see?" She drew her rusted weapon and touched its blade to Dantress's shoulder. "Alone we are weak! But together we are strong!"

Laura, Evela, Rose'el and Levena drew their swords and touched them to Caritha's blade. A flash of blue temporarily blinded Dantress, but a warm sensation of healing, restoring energy surged through her body and testified to her sisters' success. Her hands no longer felt raw, her muscles no longer felt sore.

Together the sisters faced the dragon. He reached to his right, pushing the boulder that he had carried up the mountain so that it rolled back down, creating an avalanche as it gained momentum; it crashed into other stones and finally fell into a canyon where it broke into billions of fragments.

Albino swung around, his tail cutting into the cave wall. "Congratulations, my daughters. You have passed the test."

Caritha parted the fold in her purple skirt and slid her sword back into its scabbard. "Father, why is it that Dantress can use her power without joining with ours? What happens if one of us is separated from the others? We would be powerless."

"Nay, my daughter," the dragon rumbled. He raised one clawed hand and waved it at the fog, and the moisture raced away from him. "You are all of dragon blood . . . *my* blood. Each one of you will discover the power that that gives you, but only in time.

"Dantress will forever be different but you all have the same potential as she does. Strive to exercise justice with mercy and wield with wisdom the swords that I have granted you. By so doing you will learn the things that she has learned and move on to discover things you had never known were possible."

He entered the dark cave and they followed.

"I can't see my feet," Rose'el said.

"Use your sword." Dantress drew Xavion's weapon from beneath her skirt.

But the dragon's hand settled around her shoulders, and he spoke softly into the darkness. "There is no need of those while you are with me." To the sisters' astonishment the imposing form of the dragon glowed surreal beside them, and in that pure white light every step of their way stood out clear as if lit by the light of full moon.

They followed the dragon deep into the mountain, navigating the myriad of tunnels and caves concealed therein until he brought them to a white stone bridge, broad enough for the dragon and his children, spanning a raging underground river.

On the opposite side of the bridge, carved into the solid wall of stone, a door at least a hundred feet tall and shaped like a maple leaf, stood out.

Dantress and her sisters clustered close to the dragon and craned their necks to better see the intricate patterns of vines and flowers carved into the leaf's face.

"There's no need to be afraid, my daughters." He stood on his hind legs and rested his clawed hands on the door. His body resonated with light, glowing brighter and brighter until Dantress and her sisters shielded their eyes with their hands.

The dragon dropped back to all fours, rumbling deep in his throat. Soon the sound of stone grinding against stone pulled the sisters' attention back to the door. It fell away from them into a chamber beyond with an earsplitting crash that Dantress feared would bring the mountain down on their heads.

Dantress followed her father the dragon into the chamber. He gripped a blue marble pillar that reached from the floor to the arched ceiling some couple hundred feet above them and pulled, growling with the effort. It must have taken a lot of energy for the pillar was enormous, but it began to move silently upward until its base rose above floor level, revealing a sheet of glass concealed beneath it.

Albino ceased his efforts and the pillar stayed where it now stood on the vertical sheet of glass. The glass portion beneath the pillar fizzled with energy and the dragon sprayed a torrent of searing flames into it. A portal opened, unlike anything Dantress had ever imagined. She could see, as it were, to another place. A deep-blue sea lay to the right, and to the left stretched a sandy white shore with a river pouring through it.

"Behold the River Eiderveis, the beginning of your journey," the dragon said. "Its current is full of life, and it possesses a power that will decide the fate of an entire race.

"Search along the river's eastern shore until you find a cottage . . . it is the only one on that side of the river and you cannot pass without seeing it. There you may stay without fear, for I know the tenant of that place and she is a trusted and old friend. This same individual knows what you must do. Listen to what she says and do as she instructs you."

He hesitated, looking at each of them in turn. "Do not fear, Evela. I will be watching over you even when you cannot see me.

"Rose'el, listen to Caritha and Dantress. They have more wisdom than you know, but they will need your help if this mission is to be a success."

She stiffened and resolutely looked at the portal. "Yes, Father. I will."

"Very well, I believe you are all ready to begin your journey." He stretched his tail around them and looked at the back wall. Beams of light shot from his eyes and struck it, sending a shock that seemed to shake the mountain to its foundations. If his tail had not supported the sisters they would have fallen.

In several dozen places the chamber's wall opened and semi-transparent cylinders of various sizes slid out, resting like cocoons on the wall while a soft green light lit them from above.

"What are they?" Dantress recognized the shapes of human men and women along with various creatures inside the cocoons. Yet they were distorted by dark webbing that coated each of the cylinders.

The dragon looked dreamily at the collection suspended above him. His eyes roved from one to the next, and the next. His scaled chest heaved as he let out a long breath.

"Father? What are they?" Dantress glanced from cylinder to cylinder, half expecting a corpse to fall out.

"The mightiest warriors of history, my daughter," the dragon replied. "They wait for a future day when they will be awakened by One who will claim victory and reclaim this world from the wicked. Mark this moment in your memories, my children, and remember the glory that once was and the glory that has not yet come. Fight for the innocent and use your powers with wisdom; in so doing you may one day be remembered among the honored warriors of the past."

He roared and herded them toward the portal. It fizzled louder as they approached it. "Now, go, my daughters! Speak to no one until you come to the cottage of my ally and receive her instruction!"

Dantress felt herself passing into the portal. It was like sinking into jelly, slippery and cool. She shot out the other side and rolled on the ground. A wave crashed over her and pulled back, leaving her soaked from head to toe. She got to her knees and then coughed, tasting salt.

⚇ ⚇ ⚇

The man opened his eyes and reached out weakly for support, touching the cool glass angling away from his linen-wrapped-torso with his fingers. As he applied his full weight to the glass, it gave way beneath him. He tried to grab for something, anything, but fell forward. His eyes ached, his vision blurred. Tired, he felt very tired.

Dark webbing, thick and sticky, caught him as he fell and lowered him gently to the stone floor. He rolled on his side, squinted up, trying to see, then turned away from the bright window of energy fizzling before him. A portal to another place . . . it had to be. But where had he seen one of those before?

He propped himself on one elbow and then sat up. His mind was hazy and he felt—disoriented. As his vision cleared, the chamber's dark walls of stone rose around him.

With a snap and a fizzling sound, the energy portal closed down. Soft green light shone from above, illuminating the room.

Something behind him, slid over the stones. The floor shuddered under a great weight.

He looked over his shoulder, caught a glimpse of something long and white. Something was in here with him. Hurriedly he pushed himself up and tried to stand. But his legs, bound in linen, prevented him from maintaining his balance. He fell backward.

"Whoa there," a voice rumbled. A scaled hand caught him before he hit the floor and stood him up, keeping him steady. "Rest for a moment, my friend. Your body is weak from being in stasis for so long."

The man looked up, his vision had nearly cleared. "My master," he said, reverently lowering his eyes.

Albino dipped his head in acknowledgement and then reached over to the portal with his free hand, pulling down with great force until it slid into the floor, hidden again from sight, with the blue marble pillar resting on top.

"How do you feel?" the dragon asked.

The man held his hand against his aching head, "Confused."

"But you remember?" the dragon continued. "You remember . . . everything?"

"No, just bits and pieces." The man groaned as a head splitting ache pulsed through his brain.

The dragon looked hard at him and then put a clawed hand on his chest. A white glow seeped from beneath the dragon's palm. "That should remedy the pain."

The man straightened and nodded. "Thank you, yes. That is much better."

"Good." The dragon glanced behind the man. "Have you brought the items, my friend?"

Patient emerged from a dark corner of the room. His shepherd's staff tapped the floor once for every couple steps he took. Over his free arm draped a light gray fabric, and in the crook of his elbow he cradled a long, black-handled scythe.

"Does he remember?" the shepherd asked.

The dragon clicked his claws against the stone floor. "No."

The man stared at Patient. His gaze swept from the base of the shepherd's white robes, to his bearded face and blue eyes, then on to the hooked staff. "I know you. Don't I?"

"You did," the shepherd acknowledged.

"And who am *I*?" He waited for an answer.

Patient did not say a word. He merely set the staff and the scythe on the floor and held up the gray cloth. The dragon stripped off the linen wrappings and helped the man into trousers and a shirt that appeared to be made of the same material as the one the shepherd held.

When he had been clothed the man stretched his aching legs. The shepherd stepped up to him, lifting the cloth to attach it at the shoulder. Albino touched the fabric with the tip of his claw. When he withdrew it, a crystalline clip remained in its place.

The man ran his finger along the crystal and found the form of a fire breathing dragon sculpted thereon . . . He'd seen this before.

Patient lifted another portion of the cloth, holding it there until the dragon had similarly attached it to the man's outfit.

"Kneel down," the shepherd commanded.

Dropping to his knees, a bit unsteadily, the man felt the shepherd draw the cape's hood over his head.

"Now rise!" the dragon thundered. As he did so he shoved the scythe into the man's hand.

Standing, the man looked down at himself. His apparel appeared plain, yet elegant. It shimmered for a few moments, then vanished . . . and his body vanished with it.

"From this day forward," Albino said, gripping the blue marble pillar with his claws—and his pink eyes flared—"you will call yourself and be known as Specter." He hauled up the pillar and shot flames against the energy fizzling on the glassy surface until the portal opened.

Specter looked down at the shepherd. Then he knelt before him and the great white dragon. "I live to serve, my masters. Send me where you will."

"Then go," the dragon said, "and watch over my children, my six human daughters. They are young and inexperienced. I want no harm to befall them."

"And how, my master, will I recognize these young women? I do not even know who I am."

"Yet you *will* know them, Specter. And your memory will return to you ere this mission is over." The dragon stepped away from the portal. "We have given you all the tools that will be necessary for this assignment, and you are swifter on foot than most of my children; you will have no difficulty in locating them."

Specter rose, bowed to the shepherd and the dragon, and walked into the portal.

COTTAGE ON THE
RIVERBANK

Dantress swallowed enough salty seawater to make
her gag.

"Are you all right?" Caritha knelt beside her and
wiped the sand from her face with a dry handkerchief.

"Yes . . . I think so." She looked around. The mid-morning
sun shining on the white beach radiated heat through her clothes.
She wrung water from her hair.

Evela stood in the midst of the long silvery grass ten or more
feet from the shore and pulled a thorny barb from her skirt.
Rose'el and Levena, looking dazed, sat up and held their heads
as they looked at the trunk of the broad oak tree they'd struck.
Showing neither discomfort nor surprise, Laura walked slowly
from the shrinking point of light that had been the portal. The
point of light snapped and, an instant later, the portal vanished.

"Well, we made it." Caritha rose and smiled at her sisters.

Rose'el grunted, prepared to say something, but Caritha frowned at her and she said nothing.

The Eiderveis River, to the west, poured into the sea. Its water was the clearest sparkling blue that Dantress had ever seen, as if it ran over polished sapphires. She stood and walked the hundred yards or so to the river's bank, gazing southward. The shores of the Eiderveis River stretched like narrow bands of gold from the sea, cutting through the thickly wooded hills lying in that direction until they disappeared in the distance, heading toward a group of mountains whose dark peaks somehow reminded her of her narrow escape from the basement in Shizar Palace.

Laura pointed to the west along the seashore. Wisps of gray and black smoke rose into the still, cool air. "There is smoke rising from behind the trees in that direction." A line of flat stones rose from the river. She jumped to the first, then skipped from one to the next until she stood on the opposite bank. She glanced back at her sisters. "What are you waiting for?"

Caritha shook her head and held back Levena from following Laura across the current. "Laura, come back; Father said that we are not to speak to anyone until we find the cottage on the river's *eastern* bank. Come quickly, for I think we should head south as quickly as possible. That way we may avoid contact with the residents of these parts. Be they friendly or not we should stick to the river's bank."

"What makes you think we need to go south?" Laura asked.

Caritha raised her eyebrow and pointed at the sea, for it cut off any northward trek.

Casting a longing glance in the direction of possible civilization, Laura acquiesced. She skipped from flat stone to flat stone, back across the river and stood behind Dantress.

With Caritha leading the way, they set off at a brisk walk, following the river's broad golden bank. The sunlight angled through the trees that bordered the sand. A cool and gentle breeze blew over the river.

A remarkable, wide variety of trees comprised the forests. Oaks and willow trees, ash and hickory, walnut and some elegant but unknown varieties of bright colorations stood away from the river's bank. Pine trees with their needle-laden branches, stood together in small clusters. At one point, a line of tall white birches, their bark smooth, flawless, bent over the river's edge. Their reflections mirrored in the river.

Birds flocked to the trees' branches, twittering to one another and fluffing their feathers. Ruby red cardinals, vibrant blue jays and many, many others flitted through the branches, their songs filling the air.

Around a bend in the river, while Caritha walked a short distance ahead of her, Dantress spotted a larger bird, an eagle, turn its white plumed head. Its yellow eye followed their progress as it preened its brown body feathers and spread its wings to a full span of at least seven feet.

The eagle remained silent, testing the air several times before taking flight from its perch on an oak branch. Swooping straight toward her, it glided overhead and out of sight upriver.

The sun rose higher in the sky, until it was at the zenith. At Caritha's suggestion the sisters rested, sitting on a fallen moss-covered log. They had brought wafer cakes with them, prepared specially by Elsie, Helen and Gwen. These they retrieved from the small white-cloth pouches attached at their waists and ate slowly. Dantress allowed the creamy center to linger in her mouth while she chewed the rice and grain-encrusted outer portions.

From where she sat, she viewed the river and the surrounding landscape that was foreign to her. She chewed on the wafer cake, and watched the river flow. Its surface was unbroken, except for the occasional stone. But then she thought she spotted a gray-green dorsal fin pierce the river's current. It remained in view for only a moment, but she saw enough to know it was too large to be a fish.

Not knowing how to react, she turned back to her food. Just then another dorsal fin cut the water's surface. This time she felt certain of what she'd seen, yet it had disappeared and so she hesitated to say anything to her sisters. The water's gentle current rushed toward the sea, and its surface remained smooth.

"Come on," Caritha said, rising and beating some sand off her purple skirt. "I wouldn't want to be caught out here after dark." She started off, again heading south along the river's bank. The others followed, Dantress taking the rear. She kept one eye on the river.

The farther they progressed into the forested land, the more often she spotted the gray-green dorsal fins. "Evela," she said at last, pointing at a dorsal fin weaving through the water. "Look!"

Evela called for the other sisters to halt, pointing and shouting for them to take notice.

"What is it?"

They all stood still, trying to see what kind of creatures were out there. But the light reflecting off the water's surface hid the aquatic world from their eyes.

"It's nothing," Rose'el grunted and walked away.

Dantress and Evela held back for a short while as the rest of the sisters lost interest and continued on their way.

"What are they?" Evela whispered.

"I wish I knew . . . They certainly are not fish."

Evela giggled girlishly and prodded her in the side. "If they were a lot bigger I would say they are *mermaids!*"

"Mermaids? Don't be silly, Evela. Mermaids are a myth!" She gestured for Evela to follow her as she set off after her other sisters.

"You don't think they exist? Hmm . . .?" Evela wrung her hands. "There's a book about them in Father's library. *A History of Mermaidian Encounters* I believe it was called. With all the time you spent reading I'm surprised you didn't notice it."

Dantress laughed, putting her arm around her shorter sister's shoulders. "It is a rather large library. I doubt I'll ever read through every volume." She glanced at the river. "Anyway, mermaids would be larger and, I think, they'd live in salt water."

"Then you don't think it's possible?" Evela probed.

"No."

"Well, Dantress, you're entitled to your opinion. And *I'm* entitled to mine."

❧ ❧ ❧

Twice more on the journey down river Dantress spotted the eagle, or what looked like the same one. Each time it perched on a branch and stared hard at the procession of young women before taking flight.

It wasn't until evening that they spotted a break in the line of trees on their side of the river. There, nestled between two enormous oak trees, stood the cottage they sought.

Fragrant rosebushes and white lilies lined a stone path leading from the river's golden sand to the white front door of the structure, set not in the center of the wall but to the side. A lone, four-paneled glass window was centered between the door and the opposite corner of the cottage, its bulky flowerbox overflowing with blue poppies and phlox. A chimney rose from one end of the house.

Flowers of wide varieties and colors also carpeted the ground in the area around the cottage. Butterflies flew from flower to flower. Bees buzzed merrily as they collected the pollen and swarmed back to hollows in the two trees. A faint odor of honey, pleasantly sweet, drifted from the hives.

"What do you think?" Caritha asked no one in particular. "Should we wait for someone to notice us or shall we knock?"

Rose'el walked briskly past her up the path to the door. She drew her sword and gave the wood four solid raps with its pommel.

"Rose'el, what do you think you're doing?" Dantress shoved past Caritha and Laura as they also, with eyes wide, followed their bold sister to the door. "Rose'el, put that down!" She tried to keep her voice low but her tone firm. "What are you doing with that?"

"Relax." Rose'el sheathed her rusted blade and folded her outer skirt back over it.

It was none too soon, for the door opened a crack, and a wrinkled, friendly face peered out at them. "Eh?" the woman said in a cracking voice.

Dantress remembered her manners and curtsied. Her sisters did likewise. "Please Ma'am," she said "we are here on an errand from the great white dragon. He told us that you would shelter us."

Leaving the door opened a crack the old woman scanned their faces. "Servants of the dragon, eh?"

"Yes, he said—"

"What's the password?"

"The password?" Dantress and her sisters cast cautious glances at one another. "Ma'am, we don't have a password."

A grin wrinkled the woman's face even more, and she opened the door wide. "Good! I never could see the sense in using one of 'em passwords. Wouldn't make sense. Could be stolen and used against us. Eh?"

"I-I yes, I suppose you are right," Laura agreed.

Caritha smiled at the woman. "Then it was a trick, wasn't it? You don't have a password."

"Eh, I can see you are a smart one!" She pulled them inside. "Come, you look haggard! I already made your beds and your places at my table are set. Do you like goat's milk?"

Dressed in a dirt-encrusted skirt of an indistinguishable color and a pale green blouse, the old woman stood hunched, no more than five feet tall and maybe less. Dimming gray eyes peered at the sisters from beneath stray strands of long, thick silvery hair that she brushed behind one of her small ears. What appeared to be a fresh-cut flower stem had been stuck through her hair. Her feet, bare and browned, displayed nearly as many wrinkles as her face.

When she opened the door for them, they entered a cozily furnished sitting room. But she took Dantress by the hand, without introducing herself, and led her into the adjacent room which proved to be the dining room.

She beckoned to a wash basin set against the wall. An arched entry to a long, narrow hallway opened beside it. "There're towels 'round the corner, in the hallway," she said. "Wash your faces; freshen up."

Dantress found the towels and handed them to her sisters. They all peered down the hallway and whispered among themselves, surprised at how large the house seemed on the inside.

The old woman sat them at her table.

Rose'el elbowed Dantress and said under her breath, "There were only six towels and now there are six place settings. Do you think she knew we were coming?"

Dantress gave a slight shrug of the shoulders.

Their hostess hobbled into the room and pointed at a roost in the corner. The eagle Dantress had spotted on three occasions that day perched thereon, its eyes closed. She was surprised she hadn't noticed it before.

"Herbert informed me I'd be havin' company," the old woman sang out. "Liked you from the moment he saw you, or so he said. He's been a faithful companion to me. He's been with me for a long time, too.

"What would you like, Dearies? I've got goat's milk and cheese . . . and fish in the oven." She waddled over to open the ancient-looking grating over her fireplace oven. The sisters offered to help, but she insisted on serving them, pulling a pan of fish from the oven and setting it before them. "Help yourselves," she said. "There's enough for all of you, eh?"

Indeed, the portions proved more than adequate. The tantalizing smell of lemon and breadcrumbs almost made them forget their manners as they divided the fish into portions and set them on the seven plates arranged on the mahogany table. Dantress ran her fingers over the wood, admiring its rich color, and drew back her hand as a few splinters caught in her skin.

Pulling them out, she stuck her fork into the fish meat and tasted it. The flavor was even better than it looked. The old woman must have smothered it in butter.

The woman returned from her cupboard with a great big slab of cheese. Then she knelt, with difficulty, and opened a trap door. She reached into the opening and pulled out a frost-covered glass jug filled with milk.

"Ye ladies want some milk?"

They all nodded enthusiastically and took it from her to fill their wooden mugs.

Their hostess plopped into her wooden chair and ate as heartily as any of them. She spoke little, saying nothing except to respond to the sisters' praise of her meal and flowers. The sisters offered their assistance and cleared the table and washed the dishes in no time, after which she directed them down the hallway to their sleeping quarters. "The bedrooms are small, eh? But you will, each of you, have your privacy."

"Thank you for everything," Caritha said, bowing. "We really do appreciate all you have done for us, but—"

The old woman chuckled, "I could see the 'but' coming a mile away." She smiled and patted Caritha's cheek. "What do you want?"

"Well," Caritha said, "we came here because the dragon sent us and he told us that you would tell us what we are going to do."

"Patience, child! It never harmed anyone to sleep on curiosity, eh? Sleep tonight. Tell you I will, soon enough."

At first Caritha looked ready to press the issue. However, she must have decided against it. She bowed again, said goodnight and slipped into one of the bedrooms, closing the door behind her.

The others said goodnight, too, closing their doors behind them without a word. Dantress lingered in the hallway for a moment, for she heard the old woman sigh and felt a wave of disappointment emanate from her as she shuffled back down the hall.

"Wait!" Dantress ran after her, the old woman turned, and Dantress pecked her on the cheek and gave her a gentle hug. "I thought you'd like a goodnight kiss."

Tears welled up in the woman's eyes. "Bless you, dragon child. Bless you." She kissed Dantress on the cheek, then walked away with a new spring in her step.

Walking back down the hallway, Dantress found her bedroom and closed the door behind her.

An oil lamp flickered on the elegant dresser standing against one wall. Paintings of flowers hung on all four dark green walls. Hand-carved molding covered the lower half on all sides. A small bed rested to her left against the corner, covered with a hand-sewn quilt patterned in pink and blue. A white nightgown draped one of the bed posts.

She undressed, removed her sword with its sheath, leaned it against the end of the bed, and put on the gown. It felt as soft as down and as heavy as wool, warm and cozy. The lamp flickered again and she blew into its chimney, extinguishing the flame before curling up in the soft bed.

⚜ ⚜ ⚜

The next morning, Dantress sat on the edge of the narrow bed, Xavion's sword in her hand and the point of its blade resting on the floorboards. Stained and rusted by the blood of the innocent. Ever since she had acquired it, the sword had ceased to bleed on a regular basis, as had the swords her sisters received. Though she'd scrubbed the blade the rust had refused to be permanently removed.

What had the sword looked like before it had spilled—*wait!* The dragon had never told whose blood stained the sword of Xavion. Was there a part of the puzzle that he had withheld from her? But why would he do that?

Someone knocked feebly on the door. She left her sword on the bed and opened it. Her hostess waited outside with a warm smile.

"Sleep well?"

"Yes, thank you."

"Get dressed, eh? And come to breakfast. We mustn't delay; time should not be wasted."

A fly buzzed somewhere in the dim, windowless bedroom as Dantress closed the door and undid her nightgown. Her purple dress lay neatly folded on the dresser. Apparently the old woman had cleaned the garments while Dantress slept. She shook her head, at a loss to know how the woman had managed it.

After pulling the dress over her head, she noticed a mirror in one corner of the room. She moved in front of it to study her reflection. The extenuated dress sleeves draped over her wrists, extra fabric hung out beneath.

She pulled aside the outer skirt and reached over to the bed, taking the rusted sword and sliding it into the sheath. Doing that was not easy. The blade seemed to grow in size every passing year and it fit into the sheath with difficulty. But she at last succeeded and headed for the door. Time for breakfast.

✿ ✿ ✿

When breakfast had been cleaned off the table the sisters' hostess hobbled ahead of them into her living room. The brick fireplace filled the north wall and a low fire crackled, sending a narrow band of smoke up the chimney. A long sofa, uphol-stered in flowered cloth, stood against the west wall and under the window that looked out over the flower gardens to the Eiderveis River. Two other sofas occupied the room along with five high-backed chairs, two of them rested on either side of the hearth.

The cottage had appeared to be nothing more than a small structure from outside. Now, looking around at the interior, Dantress marveled at how much more there was than at first met the eye. After all, it had enough bedrooms to accommodate all of her sisters, herself, and the old woman. There was even a little stairway in the south end, and she would not be the least bit surprised if that led to more rooms.

"Sit, my dears, and I will tell you why you have come." The old woman waited until each of the young women sat down, and then she straightened her back and held her chin high.

"Many are the years that I have lived and many are the

things that I have witnessed. I am old, eh?" She glanced from one face to the next. "Aye, I *am* old and I have served faithfully the great white dragon for all my days and will do so until my dying breath. He it was that saved this world from the wizard Hermenuedis when no other being was left to stop him.

"I know what you are, daughters of the great white dragon! You are literally and fully dragon, yet born in human form. You have come to the shores of the Eiderveis River with the weapons of the Six, and you have come to deal with the first among those who escaped justice. His name is Kesla. He dwells in the ruins of the ancient temple, Al'un Dai. Were it not for him, the prince of Prunesia, young Brian of Millencourt, may have lived . . . as would Xavion, captain of the Six.

"There are three of the Six that number among the living, three Accursed Ones who must either turn from their wicked path and repent of their deeds or pay with their own lives. Letrias departed this region of the world ages ago. He is now beyond my sight. Auron wandered these lands, but he too left, and I know not where he has gone, though I suspect he followed Letrias, for he did always seem to esteem and follow him.

"You are here, daughters of the dragon, not to discover where these last two have gone. Instead you have been sent to deliver an offer of pardon to the man who even now dwells in Al'un Dai, but if he will not repent and turn from his wickedness then you are here to take his life with the very same weapons that he once used to betray innocent blood."

For a little while the sisters gaped at her. *If he will not repent and turn from his wickedness then you are here to take his life.* The line kept running through Dantress's mind.

At last Caritha stood and frowned. "You are asking us to go and find a man that we have never met and kill him? We aren't even seventeen yet!"

"Ah! If it is necessary then yes, Kesla must be dealt with, and you are the ones whom the dragon has sent."

"He didn't say anything about killing," Dantress stood, feeling a rush of heat pass up her back and flush her cheeks. "I don't want to kill anyone! Not even if he *is* a murderer."

"What would you do, child? Eh? Would you have your father kill the man, or would you have someone else do it? Or would you prefer us to do nothing and let evil continue to spread until every innocent creature, and every man, woman, and child are enslaved because of our inaction? No, justice must be served, and the dragon's judgment is final.

"If you are able to convince Kesla of his wrong, if he repents, then he will be pardoned. *But*," she added, raising her hand as Dantress let out the breath she'd been holding, "if the man will not turn from his wickedness then he must pay the price of his deeds."

Caritha walked over to the window and gazed out. Dantress watched her, keeping quiet so as to let her think. Several minutes passed before Caritha turned to face the old woman. "We will go to Al'un Dai, as Father wished, *and* we will find Kesla."

"Now you are seein' reason!" the old woman said.

"I did not finish," Caritha said. "When we find Kesla we will deal with him as seems best to us at the time, but we will not kill him unless he first attacks us. He will be brought to justice—we will see to that—yet we will not murder him. Instead we will bring him to Father for judgment."

"Judgment has already been passed on this man, my dear. He does deserve death."

"Yet, we will not kill except as a last resort," Caritha replied firmly. "If Father gives him death, then so be it."

"So be it." The old woman smiled, hunching over again, and hobbled to the door. She held it open. The fragrant scent of flowers blew inside with a warm and steady breeze. "Go down to the river and wait there until the water divides so that you may pass to the other side. Then head west through the forest.

"Watch your step; there are foul creatures lurkin' out there that will tear you apart if you give them the opportunity! The ruins of the dark temple of Al'un Dai lie in the west. You will find Kesla there . . . Take my warning, eh? Watch your step!"

Kissing each of them on the cheek the old woman held the door open until they left and then closed it.

Caritha led the way down to the Eiderveis. When they reached the water's edge, Dantress stood next to her. "What do you think she meant, Caritha? Wait here until it 'divides?'"

"I don't know." Caritha knelt on the golden sand. "Whatever she meant, I hope it happens . . . and soon."

They did not have long to wait. As Dantress gazed into the swift moving current, a dorsal fin, gray-green in coloration, cut the water's surface. Another soon followed and another . . . and then three more. All angled toward the river's bank. Others joined these until it appeared that the river swirled a mass of scaled fins. First one of the creatures and then another breached the water's surface, giggling as they rose out of the water.

"Did you see that?" Evela pointed, her eyes wide. "They are mermaids!"

Dantress could not deny it. The creatures had long hair and shining silver eyes. Scales covered the mermaids' miniature bodies. Oversized ears twisted back from their heads. Some of them had skin as black as night, while the faces of others looked as white as paper.

One little mermaid, her white teeth smiling from her black face, flipped high out of the water and onto the shore to lie on the sand at the sisters' feet. Resting on her elbows with her chin resting on her fists, she flipped her dark hair out of her eyes and looked up. "Greetings, children of the dragon," she sang in her smooth voice. "Stand back and let the Wee Mermaids open the Eiderveis River for your passage across."

The sisters retreated a step, Dantress last of all because she felt curious and wanted to talk to the creature. She kept her eyes on it as she backed up the bank. Evela had been right; mermaids did exist.

Swimming in a large circle, the Wee Mermaids laughed merrily. Their numbers increased, and a faint melody drifted over the water. The river swirled with them, a whirlpool forming in the space of half an hour.

Moving closer to the shore, the majority of the creatures maintained the whirlpool. Two of them slid onto the sand and flopped around, pointing with delicate fingers at the exposed riverbed in the whirlpool's center.

"Come on," Caritha said. She leapt from the shore and landed in the dry riverbed.

Dantress jumped after her and Laura followed. Levena went next, and Evela, closing her eyes, sprang after her.

"Jump, Rose'el!" The sisters beckoned to her.

She harrumphed. "I think we should have made a boat." But she leapt in and the Wee Mermaids, laughing still, gradually shifted the whirlpool across the river, which at this point was about a hundred feet broad.

An hour or more after, the sisters leaped onto the river's western bank. The Wee Mermaids slid onto the sand by the hundreds. As far as Dantress could see along the shore the creatures were slipping out of the water to lie in the sun. Their fins flapped lazily in the breeze and they closed their eyes.

One black mermaid—Dantress thought it might be the same one that had spoken to them earlier—remained on watch while her companions napped.

"Do you think it is safe for them to expose themselves like that?" Dantress said as she and her sisters walked west into the shade of the trees.

"I was wondering the same thing." Evela glanced over her shoulder. "They're rather adorable, don't you think?"

"Vulnerable and foolish," Rose'el murmured.

Suddenly they heard screams rising from the river. Racing back through the trees they saw, to their horror, one of the Wee Mermaids dangling from the talons of a hawk. The hawk's wings beat furiously, trying to gain altitude.

"Isn't that—?"

"Yes, I think it is!" Dantress reached out her hand toward the burdened bird flying over the river with the blood-streaked mermaid struggling in its talons. She breathed slow and deep, calming her body, then extended her senses, threading them past the varied emotions rolling from her sisters' minds. Her mind carried her past the thoughts of the agitated and horror-stricken mermaids, up into the sky. She could feel the Wee Mermaid's pain as it attempted to free itself from the bird's talons, managing only to rip her scales.

It would only take a twist of Dantress mind, a thought, to muddle the hawk's mind and send it crashing into the Eiderveis River. But as the threads of her thought bent around the bird, she detected—not merely hunger—but a consciousness, desperate and afraid.

Her thoughts latched onto the bird's mind. *Let the mermaid go.* She applied pressure to the bird's neck. *Let her go now and I will let you live.*

Something more than basic instinct, awoke in the hawk's mind. *No, no, please no! The water creature is mine, my chicks haven't eaten . . . don't hurt me!*

I have no desire to hurt you. She relaxed the pressure on the bird's neck. *But you must realize that I will not let you eat that mermaid. She is an intelligent being, deserving of life . . . not death.*

Please, we must eat—

Hunger is not a justification for your actions. Drop her now and I will spare you.

What am I going to feed my chicks?

She reached out with her mind and sensed the presence of a rabbit nibbling on some grass by the riverside. It had no intellect, only instinct. Sighing inwardly, she threaded her thoughts down through the air, latching them onto the creature.

Drop the mermaid, she said to the hawk. *You will find a freshly killed rabbit on the shore not far from here.*

You are strong and wise, dragon daughter—for I sense the source of your strength: you are dragon blood—I will do as you say.

Dantress opened her eyes. The bird dropped its victim. The wee mermaid somersaulted in the air and dove into the water.

"Whew, what a relief!" Evela exhaled slowly.

Caritha studied Dantress with a frown on her face. "Did *you* do that?"

"I told him to let her go."

"Him?" Her sister's eyebrows lifted. "Who did you tell?"

"The hawk, of course." When all five of them looked quizzically at her she realized and frowned. "You couldn't communicate with it . . . could you?"

"With a *bird*? Dantress, since when have you been able to do that?"

"Well, actually . . . this was the first time I used my ability to do anything like this."

Caritha shook her head in amazement. "Sometimes, your abilities trouble me, little sister." She walked toward the forest and gestured that they should follow. "Come on, we should get moving."

THE GREEN-BLOODED DRAGONS

Dantress stood near the base of a large dark tree, cloven from its highest branches almost to the ground. It reminded her of something out of a fable. Its two halves bent to the grass in the clearing, shaded now by the surrounding forest as the sun set. It had no leaves and its roots anchored it to the western edge of the clearing, guarding a broad trail leading into a thick growth of gnarled old trees.

To the right of the moss-covered tree gaped the hollow heart of a log of extraordinary size. It wouldn't have fit a dragon, but it would easily accommodate Dantress and her five sisters. The log extended out of sight into the forest, extraordinarily long. Darkness descended.

One by one, Caritha leading the way, the sisters entered the log and lay down to sleep. Their feet squished into the wood like a sponge, rotting and thus moist. But they felt safer here than leaving themselves exposed in the clearing.

The hoot of an owl startled Dantress awake, but only for a moment. As the air chilled she and her sisters huddled together for warmth. She closed her eyes. Somewhere beyond the trees, beyond this quiet forest, lay the ancient temple, Al'un Dai. She wondered what it would look like. Would the old warrior who had once been a member of the Six be waiting for them? Surely he would be. But. . . .

She sat up. Something didn't feel right. But what was it? Probing the vicinity of the clearing, she found no minds apart from those of her sisters. They were alone.

Wait! Levena's thoughts were racing a mile a minute, frantic and feverish. Should she intrude on her sister's mind? No! It wouldn't be right. She willed a question into Levena's mind. *Levena, what's wrong?*

Help . . . C-can not . . . wake up! I must w–wake up!

"Caritha! Rose'el! Wake up!" Dantress crawled over Laura and Evela, ignoring their startled protests as her knees and feet landed on their stomachs.

"Dantress, what are you doing?" Rose'el sat up. Even in the dim light of the moon within the hollow log Dantress could see the scowl on her face.

She reached Levena and slapped her cheeks. Levena inhaled in short, painful swallows, her eyeballs moved rapidly to the left and right; she had entered a deep sleep.

"Stand back!" Caritha's forceful words caused all of the sisters to do as she said. They stood away as she whipped out her now-glowing rusted blade and stabbed it toward Levena's left leg.

Dantress screamed along with her other sisters. "Caritha! What're you are doing?"

Caritha's blade never touched her sister's skin. Instead its point snagged a black object and pulled it away. "Foul creature," Caritha spat as she displayed the spider on her sword's point. Its hairy, inch-long legs clawed the air uselessly. Clear liquid dripped from twin fangs that showed above its shining black eyes as it wriggled on the metal.

"How did you . . .?" Dantress did not get to ask how her eldest sister had spotted the spider and how she had managed to react so quickly. Caritha raised her hand for silence and knelt to examine the bite. "It looks bad." She shook her head. "Really bad."

"Cut it open! Let the blood flow so that it can drain the poison." Laura drew her sword and approached.

Levena groaned and choked for air.

"Cut it?" Rose'el growled at Laura and restrained her with a hand. "With what?" She glanced at her sister's sword. "With a rusted blade? You would cause more problems than you'd fix using that."

"She's right," Caritha scraped the spider off her blade with her shoe, sheathed her weapon, and slid her arms under Levena's shoulders. She glanced around. "Well? Anyone want to give me a hand?"

They carried Levena outside and laid her in the grass. The damp air wetted Dantress's skin as they drew back from the prone form.

"Any ideas as to what we should do?" Caritha asked, looking from face to face.

Dantress knelt. A shiver ran through Levena's body. Her lips turned purple, her skin paled. She looked up to find Caritha stooping beside her.

Caritha slowly nodded, deep in thought. "You understand how to use our powers more fully than any one of us. If anyone can help her, you can." She stood and stepped back, waving her hand at Laura, Evela, and Rose'el. "Everyone be quiet and stay back. Give her space so that she can concentrate."

Perspiration broke out on Dantress forehead. They were counting on her to heal Levena, and she wasn't even sure she could.

She had to get a hold of herself. She'd saved Miverē when it'd seemed impossible. Maybe she could save her sister, too. Beating her fist into the ground she gritted her teeth. No. She couldn't just try; she *must* succeed.

She reached her hand to her sister's livid face. With all her might she probed her mind into her sister's consciousness, searching for the flame of life masked by death's cloak of despair. The blood racing through Levena's body, roared in her ears, begging her not to give up.

The spider's venom had succeeded in paralyzing much of Levena's energy and now fed off of her blood, using it to convey it to other parts of her body. If she could only stop the poison from reaching the heart, isolate it, perhaps, Levena might have a chance. The blood in Levena's heart, untainted by the arachnid's venom, responded to her mental probe and the dragon side in her sister reared up, promising to fight.

"I can feel it," she murmured, ignoring her sisters' intent gazes, "I can see with my mind's eye. The venom . . . ah! Yes, it is spreading. But not for long."

With her other hand she touched Levena's leg. The spider's fangs had penetrated the skin. Swollen tissue surrounded the minute wound.

Dantress closed her eyes, willing the energy within her to heal. It worked. Opening her eyes she saw her hand glow blue, sending a shock of energy into Levena that awakened her from sleep and revealed the foreign substance poisoning her. Instinct told Dantress to rise, so she stood, squinting in the bright light emanating from her palm, streaming into the bite.

Venom works its damage from inside of the body, so she left the wound open. The spider's poison needed to be drawn out. She concentrated on the energy making contact with the spider's fang marks—it was an extension of her own self—binding the venom with a vengeance.

The sticky poison still could not resist her pull and she drained it out of her sister's body bit by bit until she saw it swirling up to her hand. Attaching bit by bit like strands of pitch, the venom gathered above her palm, hovering inches from her skin until it formed a little black sphere.

Weariness suddenly overcame her. She stumbled to her knees. Her hand ceased to glow, and the energy stopped flowing. Her vision blurred. The voices of her sisters crying out with mingled relief and concern faded. Sleep, sleep . . . she must sleep.

❀ ❀ ❀

"Dantress!" Caritha caught her as her head lolled to the side and her eyes closed.

"Is she going to be all right?" Evela asked. She drew near and helped lay their sister beside Levena.

"I don't know," Caritha said. "Maybe she wasn't strong enough for this yet; she healed the fairy once, but this task was much larger."

"Humph! If this was beyond her abilities then Levena would be dead." Shaking her head, Rose'el crossed her arms as she stood looking down at the two unconscious members of their party. "Whatever she did, looks like it worked."

Caritha listened to Levena's labored, yet steady breathing. Rose'el was correct. Whatever Dantress had done, Levena appeared better off for it.

The darkness thickened. She looked up at the sky. Not a star shone, so she guessed that a layer of clouds blocked their light. As she gazed into the darkness lightning zipped across the heavens. That instant of illumination confirmed her cloud theory, and she looked to the north. Somewhere out there laid the sea that joined with the Eiderveis River, the beginning of this strange journey.

Thunder rumbled in the distance, and she imagined a torrent of water raining from the sky in response.

"It had better not rain." Rose'el frowned. "We don't have any shelter. Unless, of course, we felt foolish and desperate enough to lie down in that hollow log again . . . But I wouldn't want to try it."

Raindrops splattered on Caritha's face. The downpour would follow. "We have no choice, Rose'el!" She ran to the hollow log's gaping mouth and drew her rusted sword. "Evela, Laura, come on—and you too, Rose'el. Touch your blades to mine!"

Smiling, as they comprehended her plan, the remaining sisters stood with her and touched their blades to hers. The blades glowed dull red. Energy sizzled from their guards and down their blades. When the energy unified at the swords' tips an explosion of orange and blue light almost made Caritha forget that they needed to control it.

Caritha felt her sisters join with her in purpose, one in mind and one in heart. The energy exploded away from them and burned out the log's hollow interior. Hundreds of arachnids fled before the wave of light, but most of them did not escape.

The sisters pulled back their swords and the energy dispelled into the air.

Prodding one dead spider with her sword, Caritha smiled. "That should cleanse it of vermin for tonight. Come on! Let's move Levena and Dantress inside before it rains."

❧   ❧   ❧

Thunder and lightning vied with each other for supremacy. Dantress awoke in the middle of the night to feel the ground quaking beneath her. Sheltered inside the log she felt safe. Caritha, Rose'el, Laura, and Evela sat against the log's opposite wall, a low fire burning between them and her. She rotated onto her side. Levena was lying beside her, eyes closed, but her chest rose and fell in healthy rhythm.

The smell of smoke hung in the air. It stung her eyes. She glanced at the small fire. Ribbons of smoke wove themselves out of the log's open end, leaving little if any residue to taint the air.

"It smells strongly of smoke in here," she whispered, not wishing to wake Levena.

Rose'el rolled her eyes. "It was Caritha's bright idea to blast the log's interior with energy."

"Well, it did take care of the spiders and any other insects holed up in here," Caritha said in defense.

Rolling her eyes again, Rose'el addressed Dantress. "It also burned the wood, leaving a bit of smoke."

Thick sheets of rain fell from the sky into the clearing outside. The lightning and thunder gradually slackened off, but the rain continued unabated. By strange circumstance the clouds thinned overhead, allowing the full moon to shine through, dimly illuminating the clearing.

A roar trumpeted with sudden force in the night. It shook the ground and a primordial scream that sounded half human and half—something else—something on the hunt, like a bird seeking prey. The dark figure of a humanoid fell from the sky and knelt in the clearing. Long, curly dark hair hung across the creature's face. Moonbeams played off the creature's ragged gray-blue dress. Bare, human feet showed beneath the frayed skirt. The figure remained in a kneeling position only long enough to shake itself like a dog and then stood. Two large, dark, feathered wings fanned out from its back, shivering.

With a bird-like cry the creature turned its face upward. Its hair fell back from its face, and it raised human arms. Its face was undeniably that of a woman, though bonier than any that Dantress had ever seen. The creature's cheekbones in particular stood out from the rest of her face, giving her a rather stoic appearance.

"Bring her down! Bring her down here now!" the woman screamed.

Roaring their assent, six serpentine creatures of large size landed in the clearing. They folded their membranous wings to their black-scaled sides and dug their broad black claws into the ground. Horns rose from their spines like protruding bones and flabby skin hung from their elongated maws. Their long white teeth stuck out over their lower jawbones as if they wore frozen, sinister grins.

Dragons!

Caritha stripped some moss off the log's exterior and threw it on their ineffectual fire. It sizzled for an instant then died out.

Another dragon landed, his fellows growling their anticipation and shifting on their grotesque feet. This one dwarfed his comrades and when he walked toward them they cowered. In his clawed hand he held a large sack. "Drusa," he rumbled to the winged creature, "I have the woman."

"Show her to me," Drusa hissed.

"With pleasure . . ." In one motion the dragon lifted the sack and flipped it inside out, sending its occupant into the mud at the feet of the winged creature called Drusa.

An old woman feebly stood. Her head didn't even reach Drusa's shoulders and her back hunched. She pulled her water-soaked sweater around her upper body and faced the winged woman. "What am I doing here—who are you? What do you want with me?" Her shoulders quaked as she coughed into her wrinkled hand.

Drusa took a step forward and kicked her prisoner in the chest. As she fell into the muddied grass, the old woman screamed. Her attacker sprang on top of her and perched on her chest.

"You are the nursemaid of Ostincair Castle," it hissed "as such you must know whether the rumors are true. Is the lady of the castle with child?" It drove its fists into the old woman's chest. "Answer me and perhaps I will end your suffering! Tell me now! Is the lady of Ostincair Castle with child?"

"Even if I were torn in half," the old woman choked as the creature clamped its hands around her throat, "I would not tell you, It'ren!"

"You *will* tell me, or you *will die*!"

The dragons circled the pair. The largest among them chortled before he spoke to the prisoner. "Torn in half . . . hmm, what an idea. What do you think boys? One of you takes the arms, and I'll take the legs?"

"Perfectly devious," another growled. "Let me at her!"

The winged woman hissed in her struggling prisoner's ear loud enough for the five daughters of the dragon to hear her words from inside their log. "What say you? Shall I feed you to Turser's dragons? Or, are you ready to divulge the truth?"

"Somebody, please, stop this madness," the old woman pleaded. "I've done you no harm."

"It will take more than your cries to get you out of this mess, old woman!" The creature struck her across the face. "Now, what will it be?"

"Creator of the universe," the captive screamed, "save me!"

Drusa screamed into the air and smote the woman again. "The Creator will not save you, old woman. Only *I* can do that! Now, you will tell me the truth!" She waited several long moments, then looked up at the largest dragon. "Glandstine, tear her in two."

The dragon and one of his companions picked up the old woman and began stretching her between them, Glandstine holding her arms and the other dragon holding her legs. Pitiful sobs sounded from the old woman, yet through them Dantress heard another prayer to the Creator.

Dantress could stand it no longer. "Enough!" she screamed, racing from the shelter of the log and brandishing her rusted blade. The anger within her fed the sword of Xavion until its blade glowed dull red. The knuckles of her right hand showed white as she clenched the sword's leather-wrapped handle. She held out her other hand, palm out. "Release her."

Glandstine laughed. "Drusa, look what we have here, a young woman . . . a *very* young woman. Should we wrap her up for the wizard to play with?" He pulled on the old woman, who cried out in pain.

"I said stop!" Quaking with rage Dantress unleashed a bolt of energy from the palm of her hand. It struck Glandstine full in his left leg, causing him to drop the captive's arms and stumble into one of the other dragons.

Spitting on the ground, Drusa pointed a long finger at Dantress. The dragons, rumbling in their throats and snaking out their thin, forked tongues, whipped their tails at Dantress. She fell backward to the ground, the taste of blood in her mouth.

"Not so cocky now, are you?" Suddenly the It'ren launched through the air, its wings spread, and pounced on Dantress's chest. With blinding rapidity the creature struck, dug its nails into her arms, and kicked Xavion's sword from her hand.

"Drusa," Glandstine roared, "look out behind! There are more of them!"

Caritha, Rose'el, Laura, and Evela clashed their swords together. Blue light rose in the darkness, sizzling in the rain, then surged like a wave toward Drusa.

The It'ren rolled off Dantress. The blast of energy passed over its head. Then it jumped to its feet, screaming such a high-pitched, horrible sound that Dantress and her sisters dropped their swords to cover their ears with their hands.

As the rain slackened, the sisters retrieved their swords and joined their blades again. Another wave of energy charged forth from the swords. This one struck two of the dragons with such violent force that they were thrown against the trees at the clearing's border. Both dragons fell limp to the ground.

"Glandstine, leave the old woman," Drusa hissed, darting past Dantress and tackling Laura. "Help—me—get-t—thisss one!"

Before any of the sisters could react the remaining five dragons dove after the It'ren and subdued Laura. Glandstine flew off into the dark sky, roaring his victory, a limp Laura hanging from his black claws. The It'ren screamed into the night and shot after him, disappearing in the darkness.

"No!" Dantress stood, grasped her sword, and dashed to the scene of the kidnapping. Before the remaining four dragons could attempt to take off, she thrust one of them through his chest and stabbed another in the neck when it clawed at Rose'el.

The remaining two dragons coordinated their attack against the sisters, yet they never blew fire. It appeared that they did not have that ability.

Tears ran down Evela's face. She fought half-heartedly, thrusting here and there but never dealing serious blows. The color had drained from her face.

One of the black beasts gathered its wings and crouched. Its muscles flexed, preparing to flee. Caritha sliced its wing.

"Back you foul thing!" Dantress stabbed it in the leg.

She must have hit an artery because exorbitant amounts of the green blood mixed with the rain-soaked mud and the monster fell.

The last dragon slipped its tail through the air like a whip across Rose'el's chest, throwing her a dozen feet. With a roar it flapped its wings and launched into the air.

"Great, we've lost him." Caritha stabbed her sword into the ground.

"Oh no we haven't!" Dantress ran to where the last segment of the dragon's black, shiny tail was slipping into the air. She caught hold of it, held on with desperate resolve.

The upward thrust of the dragon's wings loosened her grip on his wet scales. She clamped her hand tighter. The scales bit into her hands and the rain pelted her face, making it near impossible to see. She stabbed her rusted blade through the tail, and held on with all the strength she could muster. The dragon roared in pain and thrashed about in the air.

Releasing her hold on the dragon, she gripped the sword's handle with both hands. It held fast.

The dragon crashed into the forest. Branches and leaves stung Dantress's face and still she clung to the sword's handle. Someone had to make this beast pay.

When they landed on the forest floor she stood, pulling her sword from the black tail; it slurped out of the dragon's flesh. At last, wiping the rain from her face, she stood with sword held aloft. "All right," she said, "now you are going to tell me *where* your companions have taken my sister and you had better be quick about it. My patience is reaching its limit."

A shiver ran down the length of the creature's body, and it lifted its head to turn and gaze at her. She felt a shiver run through her body as she looked into its simmering yellow eyes.

"Seek out my master, the wizard, if you dare, young one! But be forewarned that you have not the power to bring him down. Dragon blood you have, but your destiny lies not with my master's death. So go, if you dare, if you are foolish enough. I care not. Mayhap he will slay thee as you have slain me."

She sheathed her sword under her sopping outer skirt as the black beast closed his yellow eyes. Green blood flowed from cuts along his legs and belly. "Farewell, beast of doom. May the Creator reward you in death for the harvest of pain you have reaped this night. It was not I who decided your fate. It was you."

ANGEL AMIDST THE DARKNESS

S pecter raced through the forest lightning quick, the scythe held with both hands. He'd gone through the portal in search of the dragon's daughters. And he'd trailed them to the clearing where he'd witnessed Laura's abduction. Only he could save her and he'd set out to do it. He didn't have to look above to know that he was still managing to tail the unsuspecting dragon. He could hear its growls and the beating of its wings.

The dragon had gone far enough for Specter to determine it still headed south and did not intend to change direction. The It'ren, Drusa, flew ahead of it. The dragon clutched one of Albino's daughters in its claws.

Specter did not want them to go farther.

A fallen tree rose into view, wedged into the ground and angling upward, creating a sort of ramp to the forest's ceiling where its branches had snagged in another tree.

He ran faster. Branches whipped at his face and scratched him, but he ignored them and ran onto the tree's wet trunk. For an instant he lost his footing, slipping on the bark. No! He had to press on. Suddenly his boot soles radiated heat. The moisture steamed off the tree's trunk and he raced up it, leaving flames in his wake. His speed surpassed that of the dragon, placing him in the lead.

Specter reached the end of the tree at the exact moment Glandstine shot overhead. The ugly scythe blade sliced through the pelting rain and barbed into the dragon's belly. Specter held onto his weapon with an iron grip as the dragon's screams filled the air around him. Lightning zipped from the sky and struck somewhere in the forest ahead of them. Glandstine crash-landed among the trees, taking one of them down on his way to the forest floor.

Before the dragon impacted the ground, Specter withdrew his blade and dropped from the log, standing unharmed. The branches dislodged Laura from the dragon's claws. He pulled his hood farther over his face, the better to watch the creature's demise. The dragon hit the ground harder than a ball of lead. His body furrowed the ground, knocked over several more trees and sprawled out, his sides heaved weakly.

Having fallen from her captor's grip, Laura now lay on the ground. Stepping over a fallen tree trunk, Specter laid one hand on her forehead and then checked her pulse. Strong. She would waken before long.

He left her there, strode up to the still-living dragon, stood by its head, and raised his scythe to strike.

"Sssoooo," hissed a voice, before he could swing the weapon forward, "another stranger invades these forests."

Specter turned slowly and evaluated the winged woman perched on a log nearby. An image flashed through his mind of a similar creature, this one a male; an Art'en. How far the

Art'en and It'ren had fallen. "There is no need for you to die, too, It'ren."

She spat a wad of filthy spittle in his direction. "Do not insult my intelligence by feigning superiority, *Ghost Man.*" Crouching, Drusa hissed carnivorously. "I know your kind: would-be heroes looking for glory and reward. Do you expect me to cower in fear?"

Specter let her eat silence.

"Answer me, Ghost Man!"

He stared at her. Standing beside a dying dragon, his scythe blade dripping great drops of green blood, such a scene would, at the very least, throw deep shadows of doubt into her mind and cause her to question *what* he was. She had no way of knowing what he was really capable of. It would be up to her to decide whether or not to challenge him.

The It'ren snarled and sprang to perch on a broken branch somewhat closer to him. "Anssswer me!"

"There is no need for you to die, too, It'ren," he repeated.

She jerked her head back, confusion, then uncertainty playing in her eyes. She crept a little closer and reached out, her overly long, dirty fingernails splayed as if considering whether he were man or ghost.

Specter willed himself invisible again and, just as the creature's fingers clawed within inches of his chest, he vanished.

Drusa's eyes bulged and she shrank away, her dark feathers shivering. She twisted on the log, looking into the woods and the shadows.

While her face turned away, Specter slipped his scythe's blade under Glandstine's neck, and cut him open jawbone to jawbone. The creature shuddered, then its maw opened and froze in place. Specter still kept a watchful eye on Drusa. The woman rose in a manner that reminded him of a spider, then she spread her wings and flew away.

Satisfied, Specter walked over to Laura. Her purple dress showed remarkably little wear, a testament, no doubt, to the fact that it had been crafted in Emperia. He stroked her brown-red hair, silky smooth. Her face, fine and delicate—yet underlain by sobriety beyond her years. The dragon would be pleased with him for saving this treasure.

Withdrawing his hand, Specter looked up at the sky. Just in time, too.

Borne on the wind, three dark, winged forms, in sync with Drusa's smaller body, angled toward him and the dragon's daughter.

Very well. If she wanted to test him. So be it.

The three dragons landed together. Drusa dropped in front of them. "He isss here, sssomewhere!" She looked at Laura, lying unconscious and, apparently defenseless. Flapping her wings, Drusa flew to Glandstine and shrieked back at her companions.

They lumbered over to her and laid their clawed hands on their fallen leader. Their beady yellow eyes darted from shadow to shadow.

"Dead?" Drusa dipped her fingers into Glandstine's wound and lifted her hand, coated in green blood. Then she slapped it across her cheeks and inclined her head toward the clouds. "I want that murderer's head on a ssspear before dawn!"

Specter did not give the dragons time enough to fulfill Drusa's wish. Slipping over to the dragon nearest him, he plunged his scythe under the creature's hide, ignoring the agonized monster's roar, and hauled back on the handle. The blade cut through several feet of flesh, its point of entry and point of exit became the edge of a large flab of scaled hide that hung off the dragon's body, leaving the tender pinkish white flesh underneath exposed.

The dragon sprang into the air, splattering blood upon its companions, and made a hasty getaway. The remaining dragons raced about the area, knocked down trees and made a useless commotion until Specter stabbed one in its leg and sliced open the other's side. Both dragons flew after their companion, groaning, growling, and roaring as if the world had reached its end.

"Ssshow yourself, Ghost Man," Drusa hissed from behind.

He spun around. Drusa stood over Laura, a dagger poised in her hand.

"Show yourself!" the It'ren rested her dagger's point on Laura's left breast. "Or I ssshall—?"

Specter spun the scythe above his head and threw it. As the blade flew through the air it slit Drusa's arm from elbow to wrist. It also struck the dagger, sending it into the woods. And the handle, as it whirled after the blade, crunched across the side of the bird woman's face.

Retrieving his weapon, Specter masked his heavy breathing beneath his hood. "There is no need for you to die, too, It'ren." He repeated the sentence deliberately. A ghost would probably have done the same.

Clutching her blood-drenched arm, Drusa bounded swift as a deer over the fallen trees until her wings spread out and lifted her out of sight beneath the southern clouds.

Specter stood on a log, prepared to face a long, watchful night. His attention wholly focused on the prone, bruised daughter of the dragon. He would stay here, her guardian, an angel amidst the darkness.

⌗ ⌗ ⌗

Darkness surrounded Laura, a cold thick darkness that freed her mind yet left her, somehow, feeling physically bound. She groaned and rolled onto her sore side. How much time had passed she could not be certain. Last thing she could remember were several large, scaly dragons and a winged woman rushed viciously upon her. They had knocked her out—after pounding her head and body with fists and claws. She could remember nothing after that.

She struggled to her feet, gazed around. The moon emerged from behind the clouds and spread its soft rays over the fallen and broken trees littering the ground for several hundred yards in all directions. A large body, black and shiny, lay sprawled to her right. A moonbeam glinted off the jagged teeth in the dragon's open mouth and she gave a start.

Glandstine! Stepping carefully over the trunk of a fallen tree, she shivered and looked down at her dead captor. Green blood dripped from a gash in his throat, three quarters of the way up his short muscular neck. From the way his body had sunk into the mud she guessed that he must have unintentionally crashed.

Where was the It'ren creature, Drusa?

There was no sign of her anywhere. There was no sign of anyone. She stood alone in the tangled mass of fallen forest trees. Who, then, slit the dragon's throat? The It'ren? No, Laura felt certain that was not the case. It would have been counterproductive for the winged woman to kill her strongest companion.

Something crashed out of the forest at that moment, hairy and hulking. Four beady, green eyes dared her to stand in its way as it placed a dragon-like foot on Glandstine's body and ripped off the dragon's scales to reveal the pink flesh underneath. Before she had time to consider what she should do, five more creatures bounded out of the trees. Four of them tore into the dragon carcass but one of them ran straight for her. It launched itself into the air and slammed its head into her chest.

She fell down, the beast made a gurgling sound in its mouth and its lips curled back to reveal fang-like teeth. Its front feet pressed her arms down before she could reach for her weapon. It opened its jaws wide enough to swallow her head and she screamed.

Suddenly the creature yelped and rolled to the side. Dark blood ran from a gash in its side and its four eyes darted around as it growled and slashed the air. The other beasts ceased feasting on the dragon and darted through the fallen trees toward their companion.

Laura did not wait to see the outcome. The clouds slid across the moon again and she ran as fast as her sore and tired legs would allow. She climbed a large tree at the edge of the undamaged forest and perched on a thick limb, holding another branch for support with her right hand.

The furry creatures jumped around their fallen companion, slashing the air with their razor claws. All of them now made the horrible gurgling sound. Then, as she watched the wounded creature that had attacked her, its head separated from its body. She blinked, unsure she had correctly judged what had happened. The creature's body collapsed, its four-eyed head rolled on the ground.

Another of the creatures dropped. Blood ran from its jaws. The remaining creatures continued to attack the air as if seeking an invisible opponent and she thanked the Creator that she was no longer down there. More of the hairy beasts emerged from the forest. They swarmed over Glandstine and, within half an hour, left little more than his bones.

The beasts left and quiet settled over the area. She drew her sword and hacked branches off the tree. She used them to build a makeshift nest in the sturdiest branch. She laid her sword in front of her and curled up, then she closed her eyes. The wind howled through the forest, an owl hooted somewhere in the distance. One of the creatures gave a gurgling call. With those creatures about it would be foolhardy to try and find her way back to her sisters' camp in the darkness. Her mind and body weary, she fell asleep.

❈   ❈   ❈

The poor old woman knelt in the mud at Dantress's feet with her grimy gray hair clinging to her face. "You have saved me from a fate worse than death," she whispered, looking up into her eyes. "The secret of Ostincair Castle is safe. The devil worshipers have fled." She grasped Dantress's skirt and smiled as Dantress set her sword on the ground and knelt in front of her, gently holding her arms.

Caritha and Rose'el walked up behind Dantress, one on either side of her. Tears welled in Dantress's eyes as she noted the cuts on the old woman's arms and the bruises on her face.

"Do not weep for me, dear children," the old woman said. "A long life—and a fulfilling one—I have lived. Look now to yourselves and beware: these forsaken lands should not be trodden lightly.

"What b-beautiful and honorable young ones you are! I have not seen your equals in all my lifetime and now, while death draws near, I thank you . . . You would have died for me. I know it, for I saw it in your eyes. And I am a mere stranger to you. Fortunate are the ones who are numbered among your friends and cursed be those that make themselves your enemies!"

Gently Dantress laid the woman on the ground and closed her eyelids with her fingers. "We couldn't save her. We were too late."

"It doesn't seem right!" Rose'el kicked her foot into the mud, spraying it on her clothes and those of her sisters. "I say we go after that creature—that *It'ren—Drusa*. She and that dragon are going to pay for whatever they do to Laura, and for this deed."

Caritha raised her right hand and shook her head. "No, Rose'el. Revenge is not ours to deal out, at least not while we have a mission to accomplish."

"But that creature and the dragon have taken Laura!"

"And we do not know *where*, Rose'el," Caritha snapped back. "Remember what Father promised: he is watching over us . . . Laura is on her own now unless we come upon her along the way to Al'un Dai.

"We have a mission to accomplish—"

"With the *four* of us?" Rose'el harrumphed. "In case you haven't noticed, my *dear* sister, Laura is gone and Levena is quite unwell and we have here the body of an elderly woman that needs burying."

"No, Rose'el. Not four of us. Evela must remain behind with Levena, that leaves you, myself, and Dantress." She walked away and whispered something into Evela's ear.

Evela set her mouth in a tight line and wiped her blade on her dress. "I will do as Caritha says," she told Rose'el.

"What? No, I insist this is foolish—"

Dantress stood up, cutting her sister off in mid-sentence. "To Al'un Dai we will go." She patted her taller, frowning sister on the shoulder and then swept past her, whispering into her ear. "Father promised to watch over us, Rose'el. Have faith . . . We can do this. We have to!"

Then she approached Evela and embraced her. "Laura may return soon. And I wouldn't think a spider bite"—she pointed into the hollow log wherein Levena slept—"can keep her down for long."

"Don't worry." Evela cleared her throat and forced herself to stand straight. "I'll take care of things here. Just you be careful."

"And please bury the old woman," Dantress wiped a tear from her cheek and turned, looking at the pitiful sight. "Poor thing. She didn't stand a chance."

⊗ ⊗ ⊗

Laura woke when the first rays of sunlight struck her nest and the cries of birds filled the forest around her. The birds' screeches were not soothing; they came as throaty threats from several hundred vultures standing on and about the dragon carcass. She pinched her nose against the smell of putrid flesh and sheathed her sword.

Little remained of the fearsome Glandstine. Shreds of black, scale-covered hide hung from the clean white bones of his ribcage. For the most part, the ground had absorbed his green blood. Already the birds had stolen his eyes from their sockets.

Still she could not guess what had happened to the creature that had attacked her. She could see its severed head lying between the fallen trees, its body next to it. Only bones remained.

Perhaps another creature roamed these forests. One that could remain unseen and yet still be lethal and cunning enough to slay the beast? She descended the tree and headed north, away from the vultures. She drew her sword and listened to every sound that reached her ears. Last night had been a close call and she did not want a repeat.

Thus she passed through the forest without incident, ever northward until she chanced upon a tree that she recognized as one that she and her sisters had passed the day before. She headed west, retracing the route to the scene of her kidnapping. Her sore body complained, but she paid it no heed; she had to find out what had become of her sisters. Were they still alive? Before she'd been knocked out she'd seen several dragons moving against her sisters. If they had been overcome—as had she . . . She quickened her pace and tossed stray strands of her long and dark, red-tinged hair out of her face.

MISTRESS OF THE RUINS

A stiff, cool wind blew in from the east. Caritha, Dantress, and Rose'el stood with their backs to it, looking upon the ancient fortress of Al'un Dai as the sun's rays peeked in and out of the puffy white clouds dotting the sky.

The black metal and stone structure rose from the midst of a vast depression, a hollow bristling with wild shrubbery, vines, and dead, twisted trees. Broken walls of stone crumbled around the structure, and the deep moat that had once formed the outside perimeter was bone dry.

The structure was enormous with jagged towers rising in defiance toward the sky. Large sections of the towers and the fortress walls stood with gaping holes in them. A heap of rubble filled the structure's center—the remnants of a much larger tower that had once stood there.

The wind howled through the trees behind them and a sudden ringing of metal caused Dantress to glance to her right. Scowling, Rose'el held up her blade and thrust it at the temple.

To Dantress's left, Caritha took a few steps forward and then bent down to part the fold in her outer skirt and slide her rusted blade from the concealed scabbard. She raised the sword before her eyes, grasping its leather handle with both hands, and looked past its blade to the fallen fortress. "Draw your sword, Dantress." She glanced at her sideways. "The weapons of the Six must avenge the innocent."

Dantress started to reach down for her sword then stopped, shaking her head, looking back up at the fortress, its ancient drawbridge lowered over the empty moat. "Violence should be our last resort, my sisters, not our first choice. We are here to find Kesla and persuade him to repent—"

Rose'el growled, "And if he does not?"

"Then"—Dantress said, hesitating—"then he must die."

"Good." Rose'el lowered her weapon. "Justice must be served, as Father wishes it to be."

Caritha lowered her sword also, indicating her approval with a nod.

They made their way into the hollow along a beaten path, Dantress leading. The path took them between scraggly trees and under the limbs of broken and dead trees. Many of them stood out stark white, stripped of their protective bark. Strewn in ghastly fashion between them, lay helms and shields, halberds and spears, chain mail and solid breastplates, tarnished and rusted—enough weaponry to arm a sizeable force.

"Spooky," Rose'el whispered. She tiptoed past a complete suit of body armor half-buried at the base of a dead tree as if afraid to disturb the dead man's ghost. "I wonder why there aren't any bones."

"Who knows," Caritha said, "this battle probably took place a very, very, *very* long time ago. The skeletons probably turned to dust ages ago."

Rose'el stepped over an exposed tree root and raised one eyebrow. "Have you ever wondered how old Father is? I mean, look around! He was here when this place was undamaged, right?"

"I suppose so," Dantress interjected. She contemplated the dark structure ahead. Only a few hundred yards to go and they would reach the drawbridge. "Father is very powerful and very wise, Rose'el," she said. "We all know that. But I believe there are some things we will never understand about him. His age?" She took another step. "I doubt we are meant to know that. What matters now is finding out if that man—Kesla—is still here. Then, we can go home."

Stooping to examine a breastplate near the path, Dantress swept the grime from it with her hand. The figure of a white dragon spewing fire from its mouth gleamed back at her. Beneath the dragon's feet flames twisted up, entwining its legs. Thick black smoke billowed around it as if it walked, unscathed, upon the surface of a lake of burning oil.

Though the image on the breastplate must have been ancient the colors appeared vivid, fresh even. Bits of the image had started to flake off, but overall it seemed unaffected by the countless years sitting out in the open air, exposed to the elements.

She walked on a little farther, in the direction of Al'un Dai, then stooped to grasp the edge of a round shield. The same image—the white dragon spewing fire and walking on a lake of burning oil—met her gaze.

The colors, the mystery behind the depiction, the magnificent creature, all intrigued her beyond anything she had thus far seen, except perhaps her encounter with the sword that had spoken to her. If the dragon shown in this painting was the great white dragon that she knew, then what story lay behind it? It was her heritage, her past . . . it should be a part of her future.

Her sisters peered over her shoulders until Caritha bid them stand. "We must move on," she said, pulling Dantress to her feet. "Come on, let's find out what's inside the temple."

⚯   ⚯   ⚯

The cold metal of the drawbridge plates crept through the soles of Dantress's leather shoes, and an equally cold chill ran up her spine when she saw what should have been impossible. The towers of Al'un Dai stood as they had in ancient times; whole and unmarred. Gratings now covered the multitude of windows set in the black stone towers that had been in ruins. The fortress's outer wall rose a hundred feet high. Its iron gates, made to look like giant, feathered wings, were closed and bound to each other by chains fashioned in the forms of enormous cobras.

They had almost crossed the drawbridge. The chains were rising slowly from the dry moat and clattering into position as they stretched from the drawbridge's end to the temple's outer wall on either side of the gate. But suddenly the chains rattled faster along their runs and the drawbridge rose under the sisters' feet.

Dantress fell forward onto the ground, and Rose'el tumbled off the side of the drawbridge. Because she too had fallen, Dantress could do nothing. She bit her lip. Tears of frustration burned in her eyes.

Caritha fell beside her and returned her gaze for a moment, then she looked back at the drawbridge. She bolted to her feet, ran to the moat's edge, parted the fold in her garment, and drew her rusted sword.

A giant serpent rose from the moat and leered down at them. Its blood-red eyes gleamed. It did not open its mouth, but two fangs dripping thick, clear liquid protruded from its upper jaw. Its eyes narrowed to near-slits.

Atop the serpent's gray head, Rose'el struggled not to fall off. The serpent bucked. Rose'el grunted, her hands holding desperately onto the creature's scales. "Are you—two—going—to—help me?" she asked through clenched teeth.

Let her down! Dantress knew as soon as she communicated her thought to the serpent that it had heard her. It jerked its head to look at her, eyes wide and Rose'el fell off.

The serpent narrowed its eyes again. Dantress thought she spotted a line of ridged hairs rise on its neck as it slipped into the murky water of the moat.

She stood. Rose'el, with Caritha's help, struggled to her feet. Dark red blood ran from several minor cuts on Rose'el's hands where she had gripped the serpent's scales.

A cold, like the one she had felt while walking the draw-bridge, crept into her back, only this time she knew it was a cold not born of temperature . . . but of something else.

A quick spin brought her to face the wing gates. They were still closed but now a rough-stone path could be discerned beyond them. A silent human figure cloaked in blue-gray cloth stood in the way. A narrow band of gold ran down the cloak's front. Long, curly blond hair showed beneath the black fur-lined hood.

The cold . . . was it coming from this . . . this person?

"Well what do you think of that?" Rose'el said.

Dantress had nearly forgotten her sisters, so intent was she on studying the stranger.

"Well, well, well. How do you like that? Here we are in the *ruins* of Al'un Dai, temple of a long-gone wizard, and it looks as if he built it yesterday." She harrumphed. "Ruins *indeed*! This place is spotless. Check out the elaborate design work—"

The pause lasted long enough to tell Dantress that her sister had finally noticed the stranger.

"What have we here?" Rose'el stepped up to the gates. Blood dripped from the tips of her fingers, landing on the stone pathway at her feet. She either did not notice this or did not care. "Hello there," Rose'el began, "care to open the gate for us?"

The stranger still stood there, silent and unmoving as if frozen in time, then flipped back their hood. Slender, tall, athletic, a blond haired woman of enviable beauty fixed her sapphire eyes upon the sisters before turning and walking to the base of a gray marble stairway. The steps wove up to the recessed wooden doors in the main tower.

There she stopped, looked back and smiled. About-facing, she ascended the stairs. The doors opened inward to admit her— revealing a long, dark corridor inside the structure lined with red columns and gray banners—and the doors closed behind her without a sound.

"We'll have to let ourselves in," Caritha said.

Whipping out their swords, Caritha and Rose'el struck at the great chain across the wing gates. Bits of rust flew off their blades, falling to the dirt beneath their feet. Their efforts did not even leave a scratch on the chains.

Dantress gazed up at one of the dark towers, considering the situation. A vulture flew, not above the tower, but toward it. The bird glided, undeterred by the walls of stone, heading straight for the tower. She cringed, expecting to see it collide with the wall of stone. But the vulture passed through it, emerging unharmed on the other side, and angled for a slow descent. She watched it shrink out of sight into the northern borders of the forest.

Her sisters still beat at the chains, blades clanging. Caritha, her long hair askew, her face beading sweat, stepped back, holding her hand up, palm outward. A feeble burst of blue energy shot against the gate and vaporized harmlessly against it.

The vulture . . . it had gone *through* the stone . . . as if it were not even there. As if it did not truly exist. What if the tower did not really exist, could it be an illusion?

This temple, Al'un Dai, had fallen a long time ago. The great white dragon had told her so. Yet it appeared whole, standing as mighty as the day it had been built. But she and her sisters had seen it in ruins only a short time before. Could they be under some kind of spell? Were they trapped in an intricate deception? She could think of only one way to find out.

"Wait." She grasped Caritha's sword arm with one hand and held Rose'el's shoulder with her other. "I don't think that will do any good."

"No?" Rose'el pulled away. "Do you have a better idea?"

Dantress smiled, releasing Caritha's arm. "If I am right, then none of this is real. It is all an illusion created to keep us away."

"An illusion to keep us away from what?" Caritha shook her head. "You're not making any sense, Dantress."

Dantress eyed the wing gates, the chains binding them gave Caritha's question merit. What would be the purpose to creating an illusion as complicated as this one? Unless to hide something? Or, some*one*?

They must be on the right track.

"That's it!" she said. "The illusion is meant to keep us from finding—not a thing, but a person—the man who was once a member of the Six, the man we have come to find!"

"That is absurd," Rose'el replied, raising one eyebrow.

"Really?" Dantress looked at her. "Why?"

The question hung in the air for a moment. Rose'el pointed at the wing gate. "Tell me," she said, "that you *aren't* suggesting my sword struck an illusion."

"Would it surprise you?" she replied, inching near the black iron bars. "If I am right then I·can walk through this . . . If not then I will not be able." She took two more steps and drew in her breath. The metal was so close to her skin that she could feel its cool surface. No! It was an illusion!

She closed her eyes, walking forward. When she felt certain she'd passed the gate, she dared open them. The towers of the temple were crumbling around her. They reverted to their dilapidated state, charred and broken. Piles of rubble rose ahead of her, with the largest pile of all where the mighty central tower had once stood. Partial walls, some with windows and doors, stood amidst the rubble. A few still supported thick roofs tiled with what appeared to be smooth metal plates worn by untold years of wind and rain.

It amazed her that some of the towers still stood after so much time and such pervading destruction. The wind howled through the ancient structures, an eerie reminder of the terrible battle once fought over this bit of land.

"Dantress! H-how did you . . . how did you do that."

She turned at the sound of Rose'el's voice. Her sister stood pointing at her with eyes open wide, "how did you do that?"

Dantress had been right. She let herself smile. Caritha and Rose'el were standing in the ruins too, their eyes darting from towers to rubble and back at her. "It was nothing more than an illusion created to keep us away," she said. She absently kicked aside a metal plate on the ground. Under it a boomerang lay. She picked it up, but it drew blood from her finger and she immediately dropped it.

Caritha reached down and picked up the boomerang. She blew dust off its silvery surface. "Strange." She twirled the object with her wrist then held it out to Dantress. "The elbow is leather," she said as Dantress took it, "but be careful, its wings are outfitted with blades. I believe it is a weapon."

Tucking the blade boomerang under her belt, Dantress walked toward the place where she had seen the woman walk into the nonexistent central tower. She could sense something nearby, a presence. Pain, sorrow, anger . . . Someone was waking, someone whose bitter memories were strong enough to enter her young mind.

The shadows of her two sisters joined her own. *We are here, Dantress. Tell us what you are thinking.*

She jerked around, searching their faces. *Caritha, was that you? Did you just—communicate—using your mind?*

But the eldest daughter of the dragon looked beyond her, and Dantress heard nothing more. If Caritha had communicated to her with her mind then she was holding herself back, unwilling for some reason to continue using that form of communication. Was there more to this sister than the dragon had said?

Silencing her own questions, Dantress gestured for Caritha and Rose'el to follow her as she sidestepped a large block of stone and proceeded toward a hole in one of the temple's standing walls. She thought she heard a wail, as of a child, echoing faintly from somewhere inside the wall. But she could not be certain.

She entered the wall and searched until she noticed a large, flat stone that stood out in the debris because it appeared clean and unbroken. Approaching, she called her sisters' attention to it. With their help she slid the stone to the side.

A circular hole gaped beneath it, like a well, with stone steps set in its walls and a railing. It led down into darkness.

A draft of warm air rose from the darkness below and passed over her face. She grasped the cool surface of the rusted iron railing, held up by support bars fashioned like king cobras, and gazed into the darkness.

For an instant she caught the scent of smoke in the air but the perfumed essence of flowers replaced it. Roses, lilacs—she couldn't be sure what kind of flowers they were because the smell tinged the air as a mere sampling, no more than a whiff or two.

Drawing in a deep breath, she reached down, parted the fold in her outer skirt to reveal the hilt of her weapon. The rusted blade protested as she slid it from the sheath. "Come on," she said, keeping her voice low so as not to alert anyone except her sisters to her presence, "he's down here."

She turned. Caritha had drawn her sword and stepped around her to start down the stairs. Rose'el squinted at Dantress, her dark eyes boring into her.

"How do you *know* that *he* is down here?" Rose'el folded her arms. Her gaze diverted for a moment. Caritha stopped to look up at her.

"Rose'el!" Caritha snapped.

"Well," Rose'el defended herself, "it seems to me that it is highly unlikely to find a warrior living in these ruins. Perhaps there may be clue here to lead us to him, but I very much doubt he is living in the basement."

Caritha waved her hand, an edge to her voice. "Quit procrastinating! Dantress was right about the wing gates and she was right about the whole illusion." She redirected herself back down the stairs, and drew her sword. "Give me light, weapon of the Six." As the words left her mouth, the blade glowed dimly with reddish-orange light, illuminating the broad stone steps.

Dantress followed her down, whispering to the sword of Xavion, "Shine, oh my sword!" Its light joined that of Caritha's and Rose'el's.

Rose'el didn't say another word until they had descended an inestimable number of steps and could no longer glimpse the light of day above them. She stayed behind Dantress, from time to time grunting when a bat or two were disturbed from their sleep. A couple of times, Dantress could have sworn she heard Rose'el scraping her blade along the wall.

When they reached the bottom, the light of their swords showed a mostly-smooth floor of stones. A few of them were broken, cracked, and worn. Dantress crouched and ran her finger along the floor. When she brought it up to inspect it under the glow of her sword, she could not see a single trace of dust.

Rose'el clacked her tongue.

"*Someone,*" Dantress straightened, "*must* be down here."

"Hmph!" she heard Rose'el respond. "Someone, or some*thing.* Personally . . . I'm not sure I want to find out which is the case."

"Someone." Dantress raised an eyebrow. "That woman who appeared while you beat the gate? She disappeared this way. And I doubt she was a tramp. Her clothes were too well-fashioned and clean."

Creeping forward, Dantress held her sword out so its light fell on the floor. The light of the rusted swords revealed stone walls on either side. Dampness filled the air around her, clinging coolly to her exposed arms and the back of her neck. A bat flew past her head toward the stairway she had just descended. Beneath her the floor vibrated. The farther she walked the worse the vibrations grew until she felt her feet slipping on the floor stones.

She jumped forward and rolled. Rose'el and Caritha did not react fast enough. As Dantress turned she saw the floor stones rotate to vertical positions and her sisters fell out of sight between them. Rose'el growled in a most unfeminine manner as the floor swallowed her out of sight and Caritha's eyes startled wide.

The stones rotated back into position. The floor once again appeared solid.

Dantress stood shakily to her feet. She was alone now. The silent darkness sealing her in.

"You *are* a smart one," a smooth, high voice stated from behind her.

Holding Xavion's sword with both hands, poising it before her, Dantress turned around.

One by one, small circlets of harsh white light flickered on in the corridor, lighting up bronze and black striped walls. She could see wrought iron cobras attached to the ceiling high overhead, their ruby eyes glowing down at her.

Far down the corridor, rising almost twenty feet off the floor and circled by spears stuck upright, stood the statue of a man. Feathered wings, like those of an eagle spread behind him. His shoulders squared and he crouched, catlike, his arms reaching out. In his right hand he balanced a large globe, polished to a black shine, and in his left he held an egg the size of a large ball.

"Impressive, isn't it?" A human figure standing in front of the statue lifted her arms, spreading them reverently. Her fur-lined hood slipped off her curly, golden hair and her smooth lips parted to show two rows of flawless white teeth. She closed her eyes, her face directed upward.

"Though he is long gone, the presence of my master dwells here still. His spirit is ever present with me, the voices of his counselors are ever in my ears." She lowered her arms and her face. The light reflected off her sapphire eyes as she opened them to gaze at Dantress. "They know who you are," she said. "They have warned me that you were coming. You cannot hide from them. The white dragon could not hide you from them . . . he could not see what lay here."

She cupped her hand to her ear, another smile forming on her lips and her eyes half-closing. "Your journey here was such a waste. I have the power of my master, the power that *they* gave him. Can you not feel it? Can you not sense it growing up around you?"

Goosebumps formed on Dantress's skin. The floor around her froze, every drop of moisture turned into ice and shattered against the stones. Her limbs stiffened as the temperature continued to drop.

"Now you see, don't you?" The woman laughed, only to stop abruptly and sigh. "It is unfortunate that you have the dragon's blood in your veins. You might have become a rather powerful ally. But as a child of the enemy"—she shook her head—"you pose too great a threat."

Drops of sweat formed on Dantress's forehead. Some ran into her eyes and froze on her eyelashes, blurring her vision.

God, help me! Almost as soon as the plea left her mind she heard the words of the great white dragon echoing in her mind: "Do not fear . . . I will be watching over you even when you cannot see me."

Father, help me. I am failing.

But you will not, my child. Draw upon the strength in your blood, my strength. Use it! It is what this woman fears.

In the depths of her soul, Dantress heard him roar, and warmth flooded her being. The cold left her, resistant and painful, tearing at her.

But then she perceived that fingers formed in the air; cold, tangible fingers that slid off her arm. She could feel them. She swung her sword but it passed without resistance through the air. Nothing was there, or, if it was, it could not be touched by mere physical weapons.

She felt as if a hundred eyes were boring into her.

The woman laughed again. "You *are* a strong one! You felt them; I saw it in your eyes! But you can do nothing. They are not of our world, nor of any other." She walked forward, her hand reaching under her cloak. "Join us, daughter of the dragon. Commune with *them*. It is an experience like no other, power unimaginable—all of it placed into your hands so that all who come against you will fear even to sound your name."

Withdrawing her hand from under her cloak the woman held out a small orb, black as coal. The light around it dimmed and indeed, darkness overcame it until Dantress could no longer see the woman but only a great darkness shielding her from sight as if it had swallowed her out of existence.

In that moment Dantress felt something strike her face, hard and fast, leaving a million needles in her flesh.

She dropped to the floor. Who or what had struck she could not be certain. The floor iced over a few feet from her. She focused on that spot of the floor, holding her hand out. As the power within her surged and her palm glowed blue she heard the woman scream. Dantress shot the energy from her hand in one sudden blast. It exploded against the wall, opening a hole large enough for a small person to pass through. She saw a richly furnished room beyond radiating warm yellow light.

"*Nooo!*" a voice rasped in her ear. And a cold breath struck her. She rose waveringly to her feet.

Something touched her arm and she screamed, swinging her sword every which way.

"*It is useless, oooh yes! Utterly useless! Commune with us! Join us in the darkness. There can be no turning back. You have come too far! You are alone, helpless. Let us in! The dragon has abandoned you, hope has abandoned you, your sisters have fled; you are alone!*"

Was it true? She couldn't help thinking that it was. She truly was . . . alone.

"Given up already?" another voice whispered in her ear. She caught the sound of footfalls behind her. "What are you made of? Fight them! Do not give in!"

Light flashed past her face, a long pointed blade with a gentle curve. It pierced the cold and darkness, snagged something dark and formless. A strong hand pushed her from behind, shoving her through the hole she had blasted in the wall.

She stumbled into the room, leaving the cold behind. Hissing, whispers and wails filled the corridor behind her. A shiver ran down her spine, but the air around her felt warm again.

The woman stumbled after her just as the hole collapsed. The stones piled on top of one another to cover the opening.

Dantress poised her sword, just in time to block a bolt of white-yellow energy sizzling from the woman's hand.

The woman stepped back and screamed, piercing and harsh. She loosened her cloak from around her shoulders and let it fall to the stone floor. Red leather wrapped tight around her torso, and a double layer of black leather hung about her shoulders. She wore matching red leather pants laced with gold. Her smooth feet were bare.

"I know what you seek, dragon daughter. But you will not have him. I will not allow it!" She approached Dantress, drawing a dagger from her belt. Its long blade materialized for an instant and then vanished.

Dantress reacted without thinking. Letting go of her sword with her left hand, she reached to her own belt, grasped the leather elbow of the weapon she'd found amidst the ruins, then spun, lashing out with it.

Blood ran from a clean cut on her adversary's cheek. The woman exclaimed with surprise and touched her hand to her wound.

"You gave me no choice," Dantress cried out. "Stand aside! I don't want to hurt you!"

Ice formed on the woman's wound and a wicked voice whispered incoherently.

"Foolish child," the woman laughed. "You may have caught me by surprise, but it will take more than tricks if you are going to survive against me. Do you not know who I am? Did the dragon not tell you? Or was he afraid you would not come if you knew?

"I am the beginning of this place. I am the reason it stands! My master called it by my name." Darkness wrapped around her and hid her. "Can the offspring of the great dragon stand alone against me?" She cackled.

Something struck Dantress in the shoulder and she fell to her knees. Another blow hit her chest and she gasped for breath.

Total darkness surrounded her. She could hear her adversary but could find nothing to strike.

"Dantress?" Caritha's voice penetrated her restricting universe, and a beam of blue energy shot through the veil of darkness.

Dantress heard her attacker cry out. The darkness dissipated, allowing her to sit up. Her eyes felt weary, and she had trouble focusing her vision.

Caritha's blurred form rushed against the woman.

Rose'el followed, making a vicious stab. "Witch! You dare to attack *my* little sister!"

The battle lasted a few moments. Dantress regained enough of her wind to stand—just as the same swirling darkness that had enveloped her enveloped Caritha and Rose'el. Her sisters fell. Blows thudded against their bodies and they writhed helplessly on the floor.

"Get away from them." Dantress advanced, though she suspected her attempt to help would prove futile. She threw the boomerang. But it sailed through the dark mass and clattered to the floor. The witch rushed at her, leaving Rose'el and Caritha where they'd fallen. The two sisters' eyes pivoted to stare at Dantress, but their bodies appeared stiff.

The witch advanced. Cold fingers clamped over Dantress's wrists. But three more figures burst into view from Dantress's left. Laura, Evela, and Levena drew their rusted blades and touched them together, sending another bolt of blue energy into the witch's shroud of darkness.

"Curse you! Curse you all!" the witch screamed. Apparently disabled, she fell to the floor. "No one stands against me! No one!"

Suddenly the woman withdrew three long darts from beneath her leather shoulder pads and flung them simultaneously. Levena fell first, a dart protruding from her arm, and Evela dropped next, stuck in the chest. But Laura twisted out of the way as the third one shot toward her.

Dantress spotted two more darts as they solidified from thin air in the witch's hand. She jumped to the side. A dart sped through the space where her head had been. She swung back to face the fallen witch. Too late, she spotted another one cutting the air in her direction.

It pricked her leg, burning it with intense pain until numbness set in. She knelt on the floor. Laura deflected yet another of the projectiles with her sword, then rolled forward, and shot up next to the witch. She stabbed, wounding the woman's throwing hand before backing off. She kept a watchful eye on the witch as she retreated to each of her sisters, pulling out the darts sticking in their flesh.

Once the dart was out of her leg, Dantress focused inward, isolating every bit of the alien substance. Gathering it together, she drew it from her system. It collected in her hand and formed into an orb. She threw it away from her and then directed her attention to her sisters.

From her hand Dantress shot narrow bands of energy that latched onto Caritha, Rose'el, Evela, and Levena. The witch's poison withdrew from their systems, collecting into another small deadly orb floating between her hands. It hovered there until she finished the process, then she cast it against the far wall where it splattered.

One by one the sisters stood, and they converged on the prone woman with their glowing blades.

9

TRAITOR'S END

The sisters drew near, the witch's face paled ghastly white, and they grasped their swords. Drops of red liquid collected at the blades' lowered tips and splattered on the stone floor.

"No, it cannot be." The witch tried to rise to her elbows, but she fell back. Her sapphire eyes fastened on the swords and she swallowed. "This cannot be," she repeated, still gazing at the sisters' rusted weapons.

Caritha's hand shook as she raised her blade, holding it over the woman's heart. A tear formed in her eye. "Please," she said, "do not make us do this. Let us continue on our way. I don't want to kill you."

"What?" Rose'el snarled, glancing at Caritha. "You're going to let her live? After—after she tried to kill us?"

"Mercy? You want to show me mercy?" The witch laughed. "You have not the courage it would take to strike me down, daughter of the dragon, and I deign not to accept your mercy. I will kill you—and your sisters—before you set one step farther into my chambers."

Rose'el reacted so quickly that she took Dantress by surprise. "Hmph!" the sister said, flipping her sword upside down and grasping it by the blade. And she struck the sword's pommel against the side of the woman's head.

The witch's eyes rolled back into her head, her body fell limp.

Rose'el flipped her sword's blade pointing it up and grasped its handle, "Now, that ought to take care of that nasty tongue of hers." She nodded at Caritha.

Her older sister stared past them to the far end of the room and did not respond. Dantress followed Caritha's gaze. A large oval bed stood in the midst of white and red strips of cloth hanging from the ceiling. Fluffy white pillows scattered over its thick quilt-like cover. Six bronze posts supported the bed, each of them fashioned in the form of a King Cobra ready to strike.

A baby cried.

Dantress's sisters grabbed her shoulders to hold her back, but she pulled away. The baby's cries led her around the bed to a crib made of dark wood. She touched it and it rocked gently, leaning over to watch life's little miracle.

"Shh, don't cry." She reached down. She had never held a baby before. Its face was red, and its tiny, tiny hands were balled into weak fists. And it had thick, dark hair.

"Dantress, what are you doing? We shouldn't linger here." Caritha walked around to the opposite side of the crib.

But Dantress reached down anyway, pulling the little one from its loneliness and holding it to her bosom. The child's cries softened.

"Can I see?" Evela approached and pulled aside the child's wrapping. "Ooh, it's a boy."

Levena smiled. "He's cute. Wonder if he has a name?"

"Girls!" Caritha bit her lower lip. "What do you think you are doing? Don't you realize what that is?"

"I think they know perfectly well." Laura stood next to Dantress and ran her finger along the infant's naked arm. "*He* is the son of a witch." She turned to point at the prone woman. "*That* witch."

Rose'el scraped the tip of her sword blade on the stone floor and then cleared her throat loudly. "And who is the father?"

When Dantress looked at her, she saw Rose'el raise an eyebrow. "You don't think"—Dantress redirected her attention to the child—"that this is the son of—"

"He is my son." There was no mistaking the strength behind the deep voice.

All the dragon's daughters gazed back at the place where the witch still lay. A man stood over her, a black metal staff balanced in his white hands. Thick, curly black hair fell to his shoulders, framing his ghastly white face.

He knelt next to her, touching her neck, then let out a slow breath and stood. He had to be at least six-feet tall. He stepped toward the sisters in one long, effortless stride. If his skin had not been so white, he might have been handsome.

Dantress looked up at him, the baby fell asleep in her arms and she held it close.

The man returned her gaze, then glanced at her feet. The rusted sword of Xavion still lay there. He appraised the other sisters one by one, his eyes lingering on their swords. Dantress's heart skipped more than one beat, waiting for him to strike at her and her sisters.

But the blow never came. The man lowered his gaze and his shoulders drooped. "He sent you . . . Didn't he? He sent you here to kill me; it was inevitable. I've been expecting this."

A tear formed in the corner of his eye and he wiped it away with his hand. "Do not be afraid, children." He turned his hand over, inspecting the tear. "I could have killed you before now, if I had wanted to do so, but I will not."

No one replied to him, but he placed his staff on the floor and stepped closer to Dantress, arms outstretched. "May I have my son now?"

She lifted the child up, astonished to see three tears form and drip down his face. He had the look of a warrior, a man hardened by his experiences, but his sorrow seemed to outweigh all else.

"You are," she heard the words whisper from her mouth, though she had not intended them to, "Kesla."

Her sisters' mouths opened, their eyes widened.

The man stroked his son's dark head and gazed upon him. "Almost a thousand years ago I was like you, my son. Innocent and good. But evil has a way of finding those it wants. It destroyed me and it will surely destroy you if you stay here.

"Your father is a bad man," he sobbed, wiped more tears from his eyes, but then smiled sadly as he looked at the infant. "My path is laid before me and I cannot turn from it, but, my son, you must not follow in my steps. You must learn goodness, justice. And you must hold to them."

He looked down at Dantress and held out the child. "With the blood of a witch and the blood of a traitor in his veins, he is more vulnerable than any other child I have fathered. There is only One whom I trust to watch over my last son; One who will teach him to love the Creator and pursue righteousness.

"Take him, servant of the dragon. Take my son. Please! I beg of you. Do not let him fall as I have! Bring him to my old master, for this is all I have left to give in recompense for my wickedness."

The child he gently laid in Dantress's arms.

Her eyes filled with tears as she gazed into Kesla's eyes. "Come with us! The dragon will forgive, I know he will! He did not send us to kill you, Kesla . . . he wants you restored."

She stepped toward him, but he suddenly picked up his staff and spun it around his torso. It thwacked into a figure to his left that Dantress had failed to notice: the witch!

As if passing through air, the staff did not affect the woman.

"Al'un Dai." Kesla grasped the woman by her shoulder. "Do not harm them. Enough blood has been spilled by us. Let it end here."

The woman evaded him and snatched her son from Dantress's arms. She retreated and pulled out a dagger. Holding this above the child's dark haired head, she glared at the sisters. "Either you leave here—now—or I will slit my son's throat! *My* blood runs in this child's veins—a witch's blood—and he will one day become the greatest wizard ever to walk the face of this world.

"*They* have foreseen it!"

Kesla raced to Al'un Dai's side and smashed his fist into her right temple. She fell and he took his son from her. He cradled him in his arms. "You would *kill* our son? I dare you! Touch him again to harm him and I will knock your head off."

Darkness gathered to Al'un Dai. She screamed a horrible, piercing scream, then she dissolved into thin air, only to reform next to Kesla, her dagger poised above the child.

Dantress froze. The fate of an innocent hung uncertainly before her, and she could not move. It was too awful, too cruel. This woman was prepared to slay her own son in order to save her life.

A figure dashed from her left. Rose'el, with sword drawn and fixed in both hands, thrust out her rusted blade. It penetrated the witch's bosom, right through the heart.

As the blade's point emerged from her back, Al'un Dai dropped the dagger. Her face contorted. Kesla, still holding his son in his right arm, caught her as she fell and tenderly set her on the floor.

Rose'el's blade remained in the witch's body.

"I loved you, Kesla," the witch whispered. "I could have killed you when you came into my chambers, but I loved you. I gave you everlasting youth."

She spat blood and cried out in pain, her back arched against the sword still stuck through her body. "Revenge me, my love. Revenge me." Her arm twitched and then she lay quiet.

The baby started to cry. Kesla leaned over the dead woman, kissing her unresponsive lips and running his fingers through her golden curls.

Ice formed on the floor around him. He stood and pushed his son into Dantress's arms. "Promise me," he pleaded. "Promise to deliver my son to the dragon."

"You are forgiven," Dantress said, glancing at the child in her arms. "Come back with us."

"Dear child, I cannot . . ." Suddenly he lunged forward. He picked up the sword lying on the floor and retreated several strides.

"Though this weapon has been diminished through my wickedness," he said, eying it up and down, "it shall be purified. Oh, Xavion, Xavion, would that I could take back all that I've done and follow you in battle again. But you are dead and your sword is a mere shadow of its former glory.

"Thus, as this sword has been tainted by the blood of the innocent, now it shall be purified by the blood of a traitor."

Kesla set the sword's hilt on the floor so that the weapon stood vertical. His tears fell onto the rusted blade, mingling with the rust, and—what looked like—blood. "Tell the dragon"—he considered the blade pointed at his chest—"that my sins caught up with me and my doom was my own choosing. Tell him that my son must not become like his father, nor do I wish him to know of his mother. He is my illegitimate son, yet a son that I have loved as dearly as any other."

Running together, the sisters cried out for him to stop, but he fell upon the sword of Xavion. Its rusted blade pierced his heart and protruded from his back. His blood pooled rapidly around him. The sword glowed white for an instant and then it absorbed the blood of the traitor.

Handing the infant to Evela, Dantress knelt next to the dead man, trembling as she pushed his body over and drew out Xavion's sword. She held it aloft as she stood. Its blade narrowed and then lengthened several inches, as if it were a living thing.

The sound of another blade slurping from its victim drew her attention to Rose'el, and she saw that her sister had taken back her sword from the witch's body. Rose'el gazed upon the witch. She pulled a gold wrist band off the woman's wrist. "For the boy," she mouthed.

A brass ring on Kesla's finger sparkled in the light. Dantress reached over and pulled it off his finger, handing it to Rose'el. "You keep them for now."

Rose'el put the brass ring on her right thumb and slid the gold band onto her wrist.

Thick ice formed over the floor surrounding the dead woman. Whispers filled the room, low cold whispers that filled Dantress with dread.

"Evela, give me the baby!" She took the infant from Evela.

Ice accumulated on the walls, sealing all openings, all avenues of escape.

Caritha, Rose'el, Levena, and Laura touched their blades together, sending a blast of blue energy sizzling against the wall through which Dantress had entered the room. But the discharge had no effect.

"Great," Rose'el said, balling her hand into a fist. "Now what are we going to do?"

Suddenly the wall trembled. The ice accumulating on it shattered. Something crashed into the wall on the opposite side. It shook, and several stones dislodged from the wall and fell to the floor. Another crushing blow struck the wall. This time the stones exploded at the sisters. They ducked, and the stones landed several feet from them. They saw that a hole, large enough for a horse to pass through, had been carved out of the wall.

"Come on!" Caritha ran through it, Dantress and the others fast on her heels.

THE PORTAL OPENS

The sisters raced into the corridor and found the stairway that they had come down when they'd entered the temple's lower levels. Ghostly whispers filled the dark corners, and hisses followed them. Dantress held Xavion's sword ahead of her, its glow had intensified so that now it blazed like a torch in the darkness. Her sisters sheathed their swords, for the light produced by their weapons was inconsequential beside that of hers.

When they emerged into daylight they ran. Hissing and whispering continued to sound behind them until they crossed over the drawbridge. Exhausted, they sat on the ground, panting for breath and sore from their battle with the witch.

Dantress kissed the infant's forehead. She couldn't get Kesla's face out of her mind. He had seemed so gentle. Not at all what she'd pictured for someone who'd helped murder a young man.

An eagle shot over their heads and screeched. Their eyes followed the golden-eyed creature as it angled back its brown wings and landed on the end of a rustic canoe. It fluffed the pure white feathers bedecking its head and neck and looked up at the old woman from the cottage standing in the canoe.

"Eh! What's this?" their former hostess asked.

The sisters were startled, for the canoe was resting on dry land.

Dantress blinked. "What . . . how did you get here?"

The old woman raised her arm, pointing to the south. "Now's not the time, Dearies. No, no time to rest. See? Another evil rises from the south. He has sensed your presence, knows you are weary from battle and seeks vengeance for his slain dragons."

Faint orange colorations marched across the early evening sky. Darkness threaded its way over the landscape. The battered temple fortress rose gloomy and menacing, as if blaming Albino's daughters for the corpses lying unburied in its ancient chambers.

A flash of light caught Dantress's eye. A greenish, unnatural thunderbolt shot from right to left, behind Al'un Dai's broken towers.

A wailing wind blew from the south ahead of the storm.

She stood up, her arms still embracing Kesla's infant as she turned to the old woman. "Will you help us?"

"Help? Eh, with what, dear?"

"Sit back down, Dantress." Laura stretched out her arms and yawned. "Take a break."

Rose'el grunted and looked up at Dantress, shaking her head. "I don't know about the rest of you," she said to the other sisters, "but I've come to believe that we should trust Dantress to judge the situation. She seems to have a bit more *dragon sense* in her than the rest of us. Besides"—she pointed south—"I don't like the looks of that."

Caritha nodded. Her chest heaved as she breathed in deep and slow. "It isn't safe here. Is it, Dantress?"

Turning back to the odd old woman standing in a canoe on dry ground, Dantress held out the sleeping child. "He would slow us down," she said, gazing fondly upon the tiny being. "We cannot bring him with us."

"Then I will bring him to my home." The old woman took the boy. "He will be safe with me."

"No." Dantress stared hard into her eyes. "The child must be delivered to my father . . . it was his father's final wish." She hesitated, picturing the place along the sea's shore where she and her sisters had come through the gate and first seen the golden banks of the Eiderveis River.

The old woman's gray eyes returned her gaze. "Very well," she said. "What is your wish, Dantress?"

With such clarity did the woman speak, that, at first, Dantress believed she'd imagined it. The hunched woman before her, with dirt encrusted skirt and pale green blouse had thus far spoken with total lack of sophistication. Now, at a time when Dantress most needed her services, the old woman had spoken with dignity, respect.

Behind her, Caritha, Rose'el, Laura, Levena, and Evela rose to their feet. They were prepared to follow her lead.

"Go quickly," Dantress said to the old woman, reaching down to part the fold in her skirt. The sword's rusted metal protested as she drew it out. The ringing of metal behind her told her that her sisters had followed suite. "Take the child to the shores of the north sea. Bring him there, within sight of the Eiderveis River, and wait for us."

"It will be done as you ask." The old woman bowed, then sat in the canoe. Her eagle flapped its wings, shrieking. "Go! Eh?" She held the baby in her arm and pointed with her free hand to the forest. "Go now! Flee while ye can and don't look back. And *I* will bring the boy."

Dantress couldn't help frowning. Was it wise? Leaving an old woman with a baby, in a canoe, sitting out in the middle of nowhere, waiting for who knew what?

Green lightning flashed. A dragon roar echoed from the south. Carried by the wind, it resounded against the ruins and echoed in the surrounding forest.

"Are you sure you want us to leave you here?" She leaned forward, her hand gently resting on the old woman's bony shoulder.

"Yes! Yes, go now . . . There is no time. *He* is coming."

"Who is coming?"

The old woman slapped her hard across the face.

Dantress stepped back, shocked by the woman's change in manner.

"Listen here, eh?" the old woman said. "The longer you dally, the greater the chance that I will not be able to leave this place. Go now, like I told ye to and no harm will come to the child. If ye stay then I cannot promise what will happen."

"But—"

"No buts, deary! If you trust the great white dragon, then trust me. Go now!"

Dantress ran from that place, not venturing to glance back.

Evela, running beside her, started to turn her head, looking back. "No, Evela," Dantress instructed. "Don't let anything distract you . . . We must reach the Eiderveis River before night falls."

❀ ❀ ❀

The cold, demonic hands slipped reluctantly off Specter's shoulders and arms, icy fingernails dug into his back. He had guarded the retreating daughters of the white dragon for as long as he could, holding back the demonic phantoms haunting the temple's sublevels. The twisted forms of men and women flitted in and out of view as he charged for the stairway leading outside, glancing over his shoulder at the half circle of would-be-captors.

They evaporated like mist fleeing before a strong wind, then reappeared, sometimes full bodies visible, at other times—fragmented as if unable to take full human form. Their fingers clawed toward him, their blind eyes showed white. Veils of cloth hung heavily off their bodies, if one could call their burned and scarred forms bodies.

Stumbling over his own feet, another one of them drew close behind Specter, latching onto his white cape with serrated teeth. Specter swiped his blade between the being's unseeing white eyes, and it split into misty tendrils and vanished.

Only a dozen more steps to the stairway.

"Waittt," the being whispered, reappearing in front of Specter. "The path, the path, the path into darkness . . . It waits for you, too. Do feel it, feel ittt. Become the new master . . . this ancient place . . . Learn its secret . . . learn its secret . . . eternal mastery of the universe."

"Light cannot be joined with darkness, demon!" Specter's gray cape twirled around his leg as he spun on his heel. He swung his scythe blade and cut the demon in half.

The being's separated torso stretched out with misty tendrils and latched onto its motionless legs.

Specter did not wait to see if the being would reassemble itself. He forced his ice cold legs to ignore the pain of a million penetrating needles. Up the stairs he ran until he at last emerged outside. A bolt of green lightning reflected off the broken towers and illuminated the shadows amidst the ruins.

In the distance the six young women ran into the forest.

Specter passed over the ancient drawbridge and approached the canoe. The old woman crooned to the baby and a tear rolled down her cheek. "It was the only way to save them, eh?" she said, kissing the infant's forehead gently.

Lightning cracked. Specter stepped closer to the old woman. "Do not be afraid."

"What? Who's there?"

Specter did not show himself, but stood still, his eyes fastened on a group of eight soaring on the wind. Drusa had returned.

He looked down at the old woman in the canoe. Something familiar about her . . . a warm, sunny day back when . . . but he could not complete the picture in his mind.

"Eh, who is there?" the old woman said, searching all around with her eyes. "Who are ye?"

"We both serve the same master, Enlightenment," Specter answered. He did not know how he knew her name, but he said it anyway, then looked southward. "Now, go! I will hold them off until you and the child are safe."

The dragons and the It'ren were close now. He turned to look again at the canoe—but it was nowhere in sight.

☍   ☍   ☍

A spot of light hovered star-like six feet off the ground, spitting out strands of energy and expanding until the portal began to open. Soon the sisters would be able to pass through to the realm of their father. Dantress scanned the sea, then the shoreline and the river behind them. The old woman in the canoe was nowhere to be found.

They should not have left her alone.

Fiercely the wind now blew, kicking up the sand and biting the sea until it frothed. Dantress shivered, half from the chill sneaking through her garment and half from the foreboding darkness gathering in the sky. Clouds covered the sun, thunder rumbled—or was it the distant sounds of combat?

She shifted her eyes from the opening portal, her way home to safety.

Green energy zipped from the sky to the southwest, targeting a portion of the forest west of the Eiderveis River.

"Something's not right." She gripped her sword's handle tight and reached out with her mind, groping through the forest for any clue as to what had happened to the old woman and the child.

Caritha's hand grasped Dantress's shoulder. Dantress looked at her. Eyebrows knitting together, lips pressed tight, the older sister shook her head. "We have done our part, Dantress. Now we must wait."

"Wait? But Caritha, what if—"

The portal opened to its full aperture and an enormous white body shot through it, wings spreading as it passed over the sisters. "Father!"

But the great white dragon did not so much as turn his head as he soared into the sky and out of sight.

The portal fizzled with energy and another figure emerged, this one much smaller. With his shepherd's curved staff in hand, the wrinkled, kindly man smiled at the sisters and spread his arms wide. A gust of wind caught his hood, it slipped from his head and folded over his back. "Well done! Well done, indeed!" He kissed each of them on the forehead and slapped the dust from their shoulders.

"Our mission *was* a success." Caritha bowed. "Yet, we have failed in one regard."

"Oh?" The man leaned on his staff, fixing his blue eyes on her dark ones. "To what failure do you refer?"

Dantress stabbed her sword into the sand. The mission *hadn't* been a success. If it had, then Kesla would have returned to her father. And she had also given up his infant son. She should have kept that boy safe. She should not have given him to that crazy old woman sitting in a land-bound canoe. Things would have been different; things would have been a lot different.

She sank to the coarse sand and struck it with her fist.

As if in answer to her inner cries, a rustic canoe slid onto the beach, half resting in the water. The old woman held out her arms. Dantress stood slowly. A tear formed in each eye, blurring her vision as she reached out and took the warm, sleeping son of the traitor into her arms. She mouthed a thank you to the old woman.

"Take care of yerself, deary." The old woman's canoe slid away into the sea. "Ye have a gift, a gift to love without consideration to yourself. Never let that go."

No oars were in the old woman's hands and the boat had no rudder, yet it moved off into the distance, carrying the curious occupant beyond Dantress's sight.

"Come." The shepherd strode to the portal's entrance and waved the sisters toward it.

Rose'el set her shoulders and stepped through without a word. And Evela followed with a bounce in her step. Levena sheathed her sword, lifted her chin proudly, then allowed the fizzling circle of light to swallow her whole. Laura walked in, briskly, no hesitation. Caritha, sword still in hand, glanced at Dantress and, with a nod, stepped through.

Patient stood beside Dantress, his arm around her shoulders. With his free hand he stroked the baby's head. "You have chosen wisely, child," he told her. "In saving this one life, you have saved many.

"Now we should go. These lands must await another day,

another savior. But for now, they fall into darkness." Thus saying, the shepherd led her by the hand into the portal.

She was sinking into a jelly-like substance, slippery and cool. All sense of time failed her, light streamed by in glorious abundance. The shepherd beside her streamed into nothingness, the light nudged her with its gentle fingers, sending her into a knee-high stream of bluish-yellow jelly. She was moving at incredible speed, diverted from the portal's original course.

❈   ❈   ❈

Six yellow-eyed, black scaled dragons dropped from the sky, enclosing Specter in a circle. Drusa alighted on the ground not ten feet in front of him. Her feathers shivered, reminding him of a buzzing bee anticipating its next nectar harvest. Her eyes fastened on him and her dirty lips curled back to reveal equally filthy teeth.

She could see him? He glanced around at the dragons, their eyes fastened on him as well. They could see him too. But—what had happened? He should be invisible.

Thunder shook the ground, another bolt sizzled from the heavens. This one cracked into the ground only a few feet away from Specter, and a dark figure descended through it. Black and brown feathered wings unfolded from the humanoid's back, and a gust of wind flipped long gray hair over one of the creature's wild, black eyes.

Drusa crouched. "Master, this is *the* ghost man from the forest!"

"Ah." The creature rubbed its hands together. "But surely this cannot be the same man? For now he is visible, exposed for all of you—my faithful ones—to see."

"I have no wish to harm you." Specter stared into the creature's eyes. "Leave now and we will all live to see tomorrow."

The winged man laughed and turned to his minions. "Did you hear him? Are you listening?" He returned Specter's stare coldly. "I fear no one, Ghost Man! I am Turser, the Art'en wizard Lord of these lands and wielder of a power beyond any I gather you possess."

Turser fished into his black, ragged shirt with his right hand—the skin was black, the hand withered—and when it reappeared it balanced a small shiny sphere, as black as the depths of night, on its palm. "Tell me, Ghost, what is *your* name?" Without any warning the wizard's healthy hand sprouted a blast of green energy, striking Specter in the chest and sending him breathless to the ground.

"Pity." The wizard held out the sphere. "I had hoped we'd get to know one another better before I killed you. But seeing how easy this is proving to be, I doubt you have much longer to live."

Standing, Specter forced himself to ignore the heat racing through his chest. He drove at the wizard with all his might, but another green energy bolt struck him down. This one sizzled longer, latching onto and lingering on his chest before it died. But he stood again and, when the wizard threw another charge in his direction, Specter jumped to the side, rolled, and stood beside the Art'en. He raised his scythe.

The wizard, energy still sprouting from his left hand, did not have time to protect himself. Specter's blade sliced open the man's face from his left eye down to his chin. He swung the handle of his weapon around to hit the creature's side.

Screeching like a mortally wounded bird of prey, the wizard crouched down and bit Specter's leg. Specter attempted to back off, but the winged man seemed transformed into a carnivorous creature.

Striking with fists and wings, Turser dropped to the ground. He balanced on his hands and kicked his feet into Specter's ribs. As he fell, Specter tried to stab the wizard, but Turser's black sphere fed him green energy and blasted from his hand, hitting Specter repeatedly until Specter felt that he would indeed die—again.

Again? What made him think that he had died before? His mind filled with images of swords and blood and a youth— wielding a white-bladed scimitar. *Betrayed!* He felt the conviction of the word, knew then what he was, *who* he was. But, *no, I am him no longer. I am Specter.*

Despite the pain, despite the multitude of attacks, Specter stood up again; he would not die today.

He twirled the scythe around his body, letting his rage build inside him like a hurricane waiting to be let out. The next time that the Art'en's wings struck at him, Specter's scythe harvested their feathers.

The wizard screeched again, his featherless wings pitifully naked.

"I did not want to kill you," Specter said. He drove his weapon's handle into his enemy's ribcage. With every blow the images of his previous life returned to his mind, making him remember, making him strong.

Holding his scythe with both hands he now struck the wizard's withered hand, knocking away the sphere. As soon as he did . . . he had the satisfaction of seeing his cloaked body vanish. But his efforts had cost him dearly. His wounds drained the energy from his body. He collapsed, invisible, yet helpless.

The clouds in the eastern sky split apart as if pierced by an enormous white blade and Specter knew what would happen before it ever did. This time salvation had come in time.

Albino dropped from the sky, directly over him. The tremendous bulk of the dragon overshadowed him. In the great white dragon's presence the other dragons cowered away, whimpering like dogs in retreat.

Drusa alone tested the creature. She flew at his neck as if to tear out his throat. But instead of touching him, the It'ren passed through him as if he were not even there. When she fell to the ground, she looked up and screeched in terror. Her master rose beside her, grabbing for his sphere.

But Albino opened his mouth in an earth-shaking roar. The sphere rose into the air and hovered before the dragon until his claws closed around it and shattered it into a thousand fragments. An explosion of darkness erupted from the ruined device of wickedness, yet the dragon's white scales glowed and the darkness dissipated against them.

Clasping Specter in his claws, Albino shot into the sky. Specter watched the ancient ruins and the wizard and Drusa shrink out of sight. And even as he rested in the dragon's clutches, he felt Albino send wave after wave of revitalizing energy into his body to heal his wounds.

PLANTING SEEDS

S hooting from the stream of jelly and light, Dantress emerged into a dark place. She could see no farther than her hands and her feet did not rest on a floor. Yet the air cushioned around her, making her comfortable and secure.

Ahead of her two doors opened silently, and a vertical line of flickering light appeared. A chamber filled with raging flames emerged from the blackness. A sword, burning fire inside of and on the exterior of its blade, rose amidst the flames. She caught her breath. Its handle twisted upward, its blade pointing down, until it rested level with her eyes.

"Once again you come to me, dragon's daughter. Once again you loosen the tongue of prophecy:

'The man child you hold, the traitor's son, son of a warrior—and of a witch. A powerful warrior he will become. He will seek vengeance for those he does not know, and his eye will be drawn to dragon blood enchained beneath the valley.'"

Dantress could not take her eyes off the weapon which had a splendor beyond compare. Where was she? And what, or who had created this place?

The chamber doors closed gradually, leaving her once more in total darkness. She felt her feet rest on a solid floor of stone.

"It is done then," a voice rumbled from behind her.

She spun around. Balancing the child in one arm she reached into the fold of her garment and touched the cool pommel of Xavion's sword. Her fingers slid over its handle, and she drew it from its scabbard. The blade blazed like a torch, and the light radiated off of the pure white scales and soft pink eyes.

"Father!"

In her excitement, Dantress almost dropped the baby, who started to cry.

She ran to the dragon's outstretched arms, feeling his warm gaze. As his strong, hard fingers pressed her against his chest, Dantress wept. The joy of reunion, the stress of the past days . . . it all welled up inside her until it forced its own release.

She could not say how long she and the dragon stood there. When she opened her eyes they were standing in the palace library.

Patient stood there too, leaning on his shepherd's staff with one hand, smiling at her from beneath his hood. And in the shepherd's arm lay Kesla's son, sound asleep. The shepherd's white robes starkly contrasted the dark bookcases towering above him. Somehow he seemed almost magnificent, even in the presence of the great white dragon.

"The boy is Kesla's son," Dantress said as the dragon released her from his embrace. She walked toward the shepherd and lowered her sword into its scabbard.

The white dragon took one powerful stride past her and fixed his eyes on the weapon. "The sword." His tone was hushed. "Patient, my friend, do you see?"

"Yes! Yes, I do." The shepherd's blue eyes shone, and he stepped in Dantress's direction, his eyes fastened on the sword's handle, which she still held. "Do you think"—the shepherd looked up at the dragon, questioning—"that this weapon might be purified?"

"It appears the process has already begun." The dragon swung his head around to address the shepherd. "But the sword will never truly be cleansed, never fully restored, until it is wielded by one who has shed no blood, whose heart is pure, and in whose veins runs the blood of humanity. Only then would it be restored to its original state."

Silence filled the next moments. The dragon and the shepherd appeared deep in thought.

"Forgive me, my daughter," Albino said at last, glancing down at Dantress, "in all the excitement I'm afraid I got distracted."

He gestured with one clawed hand and led her to the door. "Elsie, Helen and Gwen have already fixed dinner for you, so go along now. I will speak with you and your sisters later. And, dear child, you did well. You have made me proud."

Dipping a curtsy, Dantress walked through the doors. They shut behind her.

"Fairest among the dragon's daughters, you are back! Well, well . . . no cuts on your pretty face, so I see." Miverē flitted onto her shoulder and clamped his thin arms across her neck, that is, as far as they would reach.

Dantress laughed and smiled down at the delicate creature. She stroked his red hair. It had grown a couple inches longer since she'd last seen him. Miverē's transparent oval wings rustled together, and he closed his eyes.

How he had found her to greet her before anyone else in the palace? She didn't venture a guess. It was nice to be wanted, to be loved. And Miverē was certainly a true and faithful friend.

A bit of stone on her shoulder caught her eye and she picked it off. Rubble from the Temple of Al'un Dai?

"Here," she said, handing it to the fairy, "a souvenir from my trip."

The fairy held the stone, turning it over and over in his hands. His wings beat against the air, and he hovered in front of her face and kissed her on the nose. A minute tear rolled down his cheek. With a smile, he flew around the bend in the main hallway.

No doubt he headed for the fairy tree.

To her right, Evela's head popped into view.

"There you are!" Evela smiled. "Dinner is being served. Are you coming?"

Dropping royal etiquette for the moment, Dantress ran down the hall. She and Evela laughed together and embraced.

"We worried about you," Evela said, leading her into the dining room where Caritha, Rose'el, Laura, and Levena sat before the table with a fine, generous meal. "Where were you? The shepherd came through the portal without you and then he told us not to worry and he brought us to the palace.

"Rose'el was convinced you'd run off to find another helpless person to save, but I told her you wouldn't be so foolish. Oh! By the way, Father said he is going to give us another assignment. What do you think of that?"

"Evela." Elsie bustled into the dining room and forced the shortest sister into a vacant chair. "No more chattering, Evela! It is time you all ate something decent. You all look a mite thinner than when you left." She neared Dantress and kissed her on the cheek. "Sit down, child. Eat and then rest. You look famished and exhausted!"

Dantress smiled a tired sort of smile. "Thank you, Aunt Elsie." She was grateful for the woman's love, but it had been merely a few days since they'd left the castle; not a month!

"Gwen," Elsie called at the closed kitchen door. "Bring an apron out, will you? Gracious me! Can't we even serve dinner in a timely fashion today?"

"We're coming, Mum." Gwen bustled in from the kitchen with a fruit bowl in her hands and a warm smile on her face. Helen followed close on her heels with more food for the dragon's daughters.

After setting down the fruit bowls, Gwen held out a neatly folded apron to Elsie.

"Gwen, how often must I say this?" Elsie stamped her foot. "Red only. This is not red—this is white."

"Sorry, Mum." The faintest hint of an amused grin passed across Gwen's face as her long legs sped her toward the kitchen. She returned seconds later, a red apron draped over her arm.

"That's better." Elsie slipped the apron over her head and tied it around her back. "Now, dinner is served!"

⚹ ⚹ ⚹

Albino closed the library doors behind Dantress and lingered there, staring at them, before shifting to face Patient.

The shepherd, still holding the infant, returned his gaze. "I will take the child and raise him."

"No, my friend." The dragon shook his head. "If Letrias ever learns of Kesla's son, he will surely seek him out. Besides which, you are going to be far too busy to raise a child. We must hand this matter over to another, someone who will be able to watch over the boy without being seen. And we must send the boy to a place Letrias knows nothing of."

The shepherd raised one eyebrow. "Who do you have in mind?"

"Who else? Specter. He has proved to be more than capable; I would trust him with my life."

"As would I," the shepherd replied. "But *where* will you send him? Letrias's might is growing and his influence may soon reach every corner of Subterran."

The dragon snarled. "Yet for all his cunning, that wizard knows nothing of that other world. As long as Yimshi shines down, its rays bathing this world, the other is hidden."

"Yes." Patient stepped forward, smiling. "Another tool . . . I am beginning to see the extent of your plan."

"Are you? I have not yet begun." Albino rumbled in his throat. "I am merely planting the seeds. It will be up to others to water them."

"Very well, then," Patient said, waving his hand. "Bring him in."

The dragon spread his wings a little and blew smoke from his nostrils. "Specter!" His voice rose to a roar.

Patient cringed, covered the baby with his own robe. "Have a care, my friend. The child is sleeping." He frowned. "Shall I go out into the hall and call for Specter? Or are you going to scream again?"

"There is no need. I am here, my masters." In a dark corner of the library the ghostly figure of the tall man coalesced. He was young, in his mid-twenties. His head bent forward slightly beneath his gray hood. He held a black-handled scythe in his right hand, keeping it barely an inch off the floor. The light of the fireplace reflected off the narrow, long blade that bent from the handle about a foot above Specter's head as he strode slowly to the dragon and the shepherd. His blue eyes did not avert Patient's or Albino's gaze and yet there was not even a hint of a haughty or proud spirit.

Specter took the baby from Patient's arms, looking down at the child in silence. He turned to go, but the dragon held out a clawed hand.

"There is one more thing I wish to do before you go." He produced a brass ring between his claws.

Specter's head jerked up. His mouth opened as if to speak, but he clamped it shut.

"Yes," the dragon rumbled, "you do know this ring. It was Kesla's . . . now it will remain with his son so that when the time comes, we will know him."

Holding up one of the infant's tiny hands, Specter waited as the dragon slipped the ring over the pointer finger of the boy's right hand. As the brass band slid past the second knuckle, it shrank until it became the perfect size for the child's finger. "There." The dragon slowly withdrew his claws.

Without a word, Specter dipped his head to the dragon. As he spun on his heels, his long, gray cape whipped around his ankles and he dissolved from ghostlike transparency into total invisibility.

"The child will be safe with him," Albino rumbled.

"I should say so." Patient held his staff with both hands, leaning on it, looking at the place where Specter had stood.

The dragon's chest heaved, and smoke drifted from his nostrils. "Specter is an appropriate alias for him," he said, "and it suits our purposes for the time being. His past would only interfere with his mission. By giving him a new name, I have protected him from the ears of all workers in sorcery. Evil fears what it does not understand, and it may be that Letrias and Specter will one day meet. When that day comes"—Albino flexed his clawed fist—"Letrias will realize the full extent of his error."

The shepherd remained silent for a time, his blue eyes staring into Albino's pink ones. Then he let go of his staff with one hand

and stroked the spine of a large book on a nearby shelf. "Why did you do it?"

With an honest, curious expression, the dragon said, "To what are you referring?"

Patient said, "Rose'el gave you two items for the boy. One was from his mother. One was from his father. A gold band and a brass ring . . . but you only gave him the ring."

"Because *this*"—Albino opened his hand and the gold band materialized out of thin air, resting in his palm—"is the ancestry that he need not know. This is his link to a mother who neither loved him, nor loved the Creator. She chose to be the evil that she was . . . she chose to be a witch.

"And, apart from this, it was Kesla's wish. I have vowed that his son will not follow in his parents' footsteps." The dragon ground the band in his scaled palm until gold dust sifted between his fingers. With a gentle puff of air, he dispersed the dust into the room in a small yellow cloud.

A moment of silence passed between the dragon and the shepherd. A moment filled only with their individual thoughts and whatever memories their conversation had brought to mind.

"What happens now?" the shepherd asked.

"Now I must plant the most important seeds of all."

"And you are sure that they are ready?"

"The dreams will lead Dantress on the correct path, my friend. You can rest assured of that." The dragon lowered his head level with the shepherd's. "All things *will* fall into place and the world as we know it will never be the same."

※ ※ ※

Six months after his daughters returned from the lands bordering the Eiderveis River, the great white dragon emerged from a cool, moist passageway in Shizar Palace. The rough stones scraped against his scaled sides as he brushed the wall. He turned, spattering a weak flame against the door in finalization as he pushed it shut. If it had been midnight, then the doorway would have revealed itself with a glowing outline, but now, in the wee hours of the morning, it was indistinguishable from the rest of the corridor wall.

He turned and listened to the faint sobs coming from the corridor's end.

"F-fairest among the g-great d-dragon's daughters, I will m-miss you."

"I know," Dantress replied weakly. "I know all too well, Miverē. But—please—think of me often, for I will often think of you."

Taking a few gentle steps, Albino stretched out his neck, peering around the corner.

Dantress, wearing her purple dress, reached out to the lowest blue-white branch of the glowing Fairy Tree and caught one of Miverē's tears as it dripped off his narrow chin.

"I will be back," she whispered. "You can be assured of that."

The fairy's shoulders shook and his green eyes glowed back at her. "Do you promise me, fairest of the dragon's daughters? Do you promise?"

"Yes, Miverē, I *promise*." Then she let the tiny fellow kiss her nose and smiled sadly at him before backing from the tree.

Albino eased his way out of the corridor into the main hallway, placed his large clawed hand around Dantress's shoulders. And then he looked down at her, and she gazed back and firmed her lips.

"I am ready, Father."

❈   ❈   ❈

The sisters stood before the great white dragon, not venturing to say a word. Dantress felt as if the enormous throne room, with its high walls and polished marble floors and imposing twisted metal throne, pressed in on her.

"A different sort of test now awaits you," the dragon said, scraping his claw across the floor as he addressed his daughters. "You will be journeying into the east, to a forest in this world of Subterran known as the Western Wood. A cave has been fashioned for you there out of solid stone. The creatures of the woods will be your only companions, and you must dwell there as guardians of that place.

"Remember what you are: daughters of a dragon. It is my blood that runs through your veins and my blood that empowers you. Beware of humankind, for many are corrupt. But beware also because you are made in the likeness of their race and, joined with men, you are capable of bearing children. Yet yours is dragon blood. If you bear a child, then know this—you will, your own life, have to give, in order to bring that life into the world."

Tilting his head back, Albino opened his jaws. Flames leapt forth and struck the ceiling. Instead of dissipating, the fire whirled into a vortex of energy. Another portal opened.

One by one the sisters walked up the steps to the throne. Each of them grabbed hold of Albino's hand so that he could hoist them onto his back. Dantress delayed for a few minutes, wishing for a less imperfect world. A place where good reigned would be nice, free from turmoil, pain, suffering and all else unpleasant.

Why couldn't she stay at the palace and lead a peaceful life? Or, better yet, why couldn't she wait for a gallant young man to come along and sweep her into his arms? And then she would raise a family.

But no, that could not be. For it was the blood of a dragon, and not the blood of humanity, that ran through her veins. And the two could never mix—not if she wanted to live.

What was it the flaming sword had prophesied? She thought back to when she saved Miverē from certain death. It was then that she first saw the sword and heard its strange words:

"It is given to humanity to bear after their kind. Yet to the daughters of the great white dragon will be given the choice of joining with the race they resemble, the race of humanity. Their lives they must willingly give if they are to bring a life into the world. This curse is laid upon them, but it is a blessing in disguise, for in the ultimate sacrifice is proven the ultimate love, and a child born out of ultimate sacrifice will bring joy and not sorrow to the one that bears her."

So clearly did she remember the words, that she could almost hear them repeating inside her mind, like distant echoes skipping over the surface of a large body of water.

With a steady hand she reached up, accepting the dragon's help onto his back.

"We are ready, Father," Caritha said.

Albino rose into the portal and streamed to their destination in a blaze of color and light.

❧   ❧   ❧

The white dragon emerged from the portal, and it closed behind him with a snap. Dantress, astride his back, drank deeply of the crisp, flowery air. Fluffy tidbits of pollen floated on the gentle moving air, filling the flat meadows around them like a haze. It gave the scene a surreal feel, dreamlike, separated from reality.

She reached out, caught one of the elusive pollen clumps. A red petal wafted into her hand and she breathed in the smell of roses.

But the dragon shifted beneath her, and she grabbed hold of his scales. The dragon's legs methodically took step after step and the ground crept away behind her. Then he picked up speed. Each long stride brought her closer to the distant setting sun, Yimshi—and a descent to unknown lands miles below.

The dragon shot off the edge and the sisters screamed. They left the beautiful flowery meadows, flying off of the land they knew and over lands that they knew nothing of.

Glancing behind, Dantress saw clouds obscuring the meadow, hiding the kingdom of Emperia in veils of innocent white mist.

Around the dragon the meadow, clouds, sunset, and lands below blended, like mixing paint, into myriads of color and light. Nothing except her and her sisters and the dragon were visible, and she supposed that they were traveling at a speed unparalleled by any other creature.

As surprisingly as the flight had begun, it now ended. The streaming colors coalesced, resolving into trees rushing beneath them and a purplish-pink sky above. The great white dragon angled back his wings and dropped through the treetops, thudding into the forest, jarring Dantress. She looked around, disoriented, wondering where in Subterran he'd brought them.

In one unified action the sisters swung their legs over the dragon's side and sprang to the ground as he crouched to permit them an easier descent. The forest's floor cushioned Dantress's feet as she landed. She looked around at the forest.

Crooked old trees and twisted young ones almost completely surrounded her, with the exception of the spot of forest directly in front of her where wild grape vines dangled over a low cliff face. A triangular wedge cut into this wall of solid stone, no more than six feet wide and ten feet high.

Albino's claws pulled aside the vines, revealing the triangular mouth of a cave. Then he released the vines, hiding it once more.

"Your assignment here, my daughters," he rumbled, "will not be immediately apparent to you. This cave will provide you with shelter from the elements until the time comes for you to leave this place."

With a gentle sweeping gaze, the dragon looked upon his daughters. His wings spread, stretched toward the cloudless sky, his scales glowing pure white in the gathering darkness. Fastening his pink eyes on Dantress, he lifted her chin with one of his claws.

His touch felt cool on her skin and she smiled up at him. But the pink eyes did not smile back and a lone tear formed in the dragon's eye. "Be safe, my daughter."

The dragon roared, shaking the ground as he shot through the forest canopy. The first stars twinkled in the heavens and he disappeared like a comet into the western sky.

※　※　※

A few days after leaving his daughters in the Western Wood, Albino strode through a different forest. Rain pelted his scales and his outstretched wing. He glanced sideways. Rivulettes of water ran down his face, weaving over his scales while he remained dry. He lowered his head to see beneath his wing.

Patient the shepherd smiled back at him. The dragon's wing made one enormous canopy against the rain. "We are almost there?"

"Yes, my friend. It is not far from here." The dragon pushed his head through some drooping branches and emerged in a grassy field. An enormous tree rose from one corner of the field, some of its branches large enough to hold even a creature as large as he. But he had not come for the tree.

At the far side of the open land, partially hidden by a tangled mass of foliage, lay a one-story structure, its outer walls crumbling. Roots wove between its stones, separating them from the mortar, and a lone pillar stood atop the landing in front of its open entrance. White marble steps fronted it, twenty-four of them to be precise. His feet sank a couple feet in the sodden soil as he stepped toward the ancient structure. His claws gripped the lowest steps and he extended his wing up the steps so that the shepherd marched forward.

The shepherd turned to him. "Understand what it means for you to enter this place. You will only be able to do so once and I refuse to ever do so again. We will obtain the sword and the key—that will be the end of it."

Deep in his throat Albino rumbled. "Let us be done with this."

Pointing into the open, crumbling entry to the structure, Patient set his mouth in a sober line. "Fire a steady burst of flames at this position."

Flames roared from the dragon's mouth, struck the stones. The shepherd closed his eyes and mouthed a silent prayer. The flames rolled off the stones, spun around them. They tornadoed into the structure and electric energy sizzled forth. The shepherd and the dragon were swallowed in a flash of light and the world he knew receded behind him.

When the portal landed them in the place beyond the dragon looked about. Here at last, the hidden realm.

"Stay behind me," the shepherd warned. He led the way through dark ruins illuminated from above by a dim glow that had no apparent source. He slowly made his way down ancient stone streets between crumbled buildings. It took hours to reach it. At last they stood before the citadel.

The dragon gazed at the iron pedestal that rose from the smooth landing before the citadel. Against the darkness of his surroundings the pedestal glowed with clear, vibrant light emanating from a dome of energy sizzling over its surface.

On the pedestal and enclosed beneath the energy dome hovered a large, shiny, gold key with the miniature figure of a dragon wrapped around its oval handle. Flames were spewing from the dragon's mouth and entwining themselves around the key's bar and the gold appeared to burn with fire. The end of the key was composed of various prongs, evidently used to open some kind of lock.

"Beautiful, isn't it?"

Albino turned his bony, white head to look down at his bearded, white-haired friend. "Then this is it: the Key of Living Fire?"

"Yes. This is it." Patient held his shepherd's staff with both wrinkled hands and leaned on it as he scrutinized the key with narrowed eyes. "Good," he murmured. "Very good. It is safe."

"Did you expect anyone else to find this place?" The dragon growled. "It is buried from the world and only you and I know of its existence."

Patient chuckled. "One can never be certain that a secret like this will be kept safe. And this is one secret that, I daresay, any wizard would give anything to know. But the battle that was waged in this place was like no other and the collisions of demonic power with that of the powers granted by God opened many portals out of this realm. I feared that someone would have discovered one of those portals by now."

"It has been long ages since this realm was hidden from the world, Patient. If none have entered it is likely that none will." Something crunched under his rear foot as he shifted it and he spun around.

"Ah—see? It is as I feared." Patient walked over to the skeletal remains of a man and pulled the now crushed helmet off the skull and examined it. "Strange—I am not familiar with this design—it encased this man's entire head." He held it up for the dragon to see. "Do you?"

Albino shook his head and tapped the cracked, oval window in the helmet's face. "It seems you were right: others have found this place. We must act now, before our enemies learn of the key."

"Right you are!" Patient threw down the helmet and walked up the stone steps that led to the pedestal. The energy dome sparked as he approached and stretched his hand toward it. "The Shield of Purity was put here as a safeguard against any who serve darkness," he said as his fingers pierced the dome. "Only those whose motives are right and proper and those whose hearts are pure can ever penetrate it."

"What of those whose hearts are not pure?"

The shepherd laughed and pointed at the skeletal remains.

Albino clamped the claws of his left hind leg over the bones. So this was the end result of an unworthy soul touching that which should remain in its place. How many, he wondered. How many had touched this ancient shield and died? He threw the bones into the surrounding blackness. "I see. Very effective."

"Quite!" Patient's fingers preceded his hand through the energy dome and closed around the gold key. The miniature dragon spurted more flames as if fighting against him, but he drew it out and held it up. His gaze never left it.

Flames grew in the darkness and the light of several thousand towering torches illuminated the ancient stone columns of a ruined city, stretching for as far as he could see. Broken pottery lay scattered in the abandoned streets and enormous stones, dislodged from crumbling buildings, peppered the ground. The buildings' proportions indicated human architecture and he envisioned for a moment what it had been like to see the city in its prime.

One structure, alone, had stood the test of time. Before him, beyond the pedestal, rose a cathedral. Its spiked spires disappeared into the darkness far above him and its marble walls stood strong. An aura of dim energy surrounded it and he knew that the thing for which he had come was close at hand.

Patient glanced up at the cathedral's spires, the key still held in his left hand. "You understand, my friend," he said, "that this power once destroyed an entire civilization?"

Albino grasped the edge of the stone steps leading up to the cathedral and pulled himself up, carefully avoiding the pedestal. "It was you that suggested this, Patient. Not I!"

"Still, it is you that wants it now."

"Yes." The dragon craned his neck to look up then averted his eyes in disgust. "If it can be used again to avert the death of the innocent then I am willing."

The shepherd looked up again. "You don't fear what sleeps there, do you?"

"Not for myself. But for my children? Yes!" He growled and nodded at the cathedral. "If you will not let me face him, then let us proceed."

"As you wish." Patient preceded him to the cathedral's double doors, his staff tapping lightly against the stone floor and his robes trailing behind him. Engraved in ivory upon the doors was the figure of a snarling white dragon with amethyst eyes.

Inserting the flaming key, Patient gave the doors a push and they opened inward (with a growl that sounded very much like a dragon). They entered a room several times higher than its width. Ivory and black tiles checkered the floor, a stained-glass window depicting the white dragon filled a portion of the back wall, and jewel-like stones hung from the broad rafters. The stones gave off a steady, soft light.

"We have come to it," Patient said, holding up his staff and coming to an abrupt halt. "The Hold wherein we will find the living fire."

Albino checked his surroundings for an indication of where the Hold was. He felt confused. "Do you mean that this—this cathedral is the Hold? I thought you said that no one can step into it."

But the shepherd thrust out the key and turned it in the air. "Click!" Then the floor trembled and rose beneath them, raising them far above to a platform that had been invisible from the ground level. "Hurry! Get on the platform before the floor recedes."

Following Patient's advice, Albino jumped forward just as the stones on which he had been standing dropped hazardously out of reach. He found himself standing opposite a wooden door about eight feet high and five feet wide. A heavy iron chain stretched across it and an inordinately fat padlock had been fastened to it.

Patient held out his staff. "Hold this for me."

Taking the wooden stick in his claws, Albino held it gingerly. "I don't know why you bring this thing with you. It only gets in your way."

The shepherd chuckled. "My friend, if you were human then you would understand that age has a way of catching up with you and that a staff can be more than a little helpful at times." He grabbed the padlock and rattled the chains. "Hold on!" Turning the key in the padlock he dropped the chains and the wood door swung outward.

A whoosh of hot air forced Albino to close his eyes for a moment. He dug his claws into the platform as some kind of force tried to push him off.

"Stop," he heard the shepherd say. "Enough!"

The storm passed and Albino opened his eyes and relaxed his muscles. Before him lay a chamber ablaze with fierce flames. Patient stood before it and reached back even as Albino held out his staff.

"The powers of a penitent prophet never die," Patient said as he took a step toward the Hold. "They live on without him and, yet, bound to him. Once given up they yearn to return to their master, but they are not allowed to do so. Today I have come to close off this danger to the world, this threat to mankind's existence:

"A power of evil rises from the ashes of his master's doom, a threat upon the world grows in strength. He gathers the corrupted and the evil to himself, preparing for a war upon Subterran that will subject it under him. To what will men turn when this evil threatens their existence? Do they have a champion, a man who can match the evil brought against him?

"I see the youngest daughter of the great white dragon, pure and beautiful, won by a man of her choosing. She gives her life and brings a child into the world. A child of hope, an offspring of the dragon. But the enemy seeks out the offspring and draws near to snuff out her flame.

"Will none go to her aid? Will all stand and watch as she is destroyed?

"I see a sword blazing in the hands of her deliverer! Fierce and glorious, he stands between her and death. The sword given to men by the dragon prophet is in his hands. Lo! It has the living fire—the powers held from time long past. It is he, the son of the traitor.

"Take now the weapon and arm the deliverer!"

Albino beheld a mighty sword rise from the midst of the Hold. Its blade was long and elegant, double-edged. Its steel mirrored everything without flaw and flames entwined themselves around the blade, wreathing it in red and yellow fire. The sword's guard was semi-transparent, like crystal, and a gold vine wrapped it and passed below to the handle, reinforcing the leather gripping.

Patient slid his hand over the sword's pommel and curled his fingers around its handle, then drew it out, stepped back, and watched the heavy wooden door close. The chains tangled themselves across the door and the padlock fitted itself into their links before snapping shut.

"Take this!" Patient tossed him the sword. "The prophecy was meant for you and the sword is yours to give to whomever you choose."

Catching the sword in one hand, Albino waited for the cathedral's floor to return for them. As the tiles rose next to the platform, he leapt onto it and it began to descend, leaving Patient behind. Spreading his leathery wings, Albino shot up and past his friend, curling his tail around Patient's torso and flinging him onto his back.

"It is time to depart, my friend."

He streaked downward, pulled his head back and landed in front of the entry doors. Patient dismounted and opened the doors. As he did so, they saw a swirl of light and a portal opened before them.

"Our way home!" Albino roared victory but he had turned his face upward again. There, hovering in the air around the citadel spires was a host of human figures wrapped in dark veils, silent and unmoving. In their midst was a body dwarfing all others, its spiked tail wrapped around its shiny, black-scaled body. "Valorian!" he growled.

Patient slapped him across the head with his shepherd's staff. "Leave him be! We're getting out of here."

The portal grew in size and prepared to swallow them and at that moment Albino heard the faint tinkle of metal as the key slipped through Patient's fingers and fell to the stone floor. He grabbed for it but missed. The key vanished and reappeared inside the energy dome atop the pedestal. "No!"

A whirlwind of color caught him up. He felt his surroundings disappear and saw the light of day fill the darkness. Moments later he found himself standing outside of the ancient ruin deep in the forest. Rain pummeled him again and the portal vanished behind him. Patient stood next to him.

"Do not worry," the shepherd said. "The sword is what we really came for. It is the key to the future, and the Shield of Purity will prevent anyone else from obtaining the key."

"And what if someone else manages to get past that shield?" Albino growled and looked at the spot where the portal had been.

Patient furrowed his brow. "If someone managed to get past the shield—" He glanced at the sword. "Then that weapon would become as any other sword and its bearer would be left vulnerable."

"Great! So we have a weapon and a prophecy that are useless! And what if Letrias finds out about this? He is crafty and may figure a way to get the key."

"Not if we keep this incident a secret."

"You mean don't tell anyone?"

Patient started walking into the trees but he called back over his shoulder. "Yes. That is exactly what I mean!"

They left the forest. Patient kept gazing upon the mighty sword and smiling. "I always believed that Living Fire could save many lives. Today the events we will put in motion have the potential of proving me true."

The rain stopped and the clouds thinned before a stiff wind that howled through the forest. The dragon crouched as Patient climbed onto his neck, then he spread his wings and pulled himself into the sky. He soared eastward to the Western Wood. Spotting the waterfall and woodland pool, he descended, gently landing in the meadow.

Patient dismounted. Not even the starlight cascading down the high waterfall could tear Albino's eyes away from the white robed shepherd. The man stepped into the pool of water formed at the waterfall's base and waded deeper. The water rippled around him. In his hands the sword of living fire burned, the tip of its beautiful blade barely touching the water's surface.

The scales along Albino's spine shimmered as a cool breath washed over him. The trees around the presence of an unseen One blossomed and shed their leaves then grew new ones. The grass warmed and shivered.

"We are all here, Patient." Albino spat flames into the misting night air.

Another voice boomed out beside him. "Let's do it, Patient. I grow weary of waiting."

A smile snuck across the shepherd's face as a breeze pushed his hood off his head and his long white hair freely flowed behind him. "Patience, my friends." But he raised the sword by its handle, above and before him, longingly gazing upon its flaming blade, then slowly lowered it into the water, and stabbed it into the depths until it was hidden from view.

Beside him, the dragon felt the presence of the other One depart.

He nodded to Patient as he slogged out of the water and obligingly dried his robes with a wave of his clawed hand. With not a word more, the shepherd climbed onto the dragon's neck, and Albino spread his wings to depart.

PART II

MIGHTIEST OF SWORDS

MAN OF THE WILDERNESS

I t was the night of Ilfedo's seventeenth birthday. Heat radiated throughout the room from the fireplace. He dropped his hand to feel the long box set across his legs, the gift he'd been forbidden to open until after cake was served. To his left sat his mother, blond hair dancing and green eyes glimmering in the candlelight. She beamed at him, clasped his hand in both of hers, then she turned to meet her husband's lips for a quick kiss.

Rising from his rustic chair, Ilinor, his father, pushed it back from the table and stood with a pewter mug held in his hand. "To you, our friends, our neighbors." He nodded at the half dozen smiling faces looking up at him with rapt attention. "And to you, Ilfedo"—he grinned at his son—"on this most momentous day of your life, a day I hope you will look back on as *not only* the day that you entered manhood, but also the day that you recommitted yourself to uphold your family name, the name of Mathaliah, with honor, for as long as you live."

"Here! Here!" The other three men sitting at the table scrambled to their feet for a moment, and clunked their mugs to his.

"And to my wife, Larkspur," Ilfedo's father continued, resting his hand on her shoulder and looking down into her eyes, "who has raised for me a son of whom I am proud!"

At this, two women seated across from his mother raised their mugs. "Here! Here! Here!"

Ilfedo's face warmed as his mother kissed his cheek, then stood. Three lads now marched into the dimly illuminated room. They'd been his friends and playmates since childhood, ever since their parents had banded together to "Tame the wilderness" and "Get out of the overpopulated coastal towns." His father had headed the expedition, much to the horror of his fellow countrymen who'd warned him that the western parts of the Hemmed Land were no place to raise a family and certainly not the place for the descendants of the tiny nation's oldest family, the family of Mathaliah, to establish themselves.

True, the western half of the Hemmed Land was home to some old beasts that had been known to tear men in half, but it was also hunters' heaven—for those, like Ilinor, who dared explore its wild forested hills.

Ilinor preferred bow and arrows—sometimes a javelin—while on the hunt. A finely crafted, sleek long bow hung over the large stone fireplace behind the kitchen table in their three-room log cabin. The kitchen table had been stained red with the blood of Ilinor's many kills. Below the bow, on a wooden peg driven between the fireplace stones, hung the quiver full of steel-tipped arrows on wood shafts. Ilinor had acquired a large quantity of the lethal arrowheads from the smiths in the coastal towns before making his departure.

His three friends marched stiffly toward Ilfedo, carrying his cake. Ombre stood nearest him, walking sideways with both hands supporting the cake's wooden dish. His hazel eyes twinkled merrily, and the corners of his mouth twitched as if he was having difficulty keeping his face straight.

Broad-shouldered, sandy-blond haired Honer held the center of the cake dish. His gray eyes met Ilfedo's for an instant before looking to his right where sat a couple whose sandy-blond hair and matching gray eyes left no doubt that he was their son. Fletch, of the family Pithion, sitting with his wife Adara, glued their gazes on their son. Honer's seventeenth had come and gone a year and a half ago.

To the couple's right sat a solid-built man with his hands clasped on the table. Jevnar of the family Ernalia. His wife had died two years ago and, though a very nice middle-aged woman back on the coast had tried to draw his eye for a while, he'd eventually decided that no one would take his dead wife's place at his side and had remained a widower. Ombre was his only child and they lived in a tiny cabin a considerable distance south of Ilfedo's parents.

The man smiled a small smile at Ilfedo when he saw him staring, and Ilfedo smiled back, then glanced toward his cake, feeling that he had somehow intruded on the man's private affairs.

Beside Honer, Ganning held the last third of the cake dish. He was a bit of an oddity from the rest, boyish yet sober, dark haired, yet blue eyed. His parents occupied the seats beside Jevnar.

Every other step Ganning took dropped his head and shoulder down by at least a couple inches. His gimpy left leg had been with him from birth. But Ilfedo knew that the boy's limp deceived many people into underestimating his physical abilities. He had seen Ganning run over a wet forest floor with hardly a sound, notch an arrow to his bowstring and bring down a deer within short order.

In fact, all the boys hunted and fished, following in their fathers' footsteps. Though, of late, Ilfedo'd preferred hunting with a sword. Unconventional it might sound—his father at first objected—but Ilfedo liked the maneuverability the sword offered him. Swing, throw, stab—the options seemed limitless.

Slaps on the back from his friends, smiles from the adults gathered around—a thumbs up from Jevnar. Ilfedo relaxed into the party, enjoying the warm love of his home.

He cut the cake into slices . . . each one large enough for two men.

Larkspur passed out the cake, and Ombre said the chocolate and vanilla flavor was just perfect. She patted Ombre's head affectionately, then turned her back to the cabin door and passed cake to Jevnar, her smile magnetic.

The next moment a furry, black mass smashed through the door, razor sharp claws wildly cutting through the air. Never had Ilfedo seen a larger bear, nor, he vowed—as blood spurted from his mother's back and her face paled—would he ever see one alive again.

Horror froze everyone at the table. Everyone, that is, except Ilinor. Throwing himself across the table, he yelled like a madman as his wife collapsed in his arms. Her eyes closed, and he yelled wildly.

He pulled the chair from under Fletch Pithion, dropping the man to the floor, and smashed the heavy wood across the black-furred face. In the few moments that it took for this to happen, the bear shook its head and opened its mouth, latching horrifically with its fangy teeth onto Ilinor's neck and dragged him, bleeding to death, onto the floor.

Everyone sprang into action, grabbing whatever weapon happened to be closest at hand. Adara smashed the cake over the bear's head, while her husband swung his chair after it. Jevnar sprang onto the table, pulling down Ilinor's bow, slipped two arrows from the quiver, and drew it back, then released the projectiles into the beast.

The bear thrashed Ilinor around on the floor, tearing limb from limb, and it struck down the would-be-rescuers with one massive paw.

Ilfedo screamed, rage mixing with sorrow as he tore into his birthday box. The gift he had known would be contained therein, shone back at him in the firelight. Highly-polished metal glinted in the firelight. He snatched up a three-foot long sword of simple yet solid composition, its blade honed to a deadly point.

He stepped over his guests, the box falling to the wood floor, his fist gripping the sword's leathern handle. His father lay dying, his mother—already dead.

The bear swatted at him. He upswung his new blade and drove its point through the bear's paw. Then, with all the strength he possessed, he stabbed the beast's face.

Ilfedo watched the bear through blurring vision as it fell, the blade stuck through its paw into its head, and he released his hold on the black leather grip.

Kneeling beside his mother he held her wrist. No pulse. He called her name, knowing that he'd been too late. Nothing beating in the heart that had loved him as only hers was able.

Ilinor's voice called him and he wept as he held his father's hand and gazed into the glazing eyes. "Father?"

"Your mother . . . is she?"

At this, Ilfedo completely broke. He wept until he ran out of tears. Then he sobbed until his heart felt ready to break.

A tear formed in Ilinor's eye and rolled off his face. "You are—alone—my son. I am . . ." Blood dribbled from his mouth. "I am sorry."

A strong hand clasped Ilfedo's shoulder. He felt someone else's tears falling onto his neck. Jevnar said, "No, Ilinor. Not alone."

The room lay in shambles, but the weeping faces of his friends all around, shook from side to side, affirming Jevnar's statement. "Not alone."

Ilinor struggled, spitting blood as he grasped Ilfedo's shoulder. "You are a man now, my son! But—you need a father—regard Jevnar as such. He—loves you—I know that." He rasped out another breath. "Remember your Creator—honor the family name—" He breathed in one last time, and his eyes closed in death.

Hours passed. No one stirred.

Evening came, darkness fell, midnight passed. Still the mourners lingered, unmoving.

When Yimshi's first light broke upon the forest, the mourners wrapped the dead and formed a blood-stained procession, taking the bodies of Ilfedo's parents to a spot deep in the forest. They cut down one of the larger trees, carved out a rustic coffin, and placed Ilinor and Larkspur together inside of it.

Deep in the earth they buried them, covering the grave with rocks so large it took all three grown men and Ombre, Honer, and Ganning to move them.

Ilfedo remained there that day—and Jevnar stood with him, while Ombre wept almost as much as he. The emotional wounds were deep, he knew. It would take time to heal. But he *would* heal.

⚬⚬ ⚬⚬ ⚬⚬

Ilfedo accepted a large wooden mug from the innkeeper. The potent juice of the wild grapes slid refreshingly from the mug, over his tongue and down his throat. He set the mug down, sliding his hand along the slippery bar. Thanks to the crackling wood in the fireplace, heat drove the dampness from his unkempt, shoulder-length hair and the clammy clothes clinging to his skin.

"Have you come far?" The innkeeper, a towel thrown over each of his narrow shoulders, drowned the mug in soapy water and pulled it out, drying it with one hand while his dark eyes remained on Ilfedo.

Nodding his head ever so slightly, Ilfedo said, "You could say that."

The innkeeper buried one towel-wrapped fist inside the mug, twisting it this way and that. "Where're you from?"

Ilfedo straightened, absentmindedly pointing out the inn's door. "The forests."

"Near here?"

"No." Ilfedo watched a fly buzz onto an empty, used mug. "A few days' steady riding. There are only half a dozen homes out there, not all are presently occupied."

The man finished cleaning the mug and shelved it on the wall behind him. "What brings you here? We don't get many people passing through. Too many rumors have spread concerning the creatures for which the Sea of Serpents was named.

"I've heard the serpents are growing bold, even entering human dwellings. A family north of here mysteriously disappeared. Their house was a disaster." He swallowed. "Folks are saying they were killed by a Sea Serpent."

Ilfedo didn't know if he believed the rumors. Yet he didn't doubt that they could be true. After all, hadn't his own parents been slain in cold blood by a wild beast?

"Where I'm from we don't have to worry about Sea Serpents," Ilfedo said.

"Ah! But I hear that people out your way tend to stick to the forests, live off the land. And I heard tell the first settlers had it real rough." He flipped the towel from his hand, throwing it over his shoulder.

"I heard that one young fellow's parents were killed—the Mathaliah family, I believe—by one of those man-hungry bears that wander round those parts—"

Ilfedo cut him off. "*Wandered* those parts . . . but not anymore."

"*If*," the innkeeper said, leaning against the counter, "and only *if* the stories are true."

In a tired sort of way, Ilfedo sighed. "What stories?"

"Stories of the young orphan lad, the last remaining Mathaliah whose parents were killed by one of those bears." As the innkeeper spoke his eyes lighted with eager retelling. "They say the lad personally visited every cave in the forests and slew every single one of those furry beasts that he could find. They say he came out of every encounter with the blood of the beast's heart dripping from his sword and never a scratch on his body."

Ilfedo inconspicuously lifted his hand, felt the small jagged scar at the base of his neck. *Almost* without a scratch.

"Anyway"—the innkeeper stood up—"such are the stories. Though few believe them, which is probably why so few choose to venture into the wilderness and even fewer settle there."

"More will come in time," Ilfedo said, rising from the elevated stool on which he'd been sitting. "But I, for one, am thankful for the peace and quiet the wilderness offers." He paused, cocking his head to listen to the cries of vendors in the streets outside, the whinnies of impatient or bored horses, and the clattering of carts wending down the narrow streets.

The innkeeper laughed and set his towels out of sight behind the counter. "Yes, I'll admit the noise can get on the nerves. It would be a nice change to live in the country, but . . . you learn to ignore"—he drew a circle in the air with his hand as if to encompass the activities outside his establishment—"all of this."

The man held up a bronze key and Ilfedo smiled back.

"Up the stairs, second door to your right." The innkeeper pointed past six round tables in front of the bar, his eye squinting. Steps rose into the dark second floor, flanked on the side by a rickety railing. "The bed's made. There's fresh water, and you'll find a lamp on the bedside table. If you need anything else just let me know."

With a slight bow, Ilfedo turned to the stairs. The long sword at his side clanked against his leg and he glanced back from the corner of his eye at the innkeeper's furrowing brow.

"Wait, please!" the man said, running up behind him. "The sword?"

Ilfedo twisted on the stairs, one foot on the step and his hand on the railing. "I use it for hunting."

Understanding dawned on the man's face. He held his hand almost to his mouth, then closed it into a fist. "*You*? You're the son of Ilinor Mathaliah? The stories . . . they're about you?"

"Good night, Sir." Ilfedo ascended the creaking steps, adjusting his black fur coat higher on his shoulders.

He found his room without difficulty in spite of the dim light shed by a grimy lantern hanging from the ceiling in the narrow hallway. The scent of oil hung in the air with unrelenting thickness. The door groaned into the room. He shut it after him and walked over to the simple four post bed, patting the coarse, brown sheets and fluffy white pillow.

Rays of sunlight spilled through the moderate amounts of dust hanging in the air. He followed the rays to their source: a twelve-paned window set low in the wall. It looked west over vast fields of nearly-ready-to-harvest corn to the line of white sand spread between the Hemmed Land and the Sea of Serpents.

White crested breakers splashed gently onto the shore, retreating with ease to be replaced by other waves.

Five years. He shook his head, struggling not to see in his mind's eye the faces of his parents on the night of their deaths. He shed his coat and hung it over one of the bed's posts, then unbuckled his belt, grabbing his sword's scabbard before it could fall to the floor.

A lot had happened in five years. He thought back to Jevnar, who had taken Ilfedo into his own home and sheltered him with his own son, Ombre. The man had treated him with kindness, and it had been with reluctance that he'd let Ilfedo move out and build his own home in the forest. Ombre too, had built his own place—only months before another of the dreaded man-killing bears killed Jevnar in his bed.

Ilfedo leaned his sheathed sword against the bed, letting his hand linger on the weapon's cool pommel. In his mind he paid a visit to the past, to the day he and Ombre had found the bear devouring "their" father. With a hatred he'd not known he was capable of, Ilfedo'd leapt onto the bear's back, driving his sword's blade again and again and again into the fat body until rivers of red blood ran across the cabin's wood floor.

Somehow, killing the beast drove Ilfedo to go alone into the wild woodlands. He'd hunted down and slain every last one of that abominable species that he could find. None remained to impede the settling of the wilderness his father had wished to tame.

He gazed out the window, leaning against the wall as he did so and crossing his arms. Yimshi, his planet's sun, turned from pale orange to red and then to a deeper red until he could see a couple spots on its setting disc. At last, it disappeared beneath the tree-covered horizon, its last few rays spread across the heavens, reflecting off the calm surface of the Sea of Serpents as light surrendered to the darkness of night.

When the first stars peeked through the velvety dome of sky, Ilfedo settled into the bed. The soft pillow compensated for the bed sheets scratching at his legs. He kicked off his boots and closed his eyes.

If tonight repeated the pattern he'd grown accustomed to over the past year, then he would again see *her*, but not her face. He didn't know if it was healthy—and he suspected it wasn't—to look forward to seeing someone who existed only in his mind, only in his fantasy. But a part of him did not care. Though he had met several fine young women whose parents had tried to play matchmaker, he hoped to someday find someone uniquely charming . . . someone like the woman in his dreams.

❧ ❧ ❧

The tracks of a deer led Ilfedo upstream through a haze of milky white light that seemed to pull him with invisible hands along the water's edge. Not a single sound penetrated the air. He could not even hear the wet ground sucking at his boots. He sniffed a whiff of . . . nothing. Anyway, it didn't matter. All that mattered was running along the stream's bank and reaching his destination.

Miles passed effortlessly beneath his feet, miles that brought him out of the forests of the Hemmed Land and into the Western Wood, a stretch of land west of his home territory untouched by humankind.

He followed the stream to a pool of water glistening in moderate sunlight and partially shaded by trees on all sides. A waterfall fell in silence over a face of smooth stone to a pool below. Ripples spread from where the water landed in the pool, building outward a series of watery half-rings breaking around olive-skinned legs, smooth as oil.

A feeling of ecstasy overpowered Ilfedo. The reflecting solar rays painted themselves on the young woman's legs. She held her silken skirt out of the water in one small hand, fingers clutching the fabric with the grace and strength of a swan. Her hair, dark and wavy, fell down her back almost to her waist. She was short of stature, yet all the more beautiful for it, and her purple dress clothed her like a queen.

He prepared to call out, to make her turn to see him there. If only he could see her face. But the scene evaporated like mist into utter darkness, and the dreams of ordinary men took her place.

❀ ❀ ❀

The next morning dawned with a clear sky. Ilfedo rose early and sat on the edge of his bed, scratching his itchy legs. The floorboards felt warm under his feet. He listened to the flames crackling in the fireplace one floor beneath him.

He pulled on his boots, rose from the bed, stood in front of the window, and pushed against the glass panes. The window swung outward into the cool, refreshing morning air. Dragging his black fur coat off the bed's post along with his sword, he pulled it snugly around his shoulders. The coat weighed on his shoulders with comforting familiarity as he belted on his sword.

Smells of syrup on waffles drifted from below. Breakfast would soon be ready and Ilfedo smiled to himself. The empty pit of his stomach felt on the verge of a rumble. First he would eat breakfast, then he would gather supplies from his coastal countrymen and head home.

The morning light revealed mist-enshrouded cornfields beyond the town. To the left and to the right stretched a wall of tightly bound logs which, he knew from the previous day, fortified the town on all sides. Two gates—one by the inn, the other on the opposite side of town—were the only access points.

A small sailboat headed out to sea from the stone pier jutting from shore near the town, and he watched it with an unexplainable sense of foreboding. As he observed, a black tail stabbed from beneath the waves and slapped across the sailboat. Splinters the size of spears flew upward, then fell into the sea. Moments later, as witnesses on the pier ran screaming for town, the sailboat crumbled to the waves as a snakelike body raced amid the wreckage.

Suddenly a scream broke from the cornfields, high and terrified, riveting Ilfedo's gaze on an enormous black serpent head rising amid the stalks. A set of human legs struggled in the serpent's closed, beak-like jaws, then fell limp as the serpent clamped tighter.

Ilfedo sprang through the window, in his haste throwing himself over the town's wall. Over eight feet he fell, hitting the ground hard. But the wilderness had made him resilient. He rolled into the corn and stood, sprinting ahead through the rows of stalks rising a dozen feet from the ground like a close-growing forest.

The sword in its scabbard swung against his leg as he ran. Dew wetted his face. He swatted aside the long leaves blocking his view of the territory ahead.

He saw a clearing through the stalks ahead and slowed his pace. Forty feet of black snake slithered across his path. The serpent's head passed by without reacting to his presence, and he breathed relief.

But a gust of chilly breath struck his back. He spun around, reaching for his sword as he did so. Such was the speed with which he drew that sparks flew from the blade. The enormous fangs stabbed at him, he ducked to the side, and they gouged the ground where he'd stood.

Ilfedo lunged forward, piercing the creature's neck. Thick blue blood spurted from the wound. Again Ilfedo struck, this time carving away two feet of blubbery meat. As the serpent thrashed around, death overtaking it, he raised his weapon above his head and brought down the blade, severing the head from the body.

Nearby, in the clearing, three more serpents worked together, herding a cluster of farmers defending themselves with hoes and spades. The farmers struck back with their makeshift weapons, but they were too slow.

One serpent loosened its lower jaw, opened it wide and snatched a man from the bunch, swallowing him whole. Another serpent did likewise and the third followed.

Noticing an ax lying on the ground nearby, Ilfedo dashed over to it, picked it up, and sent it somersaulting through the air. The head stuck in one serpent's body. The creature opened its cavernous mouth in a hissing scream.

Ilfedo ran forward, ducking to avoid the other serpents flailing at him. Clutching his long sword in both hands, he slashed the wounded serpent's body, opening a portion of tender dark flesh to the elements. The creature shrieked. Its white eyes startled open as he struck again, jerking the ax from its body and used it to chop into its neck, ending its misery—ending its life.

"Now," he said, turning to the other serpents, "it's your turn!"

With the sword in his left hand and the ax in his right, he assailed the creatures. He took down one of them with a cut across its throat. The blue blood splattered over his face. For an instant he hesitated, wiping his sleeve across his eyes. During that moment the remaining serpent lashed out with its fangs, catching them on his shoulder.

Ilfedo felt the poison spread through his body. It flowed unhindered through his veins, immobilizing him. Through blurred vision and dulled senses he felt the serpent close its jaws over his entire body, its wet tongue whipped around his torso, pulling him into its throat.

No. No, he would not die like this! He forced his stiff limbs to move. He released his hold on the ax to grip the sword with both hands. Thrusting upward as he struggled to his feet inside the great mouth, he drove the blade into the creature's brain.

Cut off from the world outside the serpent's mouth, he could see nothing. But by the way his captor relaxed and by the feeling of the jaws impacting against something, he guessed that he had killed it. He tried to move again, to escape his slimy prison. His mind clouded with uncertainty and all turned to darkness.

PURSUING VISIONS

As he slipped in and out of consciousness, Ilfedo struggled through delirium. Time passed but not in its ordinary cycle. Sometimes moments lasted for what seemed like eternities. At other times his exhaustion forced him to sleep and time sped by, unhindered by his weary mind.

In his dreams he saw himself, back turned, holding the hand of a woman. Who she was he could not tell, though he thought he had seen her in another dream. Among women she was the most beautiful he had ever laid eyes on.

Then he found himself standing on a field, battle raging around him, men and dragons fighting side by side. It seemed that he was fighting alongside them, drenched in his own blood, the enemy closing in. He tried to discern against whom they fought, but smoke billowed up, hiding the enemy from sight.

⋇　⋇　⋇

When Ilfedo regained consciousness, he found himself lying on a large bed in a rough-paneled room. A small woodstove pumped heat from one corner, a little more heat than he felt comfortable with. Instead of one pillow, he had four.

He reached his arm from under the soft, clean sheets and touched his tender shoulder. The swelled flesh kneaded like dough under his fingers. Some sort of milky balm lay soaking into his skin, covering two narrow scars that ran parallel to one another, four inches apart.

The bedroom door opened and the innkeeper ambled into the room. A ray of morning sunlight slipped through the east window, reflected off the metallic tray in his hands, and glinted in his dark eyes. The door remained ajar as he set the tray on a stand beside the bed, placed his hands on his hips, and slowly nodded.

"You're looking much better," he said.

Ilfedo saw people through the doorway. A pair of elderly men set down their mugs and looked in his direction. A young woman with long dark hair whispered into an aristocratic, finely dressed man's ear. The man nodded, folded his arms. Three young men glanced at him from where they leaned their heads together over a table. Others, wandering around the inn, ceased what they were doing and returned Ilfedo's gaze.

Other men might have found it uncomfortable to be thus exposed to the public eye, but Ilfedo didn't care. He'd been treated as an object of curiosity ever since he'd slain that first man-killing bear in the wilderness. Though not—he admitted to himself—by this many people at once.

Taking a deep breath, Ilfedo sat up, leaned against the bed's headboard.

The innkeeper nodded again then gestured to the breakfast tray. "Do you like waffles? They're fresh . . . and I've put some apple juice here—it's cold—also some bacon." He rubbed his hands together. "We owe you a debt of gratitude, young man. So, if you want anything, just let me know."

"The serpents are dead then?" He twisted quickly to reach for some bacon strips but drew back as a sharp pang shot through his head. He held his hand to his head until a wave of dizziness passed.

The innkeeper frowned. "Still feeling a bit on the off side?"

"You could say that again," Ilfedo replied. "What happened?"

"After you slew the serpents?"

Ilfedo nodded a careful, slow nod.

"It was amazing!" The man threw up his hands and grinned. "Everyone, and I mean the *whole* town, ran out of here with anything they could grab to use as a weapon.

He jabbed his finger into his own chest. "I joined a couple others in searching for you. We cut you out of the serpent's mouth and brought you back here. You were quite a mess. The rest of the town scoured the corn fields and found one other serpent. But it slithered its black, slimy hide to the sea as soon as it saw how greatly outnumbered it was."

Slipping a piece of bacon from the tray, Ilfedo held it in his fingers, eyeing it as his thoughts wandered elsewhere. At last, setting the bacon on his tongue, he said, "How long have I been out?"

The innkeeper's cheeks puffed out, his eyes turned to look at the ceiling. "One week . . . I think." His eyes shifted back to Ilfedo. "You've been in and out of consciousness for *at least* a week."

A week! Ilfedo sat bolt upright, immediately regretting it as the dizziness returned.

"I've got to go," he said to the man. "There are things at home that I cannot leave unattended for long."

Nodding his head, the innkeeper said, "How soon do you want to leave?"

"Immediately." Ilfedo lay back on the bed. "But I'm afraid I'm in no condition to set out on foot."

"Then I'll lend you some horses. I have some of the best around, and I'll send a boy along with you. He'll help out along the way and bring the animals back when you've reached your destination."

Ilfedo started to thank the man but he was cut off as the innkeeper started walking to the door, continuing to talk.

"We've cut the serpent meat into generous portions and spread it among the people hereabouts. For you"—he pointed at Ilfedo and smiled—"for you we've set aside a load of the stuff."

"Thanks for the offer," Ilfedo began, "but the meat won't last long on the trail."

The innkeeper cast Ilfedo's concern aside with a wave of his hand. "Not a problem. We smoked it for you and packed it in an ice cellar. We'll put the ice and meat in leather bags . . . that ought to keep it for long enough.

"Now"—the innkeeper put his hand on the door latch—"I suggest that—if you wish to avoid the crowd of admirers you've picked up over the past week—you wait until dawn. Besides, I think you could use a bit more rest." The man chuckled and shut the door behind him, leaving Ilfedo to rest.

⊘ ⊘ ⊘

Ilfedo leaned against the stable's wood doorway. He felt a bit unsteady on his feet. A gentle breeze cast moist early morning air against his face. He breathed the air, deep and slow, letting it refresh his fogged mind.

He had his bearskin coat opened to the air and his long sword was swinging from just above his left hip. He glanced to his other side, to the axe tucked under his belt, the prize of his victory that the innkeeper had willingly hunted down and given to him.

Letting go of the doorframe, he stepped into the stable's long, dim corridor. The sweet smell of fresh straw filled his nostrils. Whinnies greeted his ears as he walked on the cool, dirt floor between the stalls. One stallion shoved its head over the gate and nudged Ilfedo.

He reached around the horse's nose and massaged it. "Hello there, big fellow."

At that moment a burly man ambled out of the shadows. "A bright and early morning to you, Sir," he said. "Can I help you?"

Ilfedo did not reply immediately. The feel of the magnificent creature's muzzle beneath his hand calmed his weakened body.

The man crossed his arms. "Can I help you, *Sir?*" he repeated, raising an eyebrow.

But when Ilfedo turned to face the man—

The man uncrossed his arms, dropped them to his sides, and his eyes widened. "You're the Mathaliah guy, aren't you?" Before Ilfedo could respond, the man looked back into the shadows and snapped his fingers with such force that it made Ilfedo's ear ring. "Boy!" he hollered. "Got them horses ready?"

"Just 'bout," a cheery youth replied.

"The name's Barlin." The burly fellow thrust his hand at Ilfedo with a smile that seemed to twist up on one side of his mouth and down on the other.

Ilfedo shook his hand and looked past him, tried to distinguish the lad amid the random clouds of straw dust.

Barlin did not seem to notice. He slapped one arm around Ilfedo's shoulders. Ilfedo cringed, feeling some pain. Barlin walked him away from the stall. "It was a great thing you did when you killed them serpents for us! Any time you come back 'round these parts, visit us, will you?" He pulled back his arm and slapped Ilfedo's shoulder hard.

"I can't promise anything," Ilfedo said. He looked down at the other man, amused. Did he always treat ill people in this manner, or just those who'd been poisoned in the act of saving human lives?

"Ah, very well." Barlin stood back and shouted into the stable. "Ramul! Get them horses out here now."

Without a word, a curly red-haired young man strode on gangly legs from the dim recesses of the stable. His green eyes stared up at Ilfedo from a face spotted with freckles.

"How long do you need the boy?" Barlin tousled the youth's hair and fixed a hard gaze on Ilfedo.

Ilfedo ran his hand along one stallion's neck and then down to the saddle. He checked the cinch. It was tight. Swinging himself onto the animal's broad back, he reached down to shake Barlin's hand. "It is a couple days' ride to my place. I'll send the lad back as soon as possible." He wrapped the reins around his right fist. "Look for him to return within five days' time."

He smiled down at the red-headed boy. "Your name is Ramul?"

"Yes, Mr. Mathaliah." The lad mounted the horse next to Ilfedo's and grasped the reins of the two pack horses behind him, loaded down with leather bags no doubt holding the serpent meat.

"Since we will be traveling together for the next couple of days"—Ilfedo turned in his saddle to face the doors leading to the inn's courtyard—"I'd prefer you to call me Ilfedo."

Beaming, Ramul urged his horse forward as Ilfedo rode out of the stable, into the courtyard, and down the deserted cobblestone streets. He glanced back one time to look at the sign swinging above the inn door. The Wooden Mug. He would remember that name. Maybe if he returned to this place he would look it up.

⚜ ⚜ ⚜

Somewhere in the Western Wood, Dantress slipped out of the cave, parting the vines hanging over the entrance before stepping barefoot on the moist forest floor. A thorn pricked her heel. She leaned over and pulled it out. No matter how often she'd walked without shoes, her feet seemed to remain smooth and tender.

Standing, she stepped over a moss-covered log and made her way through the thick forest growth. When she'd gone out of earshot of the cave, she untied her laces from her belt and put the shoes on her feet. Owls hooted in the darkness, no doubt preparing to swoop from the branches and catch any unsuspecting rodents in their talons.

A couple of miles from the cave she walked into a clearing. The soft starlight mirrored in a pool of water. The pool was fed by water gushing over stone polished smooth. Twice her dreams had showed her this place. Twice she had come, hoping—that he'd be there.

But no one stood on the other side of the pool, no one looked at her with adoring eyes. She sighed, chiding herself for hoping that this fantasy would become reality. That one day the dreams would prove true—and he'd stand there, tall and strong.

She recalled the warmth of Kesla's child sleeping in her arms and loneliness pricked her with one of its long, hard fingers. Someone to have and someone to hold—for even a day—would be enough. She wanted it more than anything in the world. But could she ever have that? Could she bring herself to accept the price of such a union? She was not of human blood.

Thinking that she'd wasted her time, Dantress turned to go, her head bowed.

A tall, hooded figure stepped out of the forest on the opposite bank, glowing with grayish light in the darkness. The figure walked around the pool toward her. Startled, she reached down to the fold in her skirt and leaned over to draw out her blade. But her fingers touched an empty scabbard!

The ghostly figure stood still—a dozen feet away from her—and she noticed the glowing scythe in his right hand. Its blade brought to mind a memory. She struggled to recall where she'd seen it before.

"Given up already?" the familiar voice said, almost in a whisper.

"You?" She took a step toward him. "You were there . . . in Al'un Dai!"

The ghost drew her sword from its robes and held it aloft in its free hand.

A dozen questions came to mind, but only one reached her lips. "Who are you?"

"I am the master of this sword," the decidedly masculine voice replied. "I am its first bearer—the master of the Six."

"*Xavion?*" She stared in disbelief. "But I thought you were dead—"

"Xavion *is* dead, dragon child." He strode a bit closer and starlight reflected off his scythe. "And dead he will remain. I am Specter, agent of your father . . . protector of all that he holds most dear."

Specter neared her and held out the sword . . . *his* sword. A shiver ran unhindered down Dantress's spine. "I think," she managed, "that you should keep it."

His blue eyes glowed down at her and sparked. She couldn't explain how, but somehow she knew that it had been a long time since this warrior had felt as pleased as he felt now. And she couldn't help noticing how handsome, how young he looked. But he had to be around one thousand years old.

"It is kind of you to offer me this gift," Specter said. "Nevertheless, I will not accept, and I don't want to. This sword is destined to be wielded by one other aside from myself and you, and I would not trade the future it has—through your blood—for the temporary gratification of using it against my enemies." He slid the sword adroitly into her scabbard.

"Now"—he stepped back, his robes shimmering—"do not leave this place so soon. I believe the great white dragon would advise you to stay and follow your heart to where it leads you.

His hooded form vanished as he spoke and then his voice whispered close in her ear. "And do not worry about the wild beasts while you sleep. I will stay and keep watch."

Another shiver ran down her spine. Dantress smiled and lay down on the wet grass, uncaring. The dragon had promised that he would watch over his children and, it seemed, he'd also assigned a guardian to keep an eye on them during his absence.

If Specter had been with her and her sisters during their ordeal at Al'un Dai then he must have also been with them prior to that in the forests west of the Eiderveis River.

She recalled Laura's account of the night the dragons had kidnapped her. The heads of the carnivorous beasts had, according to Laura, "fallen off as if severed by an invisible blade." Specter's blade . . . it must have been.

And then there was the moment when she and her sisters had been trapped in Al'un Dai. She'd been holding the traitor's infant son when the walls had iced over. Her sisters had touched their blades together, and the energy discharge which had never failed to crumble stone had had no effect. They'd been trapped.

But at the exact moment they needed help, the wall trembled, the ice shattered. Something had impacted the wall from the other side and the stones had exploded at the sisters, leaving a large hole for the sisters to escape through . . . and she had never known why. Now she understood what had happened.

Specter . . . he was there the whole time. She couldn't help marveling at how much sense it all made.

Closing her eyes, Dantress drifted into a dream similar to the ones she'd had the past couple of nights. She saw the man's face and felt the adoration of his gaze as if nothing else mattered to him or existed outside of them.

❖ ❖ ❖

Ilfedo tore himself from the dream. He could almost feel *her* presence melting off his body like hot wax. Why? Why did this dream recur with such persistent frequency? Where had his mind come up with such vivid detail of a woman who did not exist?

He rolled up his bearskin sleeping bag and strangled it with a leather cord to his saddle. "Ramul." He gently shook the gangly lad awake. "Time we were on our way."

The hilly terrain covered with trees prevented a speedy journey through the wilderness. Ilfedo knew the region well and navigated as direct a path as possible so that Ramul, when he returned to the coast, would be able to find his way back.

From time to time Ilfedo drew his sword and slashed the tree trunks, leaving marks the boy could follow on the return trip.

A few days after leaving the coastal areas, they rode up a long hill to a broad log home set back in the slope and stopped. A portion of the roof appeared to be open, like a window to the sky. The structure was sturdy. They led the horses through large double doors set in the side of the building.

"I don't keep any horses of my own," Ilfedo said as the redhead kicked around the meager piles of straw spread on the stable floor. "But there's plenty of grass outside, and the horses can graze on that tonight." He balanced a pile of metal stakes in his arms and carried them outside, driving them into the ground, then tying the horses to them.

Ramul surprised Ilfedo with his strength. He picked up several of the larger packs and carried them to the front door. Ilfedo was left only with a smaller pack and one large one. By the faint odor of smoke his nostrils picked up when he lifted the larger of the two bags he guessed it held the serpent meat.

"Your door's locked." Ramul pulled up on the thick metal latch to prove his point.

"Stand aside." Ilfedo stepped to the door and rapped twice. "Seivar, Hasselpatch! I'm home! Open this thing, will you?"

There was a commotion in the house—pots and pans crashing to the floor, glass smashing, along with an assortment of other small catastrophes, and the door clicked open.

Two eagle-sized, white birds landed on Ilfedo's shoulders, each stretching a long neck to nuzzle his head. The afternoon sunlight shone off their hooked, silver beaks, and their silver claws clamped over his shoulders.

Ilfedo jerked his shoulder as his injury protested.

The larger of the pair finished nuzzling its master and cawed in Ramul's face, startling him back. He tripped on the threshold and fell.

"Sorry about that, Ramul." Ilfedo stroked both birds' breasts, looking upon them with a softening gaze as their silvery eyes closed in pleasure. "I'm afraid Seivar is not comfortable with strangers."

Ramul swallowed, "Those are—"

"Nuvitors . . . and the only tame pair that I know of," Ilfedo said, nodding his head. "I chanced upon one of the nests fallen from a tree deep in the forest. They would have died had I not brought them home.

"Am I right, Hasselpatch?" He glanced to his left shoulder at the smaller bird.

She cooed at him and stretched her beak into the sunlight. "As Yimshi shines down upon us, yes, Master!"

"Yipes!" Ramul's mouth froze open in shock. "They can . . . they talk?"

"Yes." Ilfedo ducked inside the house. Ramul set the packs on the warm wood floor, and Ilfedo shut the door.

The larger of the birds, Seivar, nipped Ilfedo's ear and then jumped off his shoulder to perch on the long wooden table occupying the center of the room.

Ilfedo busied himself removing his scabbard from his belt. He set it, with the sword still sheathed, against the wall in a dark corner of the room.

"But," Ramul warily kept his eye on Seivar, "they're not like parrots. They can have a conversation?"

"Would you listen to *that*, Hasselpatch?" Seivar clipped the air with his beak. "Parrots, indeed! Of all insults—"

The smaller bird crouched on Ilfedo's shoulder then pounced, landing on Seivar's back and toppling him off the table.

"Do not listen to a word Seivar says." She said, looked up at Ramul as her mate rebalanced himself on the floor. "And if he tries anything whilst I'm out of sight, I expect you to tell me immediately." She stood still, waiting.

Ramul looked from one bird to the other, not uttering a word.

"Well?" Hasselpatch stretched out her neck to better eye the lad.

And Ilfedo subtly mouthed, 'Tell her you will.'

"I . . . I will . . . thank you." Ramul stood with his hands clasped behind his back.

The bird nodded and dropped to the floor. "Come with me. There are three guest rooms in this house. Um . . . what was your name?"

"Ramul."

"Such a nice name!" Hasselpatch led him to the north side of the house and through a door into one of the small bedrooms at ground level.

Ilfedo looked at the kitchen counter against the back wall. One lamp lay on its side, jagged bits of broken glass spread around it. Several plates were neatly stacked next to the stone sink but around them lay an assortment of pots and pans in a jumbled confusion.

He picked up the humbled bird and let it perch on his arm. The claws dug into his skin but he didn't care. "What a mess, Seivar."

Hanging its head, the bird said, "Sorry, Master, I let my excitement get the better of me."

Ilfedo smiled. "No matter. A little cleanup and everything will be right again. Which reminds me: it feels chilly in here." He glanced to the large stone fireplace set in the wall next to a stone stairway leading to the second level.

The fireplace was huge. Large enough for a full grown man of shorter stature to walk into. A bed of coals glowed inside and meager scraps of charred logs growing cold slumbered atop them. Above the mantle, staring lifelessly back at him, was the head of that first bear. He stretched his shoulders, feeling the bearskin coat that'd kept him warm for several years.

The bear had killed his parents and he had killed it.

"Master?" Seivar stretched out his wings to keep his balance.

"It's all right," Ilfedo assured the bird. "I was just remembering. . . ."

Turning away from the bear's head, he stepped around a pillar rising from the floor and supporting a broad beam running the length of the house. He slapped the rough wood. Solid as the day he'd nailed it in place.

His thigh brushed against a rope hammock, strung from one pillar to the other. The hammock rocked gently.

Outside with the cool late afternoon air surrounding him, Ilfedo grabbed the steel axe by its head and pulled its handle from under his belt. Balancing it in both hands he bent his elbows, drawing them back in preparation for the swing. The thick trunk of an oak rose before him, its first branches at least ten feet above the ground.

Seivar's weight lifted from his arm, and the bird flew to a white birch. It was out of felling distance. Cocking its head in his direction, the bird awaited the first strokes of his axe.

Hacking with strong but steady motions, Ilfedo cut into the tree until the amount of chips littering the ground equaled a wedge of missing wood in the trunk almost halfway through. He stepped around the trunk, being careful not to step in front of the carved portion of tree, and stood behind it.

Again the axe that had served him in his battle with the Sea Serpents, carved deep. The cut he made was slightly higher than the wedge cut on the opposite side. He deepened it until the wood cracked. The tree creaked, then leaned away from him with a mighty groan, and it fell southeast along the edge of the clearing.

It must have been a couple hours later, Ilfedo couldn't be sure because he couldn't remember precisely where Yimshi's disc had been when he started the job. The red-headed lad with the gangly legs ran out of the house and into the stable. At first, as the lad disappeared through the stable doors, Ilfedo thought that something must be wrong.

He rested one foot on the fallen tree's trunk. Seivar glided from the white birch, his white feathers rustling as he landed on a branch of the felled oak.

"Trouble, Master?"

"I'm not sure." Ilfedo let go of the axe with one hand to wipe the sweat beading on his forehead. His other hand still rested on the axe's smooth wood handle, the head he left embedded in the tree's trunk.

But Ramul ran out of the stable moments later, his legs seemed to almost lose their balance with every stride and an axe swinging a bit carelessly from one hand. "Mr. Matheliah, Sir?"

"It's *Ilfedo*, Ramul."

"Right! Sorry." The lad's face reddened, and his freckles seemed to triple their numbers. "How 'bout I help you with the wood . . .? If I may."

Ilfedo pointed to the axe in Ramul's hand. "Do you know how to use it properly?"

"No," the lad admitted, green eyes hopeful. "Could you show me?" Seeming to become uncomfortable with his request, Ramul bit his lip.

But Ilfedo patted him on the shoulder, pulled the axe out of the tree's trunk and raised it over his head with both hands. "If you want to help then I accept. Hold the handle like so, a firm grip but not too much; you must let the momentum of your swing do the work. . . ."

That evening Ilfedo and Ramul pulled wooden chairs up to the hearth. Ilfedo stretched his feet to the crackling warmth of the fire. Ramul leaned back in the chair and crossed his arms behind his head. Then he thrust his feet beside Ilfedo's.

A pile of split logs now stood several feet above the floor to the left of the stone fireplace. Burning seasoned wood would have been easier, but somehow the task of cutting an adequate supply had eluded Ilfedo the past few months. Or, more accurately, he had avoided it. Besides, fresh cut wood always smelled better to him than old, dry logs.

Into the orange, red and yellow glow emanating from the fire the Nuvitors strutted. Seivar took the lead, momentarily spreading his wings over the warm hearth stones before fluffing his feathers and lying down. Hasselpatch cuddled beside him. Two white beauties in the light of the flames, their feathers spotless and pure.

The birds blinked a few times, their chests heaved with deep breathing. Seivar's silver iris trained on Ramul as Hasselpatch's eyes closed.

Ramul, half-asleep himself, leaned back in his chair with his long arms draped over the chair arms.

Bringing his finger to his lips, Ilfedo murmured to the bird, "Sleep, my friend. The lad will be no trouble."

His silver eye swiveling in its socket to return Ilfedo's gaze, Seivar regarded him for a moment. Then, fluffing his feathers once more, the bird closed his eyes and drifted asleep.

For a long while afterward, as the fire burned on, Ilfedo sat in silence.

The hoots of owls mingled with a chorus of crickets outside in the deepening night. From down the hill in a small swamp, frogs croaked, some loud, others weak. He imagined that, somewhere, far from all human civilization, was a dark-haired young woman dressed in purple. Perhaps even now she was leaning over that pool with the dull roar of the waterfall filling her ears as she watched starlight dance on the water.

Rising from his chair, he dropped into the hammock and twisted onto his side. The ropes tickled his cheek a bit but he didn't care. The hammock swung ever so slightly.

For now he would sleep. Maybe tomorrow would find him feeling fresh and invigorated. He hoped so. His right shoulder still felt a bit strange, a bit swollen and numb.

He remembered the white eyes of the Sea Serpents, their fangs dripping venom. And he was glad he'd come home. Back to the wilderness . . . where the most dangerous creatures left were large cats and some bears.

Venison! He licked his lips, almost tasting fresh cooked meat sitting on his table.

Tomorrow might be a good time to round up a few of his friends. It had been a little while since they'd last gone on a hunt together.

BEFORE THE DAWN

As Specter followed Dantress through the woods, moving smooth and silent, he studied the trees around her. The damp darkness of early morning could hide any number of beasts waiting to pounce upon her.

His fist clasped the handle of his scythe with firm resolve and confidence. Nothing could see him while he remained in his gray shrouds. He was a secret guardian doing his duty out of love for his master and a desire to see the evil of his one-time-pupil, Letrias, negated.

He peered from beneath his hood at the shapely young daughter of the great white dragon.

Suddenly the girl cried out and stumbled, a stone and a log pinched her ankle between them. She laid still, a flat stone under her head. He swept toward her, observed that she was breathing, sighed inwardly with relief.

Other than hitting her head on the stone, Dantress seemed fine, and though her ankle appeared twisted it was nothing serious.

Standing still, Specter felt an icy chill creep up his arm, raising every hair on end. The forest froze into silence. Not even the crickets broke the spell.

Wispy tendrils of blackness, like smoke, snaked out of the trees beside the fallen young woman. They flowed from the shadows between the trees, entwining with each other and joining.

At first Specter thought his eyes were tricking him, for he saw hands without flesh grow from the blackness—bones as black as coal, fingers groping toward Dantress from beneath tattered black robes and a cavernous hood. And, clenched in the being's right hand, visible for only a moment, was a black scythe with an edge serrated either by wear or by design.

Though he disregarded it, Specter could not shake away the icy chill filling the air. He saw the bony fingers claw down, inches from Dantress's cheek. Her body went rigid, her face turned white.

Specter stepped forward, clenched his teeth, scythe raised. *Whatever foul creature this was* . . . but he didn't get a chance to finish the thought.

The being withdrew its hand and vaporized into nothingness. Not a trace, not even a footprint, could Specter find.

Dantress sat up, held her hand to her head for a moment, eyes half closed. Specter was tempted to show himself to her, but the color returned to her cheeks, and she soon stood and limped in the direction of the cave without his help. With a strong feeling of trepidation Specter followed, the sight of the bone-hand lingering over Dantress's face foremost in his thoughts.

❈   ❈   ❈

The chirps of birds woke Ilfedo the next morning. He opened his front door and gazed outside. Yimshi's golden light bathed the treetops for as far as he could see. Their green leaves, speckled with dewdrops, seemed to glow with warmth.

Because he had built his home on one of the higher hills in the wilderness, he could look out over most of the treetops in three directions: east, south and west. A bird's eye view.

The scenery behind the house was obscured by a row of large oak trees on his hill's crest. Like wood sentinels, the trees overshadowed his home, camouflaging it from sight as well as taking the brunt of any sudden strong winds seeking to invade his yard.

Rolling into the distance the forests of the Hemmed Land dipped and rose with the contour of the land. If one looked at the trees long enough they could spot a Nuvitor or two. The beautiful, wild creatures did not customarily soar high into the sky like the eagles did. They seemed to prefer skimming the treetops, staying near the forests' protective curtain of leaves, branches, and vines, all untended by human hands and yet marvelously interwoven with creative design.

He exited the house and fetched the horses.

A short time later, Ramul strolled out the front door, taking unnecessarily long strides with his less-than-adequate legs.

"The horses are packed and ready to go." Ilfedo ruffled the red head. "Are you all set?"

"Just 'bout!" Ramul smiled up at him, extended his open hand.

Ilfedo grasped it with his larger one and gave it a firm shake. "If you ever come by this way again, stop in."

"Why . . . thank you, *Ilfedo*!"

"It was my pleasure to have you." Ilfedo walked with the lad as he approached the picketed horses. Tying the first horse's saddle to that of the second, Ramul linked the four creatures together. He grabbed the horn with one hand, stuck his foot in the stirrup, and jumped up to the saddle.

"Take the ride slow and watch the path I led you down to get here." Ilfedo patted the young man's shoulder and then handed him the reins. "These forests are not yet free of all beasts. It would be inadvisable for you to wander away from the trail. Follow the marks I made on the trees and you'll do fine."

Ramul nodded. His green eyes turned toward the path, and he departed into the trees, the horses trailing after him.

When the last of the pack horses was lost to sight amongst the trees, Ilfedo turned back to his house. He closed the door, sank into the hammock, and closed his eyes as the fire's heat washed under him. Because he'd not bothered putting more than a single window on this level of his home, the light remained dim and flickering. Above him, in the master bedroom on the second floor, the Nuvitors cooed their welcome to the new day.

But he drifted asleep. . . .

荣   荣   荣

The tracks of a deer led Ilfedo upstream through a haze of milky white light that seemed to pull him with invisible hands along the water's edge. Not a single sound penetrated the air. He could not even hear the wet ground sucking at his boots. He sniffed at the air, a whiff of . . . nothing. Anyway, it didn't matter. All that mattered was running along the stream's bank and reaching his destination.

Miles of ground passed effortlessly beneath his feet, miles that brought him out of the forests of the Hemmed Land and into the Western Wood, a stretch of land west of his home territory untouched by humankind.

He followed the stream to a pool of water partially shaded by trees on all sides. A waterfall fell in silence over a face of smooth stone to the pool. Ripples spread outward from the falling water, building outward a series of watery half-rings breaking around olive-skinned legs, smooth as oil.

A feeling of ecstasy overpowered Ilfedo. The reflecting solar rays painted themselves on her legs and her silken skirt was held out of the water in one small hand, fingers clutching the fabric with the grace and strength of a swan. And her hair, dark and wavy, fell down her back almost to her waist. She was short of stature, yet all the more beautiful for it.

He prepared to call out, to make her turn to see him there, so that he could look at her face. But she vanished and the waterfall froze, the pool beneath it froze as well. A sphere, as smooth as glass and as yellow as polished gold, dropped from the heavens. It plummeted through the icy air and then broke onto the ice. Innumerable cracks spread from the point of impact like strands of a spider's web. The cracks covered the frozen pool, spreading up the frozen waterfall. At once the ice exploded into billions of fragments that tore into the surrounding forest.

"Ilfedo!" the shattering scene seemed to say. He heard his name pronounced several times, each time more forcibly.

❄ ❄ ❄

"Ilfedo!" The man's voice carried a note of urgency.

This time the dream dissolved and he opened his eyes. The full light of day flooded through the lone window. Outside he could see, by the angle of the sunlight through the glass, that it must be late morning.

"Hey . . . look who's *finally* waking up!" Ombre grinned down at him boyishly. His unkempt light brown hair covered his

ears and some of it spilled over his forehead. The blank eyes of
the wolf's head atop his scalp seemed to look back at Ilfedo in
silent accusation.

Two years ago, while searching out a killer bear, Ilfedo had
been attacked by the wolf. It had been one of the largest he'd ever
seen, its shoulders almost reached his hip. Fortunately, Ombre
had been with Ilfedo when the animal landed on his back. He'd
reacted with a stroke of his sword across the wolf's jugular. Ever
since that day Ombre had kept the wolf's skin with the head
attached as his personal trophy, in much the same way as Ilfedo'd
garbed himself with a coat made from the black beast that had
killed his parents.

The wolf's gray fur appeared as full as the day Ombre had
killed it. The hair was silken, softer than a kitten's.

Ilfedo shook his head to clear it and nearly lost his balance
sitting up in the hammock.

"Whoa there!" Ombre gave Ilfedo's shoulder a solid slap-
punch, a laugh on the tip of his tongue.

"Ombre . . ." Ilfedo blinked his heavy eyelids. The fire crackled warmly in the fireplace, enfolding his body in its warmth.

"What?" Ombre laughed. "Did you want to sleep the day
away?" He gestured out the window where their planet's sun,
Yimshi, rose near the sky's zenith.

Ilfedo got out of his hammock, taking a few moments to
completely wake. When he was more alert he walked into his
kitchen area. Seivar and Hasselpatch had already cleaned the
dishes, arranged them on the shelves and cleared last night's
mess.

"Have you eaten, Ombre?"

"Hours ago," his friend said, dropping into a chair by the
table. He flipped the wolf's head off of his own so that it hung
over his back. He drummed his fingers on the table as Ilfedo

retrieved a cast iron pot, filled it with water from a barrel set on his counter, and hung it over the flames in the fireplace.

When the water boiled, Ilfedo tossed in several generous scoops of oats, pulled it away from the flames, and set it on the counter. The simmering oats smelled wonderful to Ilfedo—and familiar. Much better than the food he'd received while in the coastal town. Not to say he didn't like waffles. No, he loved them. But oatmeal . . . well, it served the triple purpose of satisfying his taste buds, filling his stomach, and providing him with a healthy burst of morning energy.

Bringing one of the packs from town and setting it on the counter, he fished out a couple slices of dried, smoked snake meat.

"What is it?" Ombre caught a piece Ilfedo tossed to him, sniffing it before sinking his teeth in.

Ilfedo tasted a bit of the Sea Serpent meat. A bit tough—too dry, but otherwise rather good. Not as rich a flavor as beef. It had a slight fishy taste to it.

He pulled out another slice and tossed it too in Ombre's direction. The man caught it and repeated his question. "What is this stuff?"

"Sea Serpent." Ilfedo grinned, watching Ombre's expression turn from pleasure to disgust.

Gliding into the room from the stairway, Seivar landed on the table, across from Ombre.

"Here, take it!" Ombre tossed the jerky into the bird's open beak and rubbed his hands against his trousers as if to rid them of any residue the meat might have left. He frowned at Ilfedo. "You did that on purpose."

Chuckling, Ilfedo grabbed a large wood spoon and stirred his oatmeal. He bent his face to the pot—letting the steam wend its way gradually into his nostrils.

Ombre leaned back in his chair, folded his hands behind his head. "I should have known," he said. "Is this because of that last hunting trip we took?"

"Which one?" Ilfedo feigned innocence.

"Oh don't play that game with me!" Ombre chuckled. "Just because I led you into a little mud—" He threw up his hands. "Okay, we're even.

"But speaking of hunting . . . how'd your trip to the coast turn out? I heard rumors flying that someone from these parts got tangled with a mess of Sea Serpents and killed them with a sword." He stood, walked to the counter, peered into the bag, pulling out several long slices of meat. "What've you been up to, Ilfedo? Playing hero so that you can win some woman's heart and leave our little bachelor's club?"

"I just happened to be there at the right moment." Ilfedo picked out a large bowl from those stacked on his shelf. Dipping the spoon deep into the pot, he dished out the oats, moist and hot. With the heaped bowl in one hand and the spoon in his other, he sat at the table and ate.

"So," Ombre chuckled again, "it *was* you." He sighed loudly and rolled his eyes. "All right . . . I'm ready." He folded his hands and sat opposite Ilfedo. "What happened? And don't leave out any details."

It took Ilfedo the next half hour to relate, between mouthfuls, his encounter with the Sea Serpents. When he'd finished Ombre shook his head and laughed.

"First the bears, now Sea Serpents . . . one can only wonder what will be next. Dragons perhaps!"

"Don't be silly," Ilfedo said as he cleaned the last of the oats from his bowl. He chewed them with deliberate slowness. "Dragons are myth. Every child knows that."

"Well I wouldn't be so certain of that." Ombre paused to swat a fly away from his face. "Remember the stories my father told us of where our people came from."

"You mean"—Ilfedo pointed at him with the dirty spoon— "where our people are *supposed* to have come from."

Ombre shrugged. "I agree that certain elements sound like pure fiction."

"Yeah," Ilfedo stood, "do you think?"

"Well, the part about our ancestors flying into the sky at will—that was a bit sketchy—but what of the Chronicler of our history? No one knows what became of him. He just vanished. Not a word, not a clue, not a hint.

"But Father left the Chronicler's scrolls in my possession, and I've read through some of them. Its information often seems ambiguous, yet there are details of other places that can only be explained by either his being an out and out liar *or* that he actually did explore the lands beyond our borders."

The subject was soon dropped. They'd talked about the Chronicler on several occasions, but the truth was that no one knew the truth when it came to the Chronicler. So the conversation could only go so far.

Ilfedo served the remainder of the oatmeal to Seivar and Hasselpatch. Then, as the birds ate, he sat back down. "My food stores are getting a bit low. I was hoping you might like to start out tonight."

"A hunt?" Ombre smiled.

Ilfedo nodded casually. "Ganning and Honer'll probably want to come along. We can divide whatever we catch and give them the larger portions . . . as usual. With all the mouths they have to feed they'll need it." He stared at the wood slabs on the ceiling. "How many is Honer up to now?"

"Well"—Ombre counted off silently on his fingers—"five kids and then his wife. Ganning has a few as well."

"Yes, I'm starting to feel like an old bachelor."

"You're a little young for that, Ilfedo." Hasselpatch landed on the table and Ombre stroked her fluffy white chest. She cooed her appreciation, half-closing her silvery eyes.

Seivar landed on Ilfedo's shoulder.

After a quiet interlude, wherein the men stroked the birds' warm, feathered chests, Ilfedo finally patted Seivar's back. "Now go, my friend. Tell Honer and Ganning that, if they'd like to join us for a hunt, then they should meet Ombre and me here later in the afternoon."

The Nuvitors stretched their wings, whistling and cawing with excitement. Ilfedo let them land on his shoulders. His wound responded with sharp pain, but he ignored it. Turning to the stairs, he climbed to the master bedroom in the second level of his home. He pulled a cord hung from the overhead rafters. A portion of the room opened to the blue sky just as a small puffy white cloud passed by.

Taking flight, the Nuvitors brushed his face with their wings as they shot away in a southerly direction. Anticipating their return, he left the roof open.

He breathed in the fresh air, letting it fill his lungs before releasing his breath. He rested his palm against the bedroom's wall, feeling the vertical grooves between the smooth wood poles that he'd laced side-by-side with twine. The upright wood poles gave this room a unique feel from the rest of the house, like a tree fort. Well ventilated and brighter as a result of the skylight-style partitions of the roof.

A crossbow lay on the floor, and he picked it up, replacing it on its peg half-way up the wall. The hilts of various swords and the heads of several axes were spread to the left of the crossbow.

Their polished metal surfaces winked back at him as he stepped to the bed at the room's center. Hung on the wall above the bed was one of his father's javelins.

He rearranged and neatened the bearskins, coonskins, and other hides draped across the leather mattress. Then he picked up the soft pillow and patted it back into shape. It had required several rabbits to make the pillow. It was long—as long as his arm—and checkered with both white and brown fur as a result of piecing together several skins from various rabbits. He laid it at the bed's head and pulled the blankets over it.

A floorboard creaked ever so slightly under his foot as he returned to the stairwell. He entered the dining room, glanced around. But Ombre had disappeared.

Shaking his head knowingly, Ilfedo pulled his sheath from its place along the wall. The metal of his blade sang out of the scabbard as his hand closed around the handle, drawing it out.

Ombre rushed at him, the flat of his sword swinging for Ilfedo's leg.

Parrying with ease, Ilfedo rang his blade against Ombre's with great force. With a quick upward swing he forced Ombre to pull back and defend himself against an upper body attack.

He smiled. Ombre had fallen for his feint.

Instead of striking at Ombre's upper body, he struck the flat of his blade against the man's thigh and followed through with a spin that brought his sword around to tap Ombre's neck. He held the sword there until Ombre backed away, holding his sword by its blade and presenting its handle toward Ilfedo in the traditional Hemmed Land custom of surrender.

Ombre snapped his fingers in mock frustration. "I thought I had you this time. Oh well"—he wiggled his finger at Ilfedo—"one of these days I'll figure out how you do it. And then you will present your sword to me instead of the other way around, which, by the way, I am getting a little tired of."

With a shake of his head, Ilfedo chuckled. It seemed that Ombre was bound and determined to one day best him in sword-play. He busied himself prodding the fire with a poker and said, "The Nuvitors are on their way. If Honer and Ganning show up this afternoon then we'll be a foursome. If not, we'll head out before evening. Did you bring a bow, or just the sword?"

"I left both at home."

"Then borrow one of mine." Ilfedo nodded toward the stairs. Long bow or crossbow, whichever Ombre preferred, Ilfedo had several of them.

"Don't mind if I do, brother," Ombre patted Ilfedo's shoulder and ascended the steps three at a time.

⚮ ⚮ ⚮

Later that day two men on horseback approached Ilfedo and Ombre as they stood in the clearing. Ilfedo checked the sword hanging from his side, then nodded at Ombre. "Ready?"

"Honer! Ganning!" Ombre welcomed the other men as they swung from their creaking leather saddles. He had the longbow in his hand, and the quiver filled with wood-shafted arrows on his back. Also, he had tucked a hatchet under his belt and a sheathed sword hung from his left hip.

Ganning limped to Ombre and shook his hand, smiling. Then his eyes turned to Ilfedo. "How was your trip to the coast?"

"Ahem," Ombre said, raising one hand. "Don't ask him that. He's having a little problem"—he pointed at his own head—"a little problem with a swelled head."

"We heard about the Sea Serpents," Honer said. "Nice going, Ilfedo." He patted Ilfedo's shoulder, looking at him with his gentle

gray eyes. "Word's spreading like wildfire that you single hand-
edly killed the creatures and came out unscathed. You're a hero."

"Unscathed?" Ilfedo glanced up in time to watch Hasselpatch
glide from the trees. As her weight settled on his shoulder, her
claws gently latched on. Seivar swooped in, perching on his other
shoulder. Ilfedo cringed. The male Nuvitor had landed on his
tender spot. The long, serpent-fang wound was still healing.

A slight smile showed on Honer's face. He strode back to his
horse and mounted. "I guess it is safe to assume 'unscathed' was
an exaggeration?"

"Yes." Ilfedo ignored the pain in his shoulder. "Are we ready
to go?"

They headed northwest. Ilfedo and Ombre set out on foot.
Honer and Ganning rode for the first few hours, but the forest undergrowth forced them out of their saddles for the rest
of the journey. Honer kept a third horse in tow behind him.
Ilfedo knew from experience that the packs on that animal's
back held a few pans, extra arrows, and an assortment of hunting knives.

Taking turns launching off of Ilfedo's shoulders, the Nuvitors scouted the territory ahead. If anything dangerous lay before
their master they would warn him.

But nothing of consequence crossed the hunters' path. Darkness thickened in the forest. The evening dew fell, sparse, hesi-
tant drops gathering in the inky-black hairs of Ilfedo's bearskin
coat.

They halted a few hours after darkness and, by the light of
the rising full moon, they chopped down several trees. It did not
take them long to form a clearing from the wild forest foliage.

Laying the logs around the clearing they formed a barrier
almost five feet high. Inside of this fort, they corralled the horses
and then built a roaring fire in the clearing's midst.

As they lay down around the leaping flames, Ilfedo let the heat wash across his face while the night's cool air gently nudged his back.

"Sleep, Master," Seivar cooed in his ear. The bird stretched its wings and leapt into flight, headed for the trees.

Hasselpatch too, took flight. She rose to the opposite side of the clearing. The light of the fire flickered golden on her snowy chest.

Ilfedo closed his eyes. As on previous hunting trips, his pet birds would keep watch, ensuring that no predators would surprise him with a rude awakening. If the fire burned low the Nuvitors would stoke it. If a wild animal approached the camp, the Nuvitors would wake him.

But he blinked his eyes open moments after closing them, the star-studded heavens parted as if they'd been curtains drawn away to reveal what hid behind them. A vision played out. He could see himself, walking along the bank of a stream he remembered from a past hunt.

Delicate tracks marked the bank, leading him upstream through a haze of milky white light that seemed to pull him with invisible hands along the water's edge. Not a single sound penetrated the air. He could not even hear the wet ground sucking at his boots. He sniffed at the air, a whiff of . . . nothing. Anyway, it didn't matter. All that mattered was running along the stream's bank and reaching his destination.

Miles of ground passed effortlessly beneath his feet, miles that brought him out of the forests of the Hemmed Land and into the Western Wood, a stretch of land west of his home territory untouched by humankind.

He followed the stream to a pool of water, glistening in moderate sunlight. Trees encircled it and a waterfall fell in silence over a face of smooth stone to a pool below. Ripples spread from where the water fell into the pool, building outward a series of watery half-rings breaking around olive-skinned legs, smooth as oil.

A feeling of ecstasy overpowered Ilfedo. The reflecting solar rays painted themselves on her legs and her silken skirt held out of the water in one small hand, fingers clutching the fabric with the grace and strength of a swan. And her hair, dark and wavy, fell down her back almost to her waist. She was short of stature, yet all the more beautiful for it.

He prepared to call out, to make her turn to see him there, so that he could see her face. But she vanished before he could say a word.

The surrounding forest now seemed, to him, a cage. It imprisoned him in his loneliness. The grass beneath his feet, dissolving into dust, was replaced by a searing heat that flooded the air around him so that his body broke out in a sticky sweat. Darkness spread like inky tendrils, choking out the last rays of light.

In a flash he found himself lying on the ground, staring up at the night sky. A cool breeze rustled the leaves in the trees. An owl hooted somewhere in the forest, and bats fluttered overhead, tackling insects. Everything was deceptively normal, as if the vision or dream he'd experienced was nothing more than a trick of his mind.

He smote the ground with his fist, trying in vain to dispel the urge to rise and find out if this sequence of dreams was in fact a strange twist of his fate. Could the young woman standing in the pool . . . could she be real? No. For such foolish thinking he should slap himself in the face. But what other explanation was there? How else explain the dreams, the visions, which now seemed to haunt him every time he closed his eyes?

Ilfedo closed his hand over the cool metal of his sword's pommel as it lay next to his bedroll. Glancing to the heavens again, he waited for a further revelation. Nothing happened. He set his jaw in a firm line, threw off his blanket, grabbed his sword with its sheath and fastened it to his belt.

Either he would disprove this vision so that it could no longer disturb him, or. . . . He doubted the alternative but it intrigued him nevertheless. Could the hand of the Creator be in this, or was that wishful thinking?

Time to find out.

As he vaulted the barrier he and his friends had built around their camp, he heard the Nuvitors' wings snap against the air. They would follow. He turned and shook his head at Seivar, and the bird reluctantly flew back to its perch.

"Come, Hasselpatch." Ilfedo waited until her talons clamped over his right shoulder, then waved farewell to Seivar.

The bird dutifully saluted with one white wing.

Ilfedo would not have minded having both his birds along, but without at least one Nuvitor watching the camp, his friends would be left without warning if a beast attacked whilst they slept.

Hasselpatch didn't say a word. She flew off his shoulder and circled between the trees, her silvery eyes roving the woodland floor.

Ilfedo advanced through the forest at a half-run, ignoring the dew drenched branches that slapped across his face. He did not keep track of the time but doggedly continued on until he reached the stream in the forest that he had recognized in the vision.

Following the bank, he spotted the imprints of a deer's hoofs, set deep in the wet dirt, and swallowed hard. Kneeling, he reached out and felt them to be certain he was not dreaming. The compacted moist dirt fell apart between his fingers. He stood and eyed the prints. They followed the stream in a line as straight and true as a ruler in a northwest direction.

For a long while he followed the tracks. The stream broadened as it should, for he must be getting closer to its source.

As he rounded a bend in the stream, a wild cat screamed from beside him. Its eyes glowed yellow as it leaped from a boulder, and its clawed paws extended to strike.

A screech of fury preceded a flurry of white feathers as Hasselpatch landed on the animal's head. Her silver talons glinted in the starlight like daggers as they ripped across the cat's eyes without mercy, carving canyons through its fur into the skin. As red streams coursed through the cat's fur, Hasselpatch pulled away, her talons dragged in the cat's flesh.

Not wishing to see the animal suffer, Ilfedo drew his sword and stabbed it through the heart. The cat slumped on the stream's bank.

Hasselpatch dropped into the stream. The flowing water erased all traces of blood from her feathers, leaving her as pure white as before. She spread her wings and resumed a steady circle above Ilfedo's head.

By the time the deer's tracks ended, Ilfedo's legs were feeling sore. He gazed in confusion at the marks. A stretch of fields lay before him. The stream continued on. But the deer's tracks abruptly dissappeared. They didn't just fade onto firmer ground. Instead they ended on the stream's bank without any indication as to which direction the deer had gone. The ground was soft around the last hoof prints and moist for a distance afterward. It was as if the four-legged creature had sprouted wings and flown away.

Putting the tracks to the back of his mind, Ilfedo followed the stream still farther. It gurgled beside him, a pleasant, teasing sound that drew him onward.

Through the fields he followed it until it led him into a forest on the far side. He'd never been this far west. This territory

was unfamiliar to him. The border of the Hemmed Land must
be behind him by now.

He had entered the Western Wood.

Midnight arrived on swift wings. Exhaustion compelled him
to stop. He sat on the moist, cool grass at the base of a tree. Hasselpatch stopped circling and descended into his lap.

"Rest, my friend," he whispered.

She laid her silver beak on his leg and closed her silvery
eyes.

Idly, Ilfedo stroked the Nuvitor's feathers. He leaned back
against the rough bark of the tree's broad trunk. The stream
gurgled past him, as if laughing at him for allowing it to lead him
on this fruitless search. Crickets sang, something screeched in
the distance, either in attack or terror, a deep-throated scraping
screech. He did not recognize the sound.

The noise muffled around him as his body relaxed. Sleep
received him into its warm embrace.

␧ ␧ ␧

Specter stood invisible a mere few yards from Ilfedo, evaluating
him. It was hard to determine much about a person after a mere
few minutes of observation. But he noticed that the man, though
tall and strong, had laid one protective hand on his pet bird's
back.

He did not know why he felt compelled to stand guard.
Yet the Western Wood had seemed less than safe ever since
the mysterious cloaked being had touched Dantress. Specter
would not permit anything like that to happen again—not on
his watch.

Even as Specter thought on this, a dark figure coalesced
beside the sleeping man. Hands without flesh grew from beneath

the cavernous, tattered black hood. The serrated edge of the being's scythe cut downward, driving at Ilfedo's heart.

Before the tip of the ugly blade could come close to the man, Specter whirled his blade around, hooking it around the other. The blades met without a sound, and Specter glimpsed a skull looking up at him from beneath the tattered hood. Portions of the white skull appeared to have been singed black. The being had returned.

Any further observation of his opponent proved impossible. One bony hand swept through the air and smote him full in the cheek. His blade was thrown from his grasp, landing on the grass some distance away. Specter's opponent stepped over the man and butted him with its bone-hard head.

As the unyielding bone cracked against his skull, Specter reeled back. He fell to the ground.

The being approached him, the tatters of its cloak hiding its face in deep darkness as it drew back its scythe to strike the fatal blow.

In that instant a shepherd's staff crossed the scythe's path. The hook of the staff twisted it out of its master's hand and dropped it like a stone to the ground.

"Oh you foul being." Patient's white robe dragged in the grass as he stepped toward the revolting personage. His hood had been folded over his shoulders. His wizened, bearded head was uncovered. "Grim Reaper, you have done enough. Depart! I forbid you to take this man. Go back to your darkness and prey upon the souls deserving of punishment."

The being picked up its scythe. Silently it backed away, fading into vapors that dispersed on the still air like a rope whose strands have come unbound.

"He is gone." Patient waited as Specter got to his feet. The old man picked up Specter's weapon and handed it to him with a smile. "I suggest you do not let that happen again," he said, reaching up and patting him on the shoulder. Then he said in a quiet voice, "I'll be in the area for a little while, Specter. Go back to the dragon's daughters. Keep watch over Dantress. I will watch over the man."

"I will do as you say, Master," Specter stepped away to carry out the shepherd's command. Relief slipped over him like a woolen blanket. Now, if the Grim Reaper returned, Specter would not be alone. He rather hated to admit it, but it unnerved him how *easily* the reaper had disarmed him. In the future, he vowed, that situation would not repeat itself.

A firefly glowed in the darkness beside him as he avoided a tree stump and stepped into the forest. He glanced over his shoulder, at the shepherd sitting on a log with his staff in hand watching over Ilfedo. The eastern sky faded from purple to a soft blue, and a playful gust of wind passed overhead, rustling the treetops. Yimshi was rising.

FOREST MAIDEN

A scattering of colorful leaves lay in the grass around Ilfedo. He shook his head, lifted Hasselpatch out of his lap, and set her gently on the ground. She stirred but did not wake. The deep blue sky overhead betrayed not even a hint of cloud to dim the cheery weather. He yawned, stood, twisted his stiff back and stretched his arms.

He shook his head. What a fool he'd been. He had left Ombre, Honer, and Ganning to carry out the hunt . . . so that he could chase a silly dream. He ignored the part of his being that still cried out that it hadn't been just a silly dream. The sky had opened, had it not? And what of the repetition of the dreams? It wasn't really possible to dream all of it up, was it?

But he forced his mind to be silent, and walked a few yards to the stream. At this point the water ran out of a large pool of sparkling pure water, and the roar of a waterfall told him that he may have reached the stream's source.

At least, in the matter of exploration, this trip hadn't been a complete waste. This was his first time to the Western Wood. He should take advantage of the opportunity to investigate this territory farther. But, what about Ombre, Honer, and Ganning? They would be wondering about him by now.

No. He would not stay. He would go back to the Hemmed Land. Apologies were in order for three very good friends of his.

Kneeling at the pool's edge, he cupped his hands together and dipped them into the slow-flowing liquid. He let it chill his hands before lifting them out of the water.

As he held the water in his hands, he found himself staring at it as at a mirror. Indeed, the water did appear to form a mirror. Smooth, unerring, the liquid between his fingers reflected his visage back at him. The water was so lovely that he hesitated for a few moments longer. Then he slurped it down his throat.

Again he cupped his hands into the water, brought it to him, and again looked into the mirror that it formed. But this time he saw not his own image but rather the image of the woman in his dreams, standing with her back turned to him. She was holding her long purple skirt with one hand, keeping its hem out of the water as she waded through.

He jerked back, startled. The water slipped between his open fingers, its molecules uniting with those in the larger collection flowing from the pool to the stream.

He had to get a hold of himself. But what was happening? He blinked his eyes and breathed uneasily.

Once more he cupped his hands together. Once again he lifted the natural mirror from the flow. Once again it was not his own reflection that he saw. It was hers. But this time, as he listened to the roar of the waterfall, he glanced up.

Water gushed over a high face of smooth stone set back a hundred feet from where he knelt. Ripples formed in unending number at the waterfall's base, building outward. He opened his mouth in astonishment.

There, wading through the water and holding her purple skirt several inches above its surface, was the young woman from his dream. The dreams, the vision, they had led him here! But how could this be? He had not expected to fulfill his dream.

He stood and caught his breath. Yimshi cast its early morning rays from behind him. The rays shone upon her dark brown hair so that the tinge of red clearly showed.

Unsure what to do, Ilfedo sprinted left, circling the pool in hopes of seeing her face. Her hair, the way the water rippled around her olivine legs, the manner in which she held her skirt to keep it dry—it was all exactly as it should be. It was all exactly as he had seen it would be. Nymphean she seemed, her hair wavy long and her ears fine and delicate. Out in the middle of nowhere as if set there for him to find.

He stood still.

It seemed at first that she would never notice him. Absorbed with the water, she whirled it with her foot and waded closer to shore. A songbird flew over her head. She held out her hand and the gold and blue feathered creature redirected its flight to land on her palm.

Ilfedo did not divert his attention from her for more than an instant. He glanced to the tree where he'd slept. Hasselpatch still rested there, though she was awake now. Her head held high, the bird watched him with concern or curiosity. He could not tell which, though he guessed the latter would be a more accurate assumption.

The songbird fluttered out of the young woman's hand and she watched it go, then she cut through the water toward the shore. He took a step forward, the nerve to speak to her not quite within his grasp. In mid stride a twig snapped under his heel.

She swung around, glanced at him, and stepped ashore, her bare feet treading the green grass.

At once, she picked up a sheathed sword lying behind a small boulder. The blade protested with horrible screeches as she drew it from the scabbard. He could see a great deal of rust had accumulated on the blade.

With a speed and skill that took him completely by surprise, the young woman sped toward him and held the tip of the blade against his throat. He felt the rough steel scratch his jugular. At first he wondered if she meant to kill him, but then her face seemed to relax and her dark eyes blinked, breaking the strain of her hard stare.

Ilfedo tried to clear his throat but found it impossible with the hard cold metal pressed against it. "Sorry, Miss, I didn't mean to startle you." He held his arms away from his torso. "Don't worry—I—I'm not here to hurt you."

She said not a word. Not even a cautious question parted her delicate lips.

Believing that she knew he posed no threat to her, Ilfedo reached for his sword. He wanted to drop it from his waist, to prove he was harmless. It would only take a second.

But her eyes flashed with fear.

With surgical precision she swiped downward, the rusted blade slicing open his fist even as he succeeded in disarming himself. The sword his parents had given him dropped into the long, soft grass.

Ribbons of pain threaded through his hand where she'd cut him. Instinctively he covered the wound with his free hand, looking at her with horror. The pain of the cut was not nearly as unbearable as the look of betrayal he discerned in her eyes as he grasped his injured hand with his free one and fell to his knees.

"No, no! You don't understand!" He struggled to keep his balance. The ground seemed to waver under his knees. "Please, I wasn't trying to hurt you!" Her cut had passed deep into his hand. Already a small pool of blood formed on the ground.

"I've seen much, *Sir*," she replied, the last word spiced with indignation. "And I've learned not to trust a potential foe. Drawing your sword is usually a good indicator of hostile intentions."

"I wasn't—" He shook his head to clear it. The dizziness struck again. "I was trying to discard it—to—to show you—that I mean you no harm."

Tears formed in her eyes and under her breath she said, "And I thought you might be . . . him."

He glanced toward the water. He must clean the wound. As he looked at his hand, he knew that he would never use it again. The tendons had been severed and he could no longer feel his fingers. He glanced up at her and froze in horror as she, with tears running down her cheeks, stabbed at his heart.

A flurry of white wings and a Nuvitor's terrified cry interrupted the attack. Hasselpatch snatched the sword from her hand, tumbling it to the ground before it touched him. "No! You will not harm Master!" the bird screeched. Frantically it flew circles above him.

Feeling faint, Ilfedo laid on the grass. This was not at all how he'd expected this to turn out. He'd hoped to find a soul mate, and instead he'd scared her into killing him.

Funny, he'd never thought to die at the hand of a beautiful woman. But it was better than some of the alternatives. Better this than suffocating in the belly of a Sea Serpent, or having his neck snapped by a bear.

Then he felt her kneeling next to him, heard Hasselpatch screaming at her. Something wet splattered on his cheek. A tear . . . had she shed it for him? "I am sorry," he heard her say through a broken voice. "I only meant to defend myself—I did not see. Oh, what have I done?"

⊠ ⊠ ⊠

"He can no longer hear you," Patient said. "He is passing from this world to be with the Creator."

Dantress turned to him with tears running unimpeded down her cheeks. "What have I done? This man was not evil—and I—I have *killed* him." She raised the sword of Xavion in both hands, stabbed its blade into the ground. Releasing her grip on the handle she clenched her hands together.

"My dear child." The old man wiped away her tears with his wrinkled hand and she saw tears in his eyes as well. "My dear, dear child, you are *so* beautiful! Both in body *and* in spirit. You are a treasure fit only for the most honored and honorable of men.

"In your hands rests the future of humanity and dragons. And the choices you make, from this point on, will have consequences far greater than you can foresee."

The Nuvitor had vanished into the forest when its master closed his eyes. Now it returned, the tree line behind it filling with hundreds of Nuvitors, honing in on Dantress like a swarm of angry hornets. Their silvery eyes and claws shone in the sunlight. Their sharp beaks looked ready to kill.

Patient stepped away from Dantress, smiled sadly at her. "I cannot interfere, child," he said. "Not even to save you. You have brought this calamity upon yourself. Not even your father will intervene. What happens now is entirely in your hands."

"No," she cried, "do not leave me." Dantress wept but the shepherd turned his back to her and slipped through the swarming birds and into the forest.

One Nuvitor swooped over her head, snapping its beak in an unspoken threat. Another landed on the other side of the fallen man while the rest spiraled around Dantress and the man, a tornado of creatures that all seemed in agreement that she must pay with her life if his was lost.

"You have wounded Master and his eyes loved you," the Nuvitor on the ground said. A great silvery tear rolled down its beak as it looked up at her.

"I—" Dantress choked on the words, "I thought he was going to attack me." She touched the man's face and bit her lip. "No. No, he will *not* die! I will save him."

"If he dies," Hasselpatch trembled as she spoke, "you die."

Dantress's hands shook as she laid them on Ilfedo's bleeding one and summoned the strength in her blood. His life waned, the candle of his existence flickered. No, he must not die. He could not! She latched on, praying to the Creator for strength as she fed life into the man's body.

Another tear dripped from the Nuvitor's beak as Dantress opened her eyes. "There is good in your heart. Master would not want you killed," Hasselpatch said simply. The bird cawed at its fellows and, as suddenly as they'd gathered, they dispersed into the forest.

☘ ☘ ☘

Specter stepped into the clearing after the enraged birds had departed. Invisible beneath his hooded robes, he approached Dantress. The energy she was exerting to heal the man must have been enormous. She was hunched over him, her hand glowing such a brilliant blue that it looked ready to burst into a million fragments.

When she'd done all she could—and she *had* done every-thing possible to save the man's life—she slumped over his body. Her eyes closed.

Specter did not dare intervene. First of all, Patient the shep-herd was wise. If he believed that Dantress must do this on her own, then so be it. Secondly, the man's pet Nuvitor still stood guard, and it could apparently rally, if need be, a deadly follow-ing of its species at a moment's notice. He did not need his pres-ence revealed. That would only serve to irritate an already ugly situation.

Or had he misjudged the situation? Perhaps things were not all they appeared to be.

Beside him, he sensed the shepherd observing from conceal-ment in the trees. His face showed neither fear nor concern. Perhaps the wise old man knew best.

Suddenly the sky was rent with a thunderous sound, and Specter saw the great white dragon, with wings spread to embrace the air, descend to the pool. As he splashed into the water, Albino waved a clawed hand at the alarmed Nuvitor.

Immediately the bird collapsed to the ground, her chest heaving rhythmically as if in a deep sleep.

Towering over his daughter, yet not touching her or the man, Albino gazed upon them. "Patient," he rumbled, "it is time they see what we know."

Specter approached the dragon and bowed low. "Master."

"You have done well, Specter." The dragon's pink eyes gazed upon him. "The child is now safe and so is my daughter. Tell me . . . did you have any problems with the delivery?"

"No, Master. The boy is safe."

"Very well, then stand back and conceal yourself once again. My daughter will need you for a short while longer and then I will have a new task for you."

Cloaking himself with the garments of invisibility, Specter backed to the tree line.

The shepherd knelt next to Dantress and the man. The staff he laid on the ground while he placed one hand on the side of her head and then placed his other on the man's. His eyes closed and held his position. He was as unwavering as a statue, his head was bared.

Nothing appeared to happen. But Specter knew that inside the minds of the young couple a lesson, a truth, or some prophecy was being played out.

Patient picked up his staff some time afterward. The dragon stooped and the old man straddled his neck. Then, crouching down to the surface of the pool, Albino flung himself into the sky and shot into the northeast.

Specter waited a long while for Dantress and the man to wake. The Nuvitor did so before either of them and, by the way she waddled around, he guessed she was feeling a bit disoriented by Albino's seemingly magical power.

But Dantress and Ilfedo did not rouse for a long while.

⚊ ⚊ ⚊

At first Ilfedo thought that the fertile field stretching into the distant orange horizon was Heaven. Wildflowers of bright yellow, deep blue, and smooth ivory grew on all sides up to his knees. Butterflies, with black wings speckled white, danced from blossom to blossom, dipping long proboscises into the nectar-filled hearts of the plants. The multitude of the delicate winged creatures was so great that they might as well have been leaves falling from the sky.

Then it happened—a lone figure walked toward him through the field. Her long dark hair framed her smooth face, and tears dripped from her dark eyes onto her white dress.

Ilfedo shielded his eyes from the dress as light reflected off of it. But he did not keep his eyes guarded for long. Stepping forward, he met her halfway and faced her.

She was so beautiful. . . . Her countenance changed as she saw him. The line of her lips responded with a delicate smile, and she reached toward him. But she stopped herself as her fingers brushed his sleeve and shame clouded her inner joy.

As her eyes looked at the ground, she lowered her head. Sorrow seemed to pour from her soul, dimming the purity of her garment from brilliant white to light gray.

Ilfedo raised her chin so that her eyes returned his gaze. The feel of her skin was real to his touch, and he knew without knowing exactly how that this was not a vision or a dream. Nor was it Heaven. He had died—or nearly so. And her soul had somehow followed him to keep him from passing over the gap into the next world.

The butterflies scattered to his left, and he turned. An old man stood there now, amid the flowers. He held a shepherd's curved staff in his hand, and his blue eyes returned Ilfedo's gaze.

"A greater treasure you will never find in this world, Ilfedo," the shepherd said, pointing at the young woman, "than the treasure of a virgin bride whose eyes look to you for love."

Ilfedo redirected his gaze back to the young woman. Her dark eyes brimmed with tears. How the shepherd knew his name he did not know. At the moment—it didn't matter.

"Then why?" He picked his words with care. "Why did she attack me?"

The shepherd stepped forward. His blue eyes settled their gaze on the young woman, and his hand patted her shoulder. She gazed back, a tear rolling down each cheek. "Have no fear of her, Ilfedo," the shepherd said. "Her actions toward you were instinctual and not malicious. When you reached for your sword, she took action. When you lay dying—*she* treated your wounds.

"Now, behold!" the shepherd stabbed his staff into the ground and reached out with both wrinkled hands, taking the young woman's smooth hand in one and Ilfedo's large one in the other. "Destinies intertwined to the daughter of promise and a son of man. A future of hope mixed with days of evil and despair sprouts from the seed of love here sown."

The shepherd vanished into thin air. Not a trace of him could be seen.

Ilfedo was left alone with the young woman, her beautiful eyes begging his forgiveness even as he held her hand gently in his own. The feeling of attraction that he had toward her made this an uncomfortable situation—them, twain, alone in a field filled with flowers and butterflies—but he made no move to leave and she did not withdraw her hand from his, so he swallowed hard and looked down at her.

Suddenly, just as their gazes locked, a white light sprang from between their hands. In its midst a seed appeared, the shell dried. Spidery cracks formed upon its surface. The roots and stalk of a tree grew forth, separating him from her. He watched her fall back, thrown by the rapidly spreading tree. His own chest ached where the tree's roots struck him.

He stood, raced around the tree, and reached out to her. Her eyes widened as the roots grabbed at her skirt. He offered his arm, she eagerly grabbed it, and he pulled her clear. They stood a little distance away, his arm around her small waist.

Her arms found their way around his chest and held tight.

Warmth surged unbidden through his body. He put his other hand over her arm. He would not let go.

With marvel they watched the tree growing from the seed.

It planted itself in the earth. The branches reached the limit of their size. A single apple, small and red, appeared several feet above their heads. It swung from between several large green leaves. Crimson drops, like blood, fell from the apple's skin to the ground.

A shadow covered the field and the tree. The butterflies that had flitted from flower to flower burst apart. Their wings turned into a million small clouds of dust that drifted to the ground. Darkness rolled from the horizon.

Crimson roots spiked out of the ground where the apple's blood fell. Impaled upon them were the miniature forms of men and dragons. The men struggled and the dragons screamed, but in the end their bodies surrendered to death.

During the silence that followed, the temperature dropped a dozen degrees.

The voice of the shepherd spoke, and he appeared before them. "Do not fear." He waved his arm. "There will be light in the darkness; a hope in the time of evil."

Having thus said, the shepherd touched them both lightly on their shoulders. Immediately the field and the tree faded around them.

☘ ☘ ☘

Ilfedo had never felt as strange in all his life as he did the moment he opened his eyes to find the weight of the young woman lying across his chest. The smell of her hair draped over him was as fragrant as flowers. For the moment her eyes were closed, the arc of her dark brows sloped above them as twin arches.

With a twist of his finger, Ilfedo tucked a lock of her hair behind her ear. Though he needn't have, he felt almost guilty for marveling at how smooth her skin was. But he couldn't help noticing; it was like touching warm silk, like that sample he'd once examined in the coastal towns.

He felt his own face. Not at all the same. It seemed the wilderness had left him with little more than ruts and ditches where it had left hers without a flaw.

She was coming around now. Her eyelids blinked open, her dark eyes returning his stare. He felt like melting into those eyes, losing himself in their depths. Had she not saved his life? Had she not been there, also, at the threshold of death? By the will of the Creator they'd returned alive.

In the few moments that it took for him to contemplate these things, the young woman suddenly realized their awkward situation. She rose, a bit of color painting her cheeks like twin cherries. Standing, she clasped her hands before her until he propped himself on his elbows.

Surprisingly, he felt no queasiness or dizziness when he sat up. Beside him Hasselpatch stirred as if from sleep. Her beak gaped open in a yawn that allowed him a clear view into her pink throat.

Ilfedo stood and dusted off his pants. He gave the young woman a gentle smile. He still felt uncomfortable about the strange interest that fate seemed to have taken in his life, but he wasn't about to let that stop him from getting to know this forest maiden better.

"What happened?" He cleared his throat in as unobtrusive a manner as possible. Only moments ago he had held her in his arms; only moments before that she had attacked him.

"A prophecy, I think." She hesitated for a few moments, something else on the tip of her tongue. "I really am sorry about your hand, Ilfedo."

"It feels fine now," he said, clenching and unclenching his fist, then spreading his fingers. "Whatever you did—it worked."

"I'm glad." A smile lit her face.

"Wait!" He shook his head, confused. "My name . . . how do you know my name?"

"But surely you know." Her eyes seemed to dance. "When I came to you in the field . . . the prophet called you by name."

That had not occurred to him. He chuckled at the simplicity of it.

"You find that amusing?" she asked.

"No. Just too easy." He scratched his chin. It needed a good shaving. "That explains how *you* know, but it fails to explain how the old man did."

"Have you met a prophet before?"

He smiled again. "No, I suppose not."

"Then there you are!" She poked him suddenly in the ribs and laughed. "A true prophet *would* know your name. And he wouldn't have to ask you because he receives revelation from the Creator."

Prudence kept Ilfedo from poking her back. Instead he made a slight bow and fastened her eyes with his gaze. "Now that you know *my* name . . . may I know yours?"

"Dantress," she said. She looked down at her sword stuck in the ground. Pulling aside the fold in her outer skirt, she revealed the concealed sheath. Grasping the hilt of her weapon she forced its rusted blade into the scabbard.

"*Dantress*." Ilfedo picked up his sword as well and buckled it around his waist. "Walk with me?" His words came out soft, hopeful.

Closing the purple fabric of her outer skirt over the sword, Dantress looked back up at him. "I'd love to."

Ilfedo reached down to the ground, scooped up Hasselpatch. "Master, oh Master!" A silver tear rolled from the bird's eye. "It is good to see you alive and well." Her talons clasped his arm as he raised her level with his shoulder. With short strokes he massaged her feathered chest.

The bird snapped its silver beak at Dantress. "He'll not fall for your charms, Witch!"

"Hasselpatch!" Ilfedo frowned. "This was all a misunderstanding. Don't speak to her that way. This is Dantress—"

"A name?! You asked her for her name?" The bird screeched. Her talons bit into his arm, and he cringed.

But the bird's demeanor changed. Her grip relaxed on his arm, and she cocked her pure white head to look at Dantress. Ilfedo was puzzled. The bird and the young woman seemed to communicate in silence for the better part of five minutes.

Fluffing her feathers, Hasselpatch seemed to end the conversation. Dantress reached out with one hand and smiled up at Ilfedo. Her fingers stroked the bird's chest, and Hasselpatch cooed approval.

"Hasselpatch." Ilfedo stirred the bird from its trance. "I'm going to be staying here for a while. I need you to return to the others and let them know I'm all right." The bird spread its wings to their full span. He threw her into the air and called after her. "Tell no one where I am and tell them nothing of what has transpired here."

Flapping her wings and tucking her silver talons into her feathered underbelly, Hasselpatch circled. "As Yimshi shines upon us all, it will be as you say, Master." She flew east over the trees.

Ilfedo turned to Dantress. "I don't know what you did, but it seems to have worked."

"I have the ability to communicate with creatures, my mind to theirs." She said it with such nonchalance that he marveled. It sounded like an incredible lie, but her eyes were sober and honest.

He shrugged it off, reminding himself that, crazy as it would have sounded to his friends, he had been led to this encounter by a series of visions and dreams. There was something different about Dantress. She looked human enough and the legends of his ancestors included people who were endowed with special powers by the Creator. If it was true that she possessed powers, then the Creator must have given them to her for a reason.

Who was he to question the will of God?

"Are you all right?" Dantress stepped even closer. He could smell her hair.

"Sorry, I was just distracted for a moment." Gesturing toward the sky he swallowed. "It's a beautiful day."

She laughed and something inside his heart loosened as if ensnared by an invisible rope. It felt good. He laughed with her at his own clumsy start to their conversation. "There is a trail in the forest here, to the north, and a field beyond," she said, starting to walk. "Have you eaten, Ilfedo?"

Eat? What did hunger matter? "Maybe later."

As they walked through the woods, Ilfedo took Dantress's hand. Using his free arm, he held aside branches in her path.

What remained of that day, passed in what felt like a moment. They explored the wildlife-rich territory, startling birds and deer as they wandered. On a few occasions Dantress held out her hands toward the treetops. Songbirds of wide variety flocked to her, landing on her arms and shoulders.

Ilfedo tried to gain the creatures' trust, but he succeeded in befriending just one blue jay and a chickadee. All the other birds scattered at his approach.

As he watched Dantress move about and observed her interaction with the birds, he could not take his eyes off her. She was so beautiful, not only in body. There was a peace about her face, a confidence in her walk. Dignified yet humble, she had stolen his heart before the day waxed old.

When evening came they were loath to part. He looked down at her. Bits of dirt speckled the hem of her purple skirt and strands of her hair hung out of order. "Do you have family hereabouts?" he asked.

"Yes, I live with my sisters but I'm afraid they are rather reclusive."

He squeezed her hand. "What about your father and your mother?"

"The old man"—she gazed into the forest—"the prophet . . . he looks out for us. If it is approval you seek, then don't worry. You have his."

He guided her back toward the place he'd found her. "Then, will you meet me at the waterfall tomorrow?"

She nodded. A smile lit her countenance and her dark eyes glanced up at him before looking at the ground before her.

Not only did she keep her word, returning to him the next day. Dantress came to the pool by the waterfall the next day and the next as well. In this manner a week sped by.

They learned about each other. She asked him of his family, how he'd been raised. He told her of his parents and the struggles he'd gone through to move on after their deaths.

"What about you?" he asked when he'd finished.

She hesitated a moment, her brow knit in concentration. Some kind of struggle waged within. "My family," she began slowly, "is bound by secrets that keep me from telling you everything. Nothing bad," she added, grabbing his arm and looking into his eyes for reassurance. "Far from it, in fact. My father is a great . . . one . . . who raised me with more love than I could have hoped for."

⚜ ⚜ ⚜

Then, choosing her words with care, she told him that she'd come from a distant land over which her father ruled. The details of the palace and of her father she carefully avoided. She chose to tell him mostly of Helen, Gwen and—of course—she told him at length of Elsie, who treated her as if she'd been her own daughter.

They sat on a moss-covered log, his arm around her. "My father trained my sisters and me to fight with these." She drew out Xavion's sword and fingered its leather-wrapped handle. She then told him that she'd traveled to a distant land and fought a small war to rescue a fallen hero.

"We failed. Instead of accepting pardon from my father, the traitor took my sword." She swallowed. A tear formed in her eye. "He killed himself with it because he had killed someone he'd loved. It didn't make sense. He should have accepted Father's forgiveness . . . in fact it didn't make sense that he ever fell at all.

"Father would have taken him back. He's just that way.

"There must have been a reason that the man did what he did, but . . . it eludes me."

Ilfedo drew her into his arms, ran his fingers through her hair as she sobbed. "It sounds to me," he said, "as though the man became depressed. Whatever happened to him must have been awful. But you can't look back and wonder what you could have done to save him. That only leads to more heartache because you can't change what has already happened.

"Trust me, I know. After that bear killed my parents, I would sit up late into the night imagining different scenarios, trying to determine whether or not I could have saved their lives, if I had done something differently.

"It took me a long time but I eventually realized that if I didn't let the past be the past it would ruin my future."

"Thank you," she said after a time. "I think I needed that."

"What happened then?" he asked as she looked up at him.

"We returned home, to my father's lands. As the traitor had requested, I gave his son to my father. And, not long after that, Father brought me and my sisters here to live in the forest.

"It has been a wonderful change; the birds, the trees and everything else. It's peaceful here. And then you came along." She smiled and wiped away her tears with her sleeve.

They sat there a long time. She leaned her head on his shoulder, and they watched the sky turn orange as evening approached.

Ilfedo let the silence remain for as long as it took to gain his courage to say what had been on his heart ever since their first week together.

"Do you—" He cleared his throat. It felt as if a stone had fallen in and wouldn't come out. "I mean to say . . . Dantress, I think . . . I mean . . . I *have* fallen in love with you. Please, will you marry me?"

Her eyes looked back into his, and she nodded slowly, smiling all the while. "That's not exactly how I pictured you asking me . . . but it'll do! Though, I must ask for my father's approval."

Without hesitation he agreed. Her hand trailed along his fingers as she rose to go. "I will meet you by the waterfall."

"Shouldn't I come along and speak with him, too?"

"No, Father would not want that. Very few people ever see him, and he prefers it that way." She took a few steps away, leaned on a tree and looked back at him. "I love you, too!" She flitted quick as a deer into the forest and was gone.

BENEATH THE STARS

awn broke over the Western Wood. Yimshi's first rays made the early morning mist glow where it nestled between the tree trunks. Dantress hiked through the forest, following a narrow trail until a wall of hanging foliage cut it off. She hesitated and took a deep breath before parting the vines. Stepping past them, she saw the trail was again visible as it cut through the grass to the cave entrance.

The cave appeared lifeless and black as pitch.

"Caritha, Rose'el, Laura, Levena . . .? Is anyone in there?" She could not hear her sisters moving about, and not a single flicker of firelight illuminated her way. She took a couple steps forward. A stone slipped under her foot, and she almost tripped. "My sisters, answer me."

Somewhere in the darkness metal rang and a spark flashed. Had someone drawn a sword? The spark caught, illuminating a small pile of dry wood. The spark grew into a flame that spread amidst the wood until it crackled pleasantly. One of the youngest sisters must be in there. If it were Caritha, Rose'el, or Laura they would have said something by now. "Levena, is that you?"

Someone sighed quietly. "No, it's only me." Evela stared into the fire.

Dantress sat beside her on the moss covered log. The sisters had added layers of natural green cushion to the makeshift seat in order to provide a little comfort. The cave wasn't nearly as accommodating as Shizar Palace. Nothing fancy—just a floor of dirt and stone and beds of straw that Albino had provided when he'd left them here.

"Sorry, Evela." Dantress smiled apologetically. "I couldn't see your face at first." Gazing into the shadows, she searched for her other sisters.

"No one else is here." Evela picked up a twig, tossed it into the fire. "I think they went looking for you."

"I told Caritha not to expect me back before morning." She shook her head. "What's the matter with her lately anyways? It is my choice to associate with whomever I wish."

"But he is a *man*. Even I can see that. And he is a very *good looking* man. We are not blind to your desires." Evela looked at her, not quite smiling, not quite frowning.

Dantress pulled her hair over her shoulder and ran her fingers through it. Never had she felt as happy as she felt at this moment.

Evela touched her arm. "What's happened to you, Dantress? It's been two weeks. We hardly see you anymore. You hardly say a word to any of us, and when you do, all we hear is Ilfedo, Ilfedo, Ilfedo and more Ilfedo."

Dantress squeezed her sister's arm, then stood, her back turned to the flames. "I'm in love with him, Evela. Things are bound to change when that happens."

For a long time her sister was silent. Then, when she spoke, it was with hesitation. "Caritha feared you would say something like that. She says this needs to stop before you go too far and we lose you—"

"It is already too late." Dantress smoothed the front of her dress. Turning, she faced her youngest sister and got down on her knees, grasping Evela's hands. "He asked me to marry him!"

Evela paled and jumped up. "No . . . no . . . you can't!"

"You're wrong, Evela. I can and I will."

"But how will you? I mean, you heard what Father said; we are dragon blood and—"

From the mouth of the cave, Caritha's voice finished the line with great authority. "And if you bear him a child then you will die." She emerged into the firelight. Behind her, Rose'el, Laura and Levena followed.

"If that is what must be, then so be it." Dantress held out her hand, directing her words at the eldest sister. "Surely you don't expect me to live out the remainder of my years trapped here in this cave? I do not believe that is what Father would have wanted for me . . . nor for any of you."

"Have a care what you say, Dantress." Caritha's eyes looked cold. "The great white dragon placed us here, and *here* we will stay. It is not our place to question his decision, only to abide by his word. *Marriage* does not have a place in our lives and, though I doubt not that you have fallen in love, I believe that time away from the man will make you realize your mistake.

"You say that you are willing to accept death. But are you truly? I doubt it, my sister. I think your vision is clouded by pleasure. That man"—she stabbed the air with her finger, pointing out the cave entrance—"has *corrupted* you!"

"And for that"—she reached into the fold of her skirt and drew her sword—"he must die.

"Are you with me, my sisters?" She looked around into the others' stolid faces. "We must save Dantress from herself."

"What? You would kill him?" The ringing of her sister's swords drowned Dantress out.

"I'm sorry," Evela whispered, "but Caritha is right. We will not let you destroy yourself."

"Yes," Rose'el growled, "Ilfedo must die."

The fire flared. Crimson reflected in the sisters' dark eyes.

"You would mix the dragon's blood with humanity, and that we cannot allow." Caritha stabbed her sword into the air above Dantress's head. The others followed her example, their blades ringing against hers. "I am sorry, my sister, but the man is responsible for your downfall. Thus, he must die."

Horror filled Dantress. She looked at her sisters as if seeing them for the first time. Rage cried out within her soul, to think that they would even think of such a thing. Whipping Xavion's superior blade from its sheath, she struck the swords above her head with brute force. The captain's blade glowed with holy wrath, and the blood of the innocent fell from its rusted metal.

Such was the might of her attack that all five of her sisters jerked back their hands as if stung, and all five swords clattered to the stone floor.

"For shame!" she spat at them. "For *shame*! You accuse *me* of corruption when your own hearts are filled with selfish malice toward a man you do not even know.

"Look at yourselves! Look at us! *We* are agents of justice, the pride of our father. Yet while you spout piety with your mouths you desecrate his most noble name by your actions."

Twisting to face Caritha, she held Xavion's blade to her sister's left breast. "Ilfedo is a good man, kind and gentle. I want him . . . and he will be mine! A child will be mine, too, if the Creator wills it.

"Are you so blinded by your desire to keep me safe that you do not see that this is the path I must take? Even the shepherd has blessed this union. Surely you are not so blind as to deny *his* wisdom?"

She felt hot tears sting her eyes as she looked about. Their faces did not yield compassion. She could plead with them for eternity and not breach the barriers they'd erected to keep their ears from listening.

"It would have been better," she said, lowering her blade, "if I had left with your blessings as well. But since you will not hear me I must go. There is One whose blessing I must seek before I take the final step. If his blessing is given, then I will be departing from this land."

Forcing her sword back into its sheath, Dantress walked to the cave's exit. With one final look back, she spoke in an even tone. "Be forewarned, my sisters. My heart will belong to my husband. . . . Any of you who takes aggressive action toward him will pay, I swear it, by my own hand.

"I have weighed the consequences of my decision. I would rather have you rejoice with me . . . but if you will not, then maintain a safe distance. If you harm my man, then *I* will harm you."

She strode out of the cave, leaving stunned silence in her wake.

❊ ❊ ❊

Upon the brow of a hill in the Western Wood, Dantress fell to her knees in the cool grass. The trees rose around her in a protective circle. She leaned back and spread her arms. The love in her heart for a man she hardly knew wildly cried out against all reason, begging her to forsake counsel and take what she wanted without giving ear to the wise.

But she'd made her choice; she'd chosen a path away from Ilfedo and away from her sisters. There was only One to whom this matter should be brought now, only One who cared for her without condition and yet could judge the matter without partiality and had the authority to give her hand in marriage.

A cold wind swept her long, dark hair off her shoulders, flipping it wild and free into the night and slapping it across her face. She combed it back over her shoulders.

Father! Father—I need you! Still kneeling, she looked to the heavens. "I need you!" She said the words aloud, forcing them into the night with all her strength.

And the night split apart with a sonic boom, a ball of fiery white light shooting out of the west and exploding into the ground before her. The great white dragon rose from the point of impact, as if growing from the smoke billowing around his clawed feet. His wings spread to their full span, and his pink eyes blazed as they espied her.

She rose to her feet, small and childlike.

He flexed his powerful muscles. The starlight seemed somehow enhanced by his presence as it twinkled over his glowing white scales.

"Father . . ." Albino rested one claw on her shoulder and she let out a long sigh of relief.

"You called for me, my child?"

Though she tried to, Dantress could not reply. Everything had happened so fast that now, with his wisdom at her disposal, she could not find the words to explain what she felt in her heart.

But there was no need to ask his counsel.

Albino rumbled in a deep, satisfied way, his pink eyes seemingly mesmerized by his youngest daughter. "You have reached a crossroads, Dantress, a crossroads in your life that will determine your future . . . and the future of an unborn child.

"You may, at this time, fulfill your love to this man, and he will become your husband. Should you choose that path, remember the prophecy of the sword. For, though this path will lead to your greatest happiness, it will also lead to your death and Ilfedo's greatest sorrow.

"Nine months you will have from the day of conception, and then you must give up your life to bring another into the world."

He withdrew his claw from her shoulder and rested his hand on the grass.

In her mind's eye, Dantress remembered the sword that had risen from a chamber of flames and the name written for her eyes alone to see. "*Oganna.*" She said it softly as if pronouncing the name would bring calamity upon her own head. But there was a sweetness to the vision that she could almost taste. It was a vision of an infant born from her blood, of dragon blood—and of Ilfedo's blood.

Could she do it? Could she go to Ilfedo knowing that after such a short while she would leave him to bury her and raise the child on his own? Was she really willing to give up her life just to be with him for so short a time?

She remembered Ilfedo's eyes gazing into hers, letting her know that everything that he had, all he could give, his very life even, would be hers if she asked him for it. In return for that kind of love she *was* willing—even—to give her life.

The dragon looked down at her, and she saw tears in his eyes. Yet he did not sway her against that path as she'd feared. Instead he spoke in a voice that betrayed neither fear nor hope. "You have my blessing, my child, if you wish to wed this man. Be to him a good wife, and he will love you till the end of his days, but beware that your love—fleeting as it will be—will rend his soul in two. In bonding with you he will join the destiny of your blood and the sorrow that accompanies it.

"The bond of your love will hold onto him so that he will be forever torn between this life and the life to come. And, believing that death will reunite him with you, he will wait for death and hope for it so that his suffering may end."

Realizing what he had said, Dantress felt the burden of doubt ease off her shoulders. She had her father's blessing . . . and that was all that mattered to her.

"Do not tell your sisters of this conversation," Albino instructed as his body blazed with light. He snapped his wings against the air. "Specter has told me of their actions toward you on this day. I fear they are confused, fearful. Their trial will soon come, and they must prove themselves to me."

As if out of nowhere, Patient appeared beside her. "Come child!" The broadest and brightest smile she'd ever seen on his gentle face warmed her heart. "This is a moment of celebration! Joy, joy . . . joy for you *and* for the young man! And"—he laughed—"You have made me proud, my daughter. I daresay this man is getting the better end of this union." He winked, and she blushed.

The great white dragon's pink eyes shone down at her. His scales glowed even brighter. "Patient is right. Congratulations! Go now and do as your heart has told you. Love unconditionally and receive love in return." Flexing his wings, the dragon angled his bony face to look upon the shepherd. "Patient, perform the marriage rite for me, will you?"

"Of course." The shepherd waved as the dragon spread its wings. "I'll be happy to, my friend."

Albino leapt into the air. "Farewell until we meet again, my daughter." Then he was gone.

Coming alongside her, Patient cheerfully strode into the forest at a pace she found difficult to match. "Hurry now, child. I want to marry you beneath the stars whilst they shine the brightest." He began whistling a pleasant, upbeat melody. Frequently she caught him glancing back at her over his shoulder. Every time their eyes met, his blue ones would twinkle back at her, and he'd chuckle softly, amusedly, and resume whistling.

A wedding beneath the stars! She blushed at the thought of Ilfedo waiting for her to return with her answer and then quickened her pace.

⚬ ⚬ ⚬

Ilfedo took the hand of his bride beneath night's starry dome, in a field within the Western Wood, while the hoots of owls sounded like music from the surrounding darkness. A coyote howled in the distance. The cool, moist air left little doubt as to the lateness of the hour.

The prophet shepherd, his arms spread wide and holding his staff upright in one hand, smiled at the young couple. His blue eyes appeared to glisten in the starlight like sapphires beneath his bushy white brows. The clean white beard framed his smiling, wrinkled face in a dignified manner, and his hood rested over his back, leaving his head uncovered.

"Ilfedo, do you take this woman—who loves you with all her heart and trusts in you to love and protect her in return—do you pledge to stand by her through the good times and the bad? Will you care for, nourish, honor and give yourself wholly and only to her as long as you both live?"

Not taking his eyes off of Dantress, the starlight flickering in her eyes, Ilfedo solemnly nodded. "Yes, I so pledge."

"And, Dantress"—the shepherd brought his arms together, clasped the staff with both hands—"do you vow, whatever lies ahead in your marriage, that you will stay true to this man? Will you honor him, love and obey him as long as both of you live?"

"I so pledge." Her eyes did not leave Ilfedo's.

"Then let the blessing of the bride's love, and the groom's love and commitment shine as a beacon for all others to see. Let your love for one another be without condition, and let the time you share in one another's arms be filled with passion, holy and pure."

Stepping back, the shepherd knelt and lifted his face toward heaven. "Creator of the universe, now that these two have pledged to one another, committing themselves to this marriage, I pray that you will grant them a sign of your favor that they might never forget their vows this night."

Suddenly there appeared a pillar of light, shining from the sky. It shone on Ilfedo and his bride, but the ground around them remained in shadow. Something burned Ilfedo's finger, and he looked down at his hand to find a silver ring thereon. The light glinted off of its etched surface, and a tiny flame burned behind an oval window on the ring's surface.

Dantress flinched and grabbed her left hand. Then she glanced at her finger. Surprise then delight spread over her face and she held it up. An identical ring to his wrapped its band around her finger.

The pillar of light faded around them until it disappeared altogether. All that remained were the glowing rings with the tiny flames burning behind the little windows.

"You have both been given an extraordinary gift," the shepherd said. He rose from his knees, leaning heavily on his staff for support. "A wedding like this I have never before seen. These rings will never leave your fingers for as long as you both live. They are known as Eternal Bands, the rings of binding love. Their flames will burn for as long as you both live. If the light of one of your lives is extinguished, in like manner the flames in the rings will also die.

"I wish both of you happiness and long life. May your love for one another fill and overflow so that it touches those around you." He stepped through the short space of grass separating him and Dantress. Kissing her on the forehead, he said, "You will no longer need your sword, child. Go now with your husband but leave the weapon here."

She hesitated a moment, reached down under her skirt, unbelted the sheath and held it out to him. The handle of the curious weapon seemed to beg the shepherd to take it.

"No." The shepherd pointed to the ground. "I have no need for it. Leave it here."

In response, she crouched, cradling the weapon in her outstretched hands. Without a word she set it in the grass, stood, and took Ilfedo's hand. As an afterthought, she also reached to her side and slid a crystalline boomerang from under her belt. She placed it on the ground alongside the sword and then, turning away, followed Ilfedo to a hill where the shadows were deepest beneath a lone tree in the midst of a field.

THE OFFSPRING
OF THE DRAGON

I lfedo returned to the Hemmed Land with his bride at his side. No one outside their home saw them apart at any moment. Except for an occasional foray into the woods for fresh game, Ilfedo did not leave Dantress alone. They could not get enough of one another.

Hasselpatch and Seivar mirrored their master's infectious jubilation. They dutifully and willingly assisted Dantress with household chores. Seivar was slower to accept the change, and it became the larger bird's habit to stick with his master while his mate watched over their new mistress.

Talks around the fireplace at night, when Dantress and Ilfedo cuddled in the hammock with the birds nestled on top of them, softened the male bird until he accepted her as a member of the family and treated her as such.

Ombre had never been one to deny Ilfedo happiness. But Ilfedo noticed that his friend felt jealous—no, envious would have better described it. Rather than joining in with a laugh, as he'd been apt to do before when he wasn't the only bachelor in their circle of friends, Ombre distanced himself, choosing instead to stand back and smile as Ilfedo and his wife enjoyed each other's company.

Both Honer and Ganning on the other hand visited with greater frequency than they had in the past. "A married man! Finally! Now we're only waiting on Ombre," they'd say.

With her winning manners, Dantress won the hearts of all Ilfedo's friends. Honer's wife, Eva, became her close friend, and together they'd sit for hours at the table discussing gardening and sewing.

Once, between sewing stitches on a quilt, Eva asked Dantress where her family was. Politely Dantress requested that they not discuss it. Eva honored the request and changed the subject with hardly a pause.

And so three months passed. Ilfedo settled into married life. Every morning he awoke to find that his dream had not ended. He'd touch his wife's shoulder, caress her hair, and wake her with a tender kiss. The Nuvitors would drop from the rafters above the bed and settle on the posts, fluff their feathers, stretch their wings and fly downstairs. The rattling of pots and pans would sound from below as the birds prepped the kitchen for breakfast.

Turning on her side, Dantress would smile back up at him. She was, truly, his dream come true.

Then one day, upon returning empty-handed from a hunt hampered by sheets of cold rain, he entered the house and warmed himself by the fire. "My love," he called, thinking she must be upstairs, "I think we'll have to make do with what remains of the rabbits I caught last week. Rain's coming down hard—*too hard* in fact. I couldn't see a thing; even the bow and arrow proved useless.

"As long as you have no objections, I'll wait until it lets up a bit. We should have enough meat left from my trip last week to tide us until dinner tomorrow."

When she did not answer, he dried himself as best he could. Leaving his bearskin coat hanging on a peg by the fireplace, dripping water on the floor, he climbed the stairs.

There she was, soft in the light of the lanterns glowing around the warm bedroom. Seivar and Hasselpatch were staring at her intently. A tear ran down Dantress's cheek. She did not wipe it off.

"Please"—she stroked the birds' chests one by one—"a moment in private?"

"What's happened?" Ilfedo searched her eyes, but they did not look into his.

The birds spread their wings, flapped once, and glided over his head and down the stairway.

Fingering her ring, Dantress watched the flame burn therein. "Ilfedo"—she sniffed—"I . . . I am pregnant."

"Pregnant? Are you serious? Of course you're serious!" He held out his arms, spread wide. "But that means . . . I'm going to be a father!" Laughing with delight, he sat beside her. The bed bounced beneath his weight. Smothering her with kisses, he clutched her face to his chest and laughed again. "I can't believe it. I mean, I know I should have expected it . . . it's just . . . wow . . . we're going to be parents!"

For a moment she laughed with him, overcome with his happiness. "Yes. We are."

"I'll have to get started on the baby's room," he said, scratching his head. "I hope it's a girl . . . just like you."

Then he saw the cloud of sorrow pass over her face and he stroked it. "What's wrong, my love? You always said you wanted to have children. Why are you crying? Come now, what's wrong?" He sat down.

"I am not what you think, my love," she said, sitting in his lap and looping her arms around his neck.

"What do you mean?" He chuckled and kissed her on the lips. "Are you playing with me?"

"No." She frowned. "No, I am not playing with you. There is something you must know about me, something that will sound"—she sighed—"a little strange."

He stroked back her hair and waited for her to continue. Outside, the rain pounded on the roof with a thousand hammers.

Never had he seen as sober a look as she gave him now.

"Ilfedo, I am not what you think. I am not . . . human." Another tear formed in her eye.

"You can't . . . what do you . . . are you serious?"

She nodded.

A drop of water leaked through the roof and splattered on his shoulder. Ignoring it, he gazed into her eyes. "You *are* serious. But why tell me this now? It doesn't matter to me what you are. I love you for your soul . . . you know that better than anyone. Besides"—he ran his finger down her arm—"you look human enough to me. Unless this is only an exterior shell and something else hides beneath."

"No, you don't understand." She fingered the back of his neck. "I am what I am: human in form, but not by blood."

He cleared his throat. "By blood?"

"Yes." She rose from his lap and stood back a few feet. "I look human because I was made this way, but my blood is that of another race."

"What race?" The question seemed so simple he expected a simple answer.

But Dantress held out her hands and they glowed. He held his hand up to shield his eyes. When the light dimmed, he uncovered his eyes and looked up at her.

"My hands can *heal*, my love," she said. "That is how I saved your life the day we met. Special power has been given to my race, power to heal and also power to destroy.

She glanced at the floor. "But with this blessing . . . there also came a curse."

Standing to his feet, Ilfedo frowned. "And what is this curse?"

"I am so sorry, Ilfedo. I should have told you sooner. But I was afraid. Afraid you wouldn't want me if you knew or wouldn't let me bear a child if I told you."

He felt as though the distance between them was growing in proportion to her regret.

"In order to bear a child . . ." She put her hand to her mouth and began to weep.

Drawing her to himself, Ilfedo comforted her. When at last she quieted, he kissed her on the forehead. Her arms entwined around him.

"Ilfedo, in order to bear this child, I must die. I must give my life in order to bring another into the world. . . . *This* is my curse."

Suddenly his legs felt weak, his mouth refused to speak, his body numbed. With her help, he sat back on the bed. This time it was her turn to comfort him.

When he spoke, it was to search for a way out. He would not lose her. Not after the term of her pregnancy had been fulfilled, not in a decade, not until he was old and gray. She would live to see their grandchildren. She must!

Yet his heart told him otherwise and despite his best efforts to find an alternative he came up empty.

For a brief moment Ilfedo found himself hoping the pregnancy would end prematurely. Tears welled in his eyes at the thought. One life, an innocent one, in exchange for another . . . he was wrong to even think it.

"I found myself thinking the same thing," Dantress whispered in his ear, having read his thoughts as if he had spoken them aloud. "It seems so simple. Trip down the stairs and the baby would not survive . . . and you and I could have each other forever.

"But then I realized, with shame, what right do I have to live if the cost of my life is the blood of an innocent? None!

"I want this, my love. I want this life to grow inside of me and, when the time comes, I want you to let me go in order to devote yourself to raising our child."

Ilfedo sobbed, but he felt no shame. "I will not lose you!" He clutched her tight. "If you do die, then I too, will die. Perhaps not in body at first, but I have given my heart wholly to you and with you it will go."

"No, no you must not think that way." She caressed his face, sat in his lap. "We still have each other for many months. That time is ours. No one else's, it is ours."

Their kisses turned passionate, salty because of the tears. Ilfedo rose and extinguished the lamps.

⚜ ⚜ ⚜

Seven months passed. As her due date drew near, Dantress watched Ilfedo's vigor dissipate and his countenance sadden. It had hurt her to tell him of her impending death. It had hurt even more to pass over his question and avoid telling him that she was the daughter of a dragon. But it had been necessary. If Ilfedo was to know the whole of her heritage then it would be up to the great white dragon to tell him.

She was losing strength; the life inside of her was feeding off hers. Often she found it necessary to take long naps during the day, and she climbed the stairs to the bedroom early each night, rising late each morning. Ilfedo stayed with her more often than not, leaving the house only when the lack of food obligated him to.

One day, after wishing him a good hunt, she laboriously climbed the stairs and laid on the bed. The female Nuvitor watched her from its perch on the bedpost and cooed softly to ease her asleep. As she closed her eyes, Dantress asked where the male bird had gone.

"He is with Master, Mistress," Hasselpatch preened her wing feathers. Dantress heard the bird speak in her mind. *Sleep, Mistress. Master will be back by evening.*

Thank you, Hasselpatch. I think I will. . . .

She laid back. In her dreams she stood with her father, the great white dragon. He stood in a forest, pink eyes looking out over a vast field shadowed by dark clouds. She saw men and dragons tangle with each other in fierce combat. The dead fell everywhere and a crimson dragon rampaged through the field, unopposed. His eyes were evil and she felt as though she were right next to him, a sword in her hand.

With a start she awoke from sleep. Sweat had soaked her sheets. She looked at the bedpost from which the Nuvitor kept watch. But the post was empty.

She tried to sit up, but exhaustion forced her back. She closed her eyes and shook her head, recalling the vivid dream. Opening them, she looked again at the bedpost—something was wrong with it. She forced herself to a sitting position. Was that . . .? Yes, a red stain on the wood. Blood!

She felt the presence of five individuals in the room and knew before she saw them who they were and what they had come to do. The five forms emerged from the shadows around the bed. Caritha and Rose'el stood at the foot of her bed, their mouths set in firm lines. Emerging to her right, Levena and Evela looked down at her. Evela's cheeks were streaked with tears, her hair unkempt. Laura glided from the left and stood in silence. In the sisters' hands the swords of the Six glowed rusty orange.

Drops of red blood fell from the tip of Caritha's sword and a telltale white feather hung from it. "Caritha, how could you?" She felt ready to cry. "The bird was here to protect me."

"And to protect your child." Caritha's hand clenched her sword.

The warm air chilled around her as the realization settled in. "You have come to save my life by taking that of my child?" Hot tears rolled down her cheeks. "My sisters, what has happened to you? I feel that I am losing you to darkness, and I do not know why. You have fallen far indeed if you would kill one innocent life to save mine."

Caritha's eyes filled with tears. "This is not what we wanted, Dantress. It is you that chose this path. Once the child is dead— *you* will be free to live."

A nudge from within her womb drove Dantress to desperation, and she screamed at them at the top of her lungs, "No! The child is mine! I will not let you take it!" Raising her hand toward the ceiling she cried out, "Life you gave me and life I will give to another. Stop these murderers in their tracks and empower me to save my child!"

The rafters opened to reveal clear skies above and a column of fire fell through the roof and entered her body. The sisters backed away, their eyes wide. "What kind of power is this?"

Strength filled Dantress. She rose from the bed, the burden of her unborn child hindered her movements more than she would have liked, but she nevertheless threw out her hand. A wave of energy swept out from it, throwing Laura and Rose'el to the floor.

Dantress stumbled, grabbed the bedpost for support. The drain of power required to knock down two of her sisters had been greater than she'd anticipated.

At her feet lay Hasselpatch. The faithful bird's silver beak was open, its eyes were closed. A trickle of blood ran from a hole in its chest, painting a line in its flawless plumage.

Bending down, she picked up the fallen Nuvitor and set it on the bed. Just in time, she spotted Caritha with sword aimed at her womb. Dantress held up her hand, closed her eyes and placed her other hand on Hasselpatch's chest. She didn't have much strength left. This struggle was taking its toll on her body. With all the strength she could muster she sent a beam of energy from her hand, striking Caritha a blow to the chest.

As the eldest sister stumbled back against the wall, Dantress searched Hasselpatch for signs of life. Just as she'd found in the fairy whose life she'd saved, she now found a kernel of the bird's life force remaining. She fed that kernel until it grew.

Hasselpatch stretched her wings and stood, moving across the bed to attack Evela and Levena. But she toppled on her side, breathing heavily, before coming even close.

Leaning against the bedpost, Dantress watched Caritha beckon the other sisters to her side.

"You dared to take the life of this innocent creature, and see? Power was given to me to restore it! My sisters, I beg you"—Dantress sat on the bed, doubling over with pain—"I beg you . . . do not do this. Do not become the evil we despise."

"Caritha, listen to her," Evela wept. "What if she is right?"

"Steady, little sister." Caritha touched the tip of her blade to Rose'el's. "The right thing to do is not always the easiest thing to do, but do it we must. We cannot let her die."

The five sisters touched their blades together. Blue energy sizzled along them, joining at the blade's tips. The beam shot against Dantress with tremendous force, knocking her helpless and breathless on the bed.

"No, no, my sisters. Do not do this thing," she pleaded even as tears and darkness clouded her vision. She quaked, knowing what they were about to do. At the edge of her consciousness she felt them raise their swords to extinguish the life that she and Ilfedo had created. She wanted to rise, to break their necks with her own hands. But she was helpless and alone and in a moment she blacked out.

✨ ✨ ✨

Standing invisible in the crowded bedroom, Specter slipped into position beside Laura. As the sisters' joined their swords once again, another beam of energy sizzled toward Dantress's womb.

With his hand, Specter intercepted the beam before it reached its target. The energy burned his flesh and yet the pain was nothing compared to the joy of knowing he had saved another innocent life.

The sisters looked dumbfounded. All they could see was the beam of energy stopping mere inches above Dantress's womb. The hand that intercepted it was invisible to their eyes.

All of them, with the exception of Caritha, lowered their swords and backed against the walls. The eldest sister, tears streaming down her face, raised her sword and aimed the point at Dantress's womb.

Enraged, Specter stood to his full height and looked down upon her. His fingernails dug into the handle of his scythe as he swung it upward. Its blade clinked against Caritha's, twisted it out of her hands and cast it to the far side of the room.

Noticeably shaken, Caritha stepped back. Her eyes searched the room in vain, seeking her invisible assailant.

Specter had not finished. Using the handle of his scythe like a club, he struck her on the shoulder. As she cried out and fell to her knees, he followed through with another blow to her back.

"Mercy!" she gasped. "Whoever you are, please have mercy!"

The other sisters attacked the air. Some of their strikes might have hit him, but he beat them down. Then, with all of them fallen to the floor and weeping, he spoke to them in a voice as low and deadly as a serpent's.

"If another finger is raised against the child, that finger's owner will meet a sudden end. Do not test me, daughters of the dragon. I have slain more men than I can count and seen more wickedness than I care to enumerate. This day you have shamed your father's name and from me he will hear of this.

"You cry for mercy when what you need is a scourging. Go now . . . before I decide to be less forgiving and treat you accordingly!"

Either they were too weary to test him, or they recognized the authority and justice behind his words. From his presence they fled, taking their weapons with them but, he thought, leaving their pride in the dust.

When all was quiet, he smoothed Dantress's hair and laid her in a more comfortable position on the bed. "Rest, Dantress. Your father is pleased with you."

Before leaving, he waved his healthy hand over the Nuvitor's head. "I think it will be best if you do not remember what transpired here, my little friend."

He strode to the stairs, looking back once again. His chest felt ready to explode with contentment. The life of the unborn child was safe, he'd seen to that. Now the wait began. He marveled at a mother's love. The skin of his hand still burned from the sisters' attack. In fact it looked black. But he did not care. The child was safe and that was all that mattered.

❈ ❈ ❈

Ilfedo stepped through the doorway. The fire was blazing hot and Hasselpatch struggled to throw another small log into it. Seivar flew from Ilfedo's shoulder, grasped the log and helped her throw it into the fireplace.

Taking off his boots and setting them on the hearth, Ilfedo warmed his feet by the fire. "How's she doing?" he asked Hasselpatch, patting her back.

The bird hung its head. Its silver talon scraped the hearth stones with sad persistency. "She is not looking well, Master. I brought her extra blankets. It seemed chilly upstairs, but her body felt cool."

"It does seem a bit chilly in here." He looked at the stairwell. "She's in bed then?"

Slowly the bird raised its silvery eyes to his. "Yes, Master."

He ascended the stairs, being careful not to disturb Dantress by rushing up the steps. The chill he felt was not wholly in the air, some of it was his own trepidation. The smell of burning oil smarted his nostrils. Portions of the roof remained open to the sky. Mid-day light flooded the room. He pulled on the cord hanging from the rafters. The portions of roof closed.

Dantress's skin was pallid, making her eyes seem like oases in a desert. Kneeling beside the bed, he took her hand and kissed it. "How are you feeling?"

"Not well." She swallowed and closed her eyes as if this simple action caused her pain. "I need water."

Fetching a mug of fresh, cool water, Ilfedo propped her up with rolled blankets. She drank with delicate sips. "Thank you, My Love," she forced a smile. "I think . . . I think my time is almost here."

That evening he cooked a meal of rice with rabbit and served her at the bedside. By his invitation the Nuvitors ate with them as well. Later, when Dantress had fallen asleep, he washed the dishes. The meal he'd made had seemed tasteless to him. His heart was heavy, burdened by the knowledge that this happy part of his life was coming to an inescapable end.

The fire died. He allowed it to.

Sitting in the hammock, he fastened his gaze on the embers and rested his chin in his hands. He could hear the Nuvitors putting the dishes into the cupboards. After a little while, when the birds had finished organizing the kitchen, they snuggled with him in the hammock. He threw a log on the fire and stirred the embers until the fire once again burned. But the heat provided no comfort.

Returning to the bedroom, he opened the roof. Starlight streamed inside. Dantress rested in a deep sleep. Her face bore a beauty born of heaven.

Lying beside her, he gazed up through the opened roof at the stars shining like a multitude of unclaimed jewels set in a velvety curtain. Eternal they seemed. They glowed amidst the darkness, undying—timeless. Soon he would be like one of those stars; isolated in an ocean of black loneliness. He closed his eyes and slept through the night.

He awoke the next morning to a golden dawn. Dantress gave birth to a healthy baby girl. He forgot his sorrow and wrapped the child in a soft white sheet. Placing the child in its mother's arms, he knelt at the bedside aglow with ecstasy. The child uttered her first cries. Her eyes were blue like most newborns with one exception: a hint of gold rimmed the pupils.

His happiness was short lived. Dantress fought back tears, her face began losing color, and her eyes grayed. "We did it, my love," she said. "We created a new life. . . . Her name will be Oganna." Her words trailed off as she looked at the child in her arms. With great care she let the child down into the blankets by her side. Then with great effort she propped herself up on one arm.

Wonder filled Ilfedo as he watched. Dantress held her hand over the infant's forehead. A beam of blue and white light wove through the air from the mother into the child.

"Goodbye, my love," Dantress smiled at him.

He pulled her to his breast, hugged her tight and put his lips to hers in a last kiss.

As he released his hold, she collapsed against the pillows. Her body glowed so that, for a moment, he could not look anymore. When the light faded, he saw threads of it leaving her body, arcing into the child. The infant glowed as if filled with some kind of power, yet slept as if unaffected by the transfer.

The flame in Dantress's Eternal Band flickered and faded into blackness. He watched as his ring, too, became nothing more than an ordinary band of silver around his finger. The prophet's words came to mind:

"These rings will never leave your fingers for as long as you both live. They are known as Eternal Bands, the rings of binding love. Their flames will burn for as long as you both live. If the light of one of your lives is extinguished, in like manner the flames in the rings will also die."

Another tear rolled freely down his cheek and fell on her ring as he looked upon her still body.

Yimshi's rays drove the shadows out of the room. The infant awoke crying. Ilfedo stood and picked up his child. He kissed her forehead and smiled despite his sorrow. He glanced at the bed. The strength in his legs failed him. He knelt again, caressing the silken hair of his love. His shoulders quaked as tears spilled down his face.

She was gone, gone forever. Only his own death could bring him to her now. Her skin, once warm to his touch, started to cool. He drew back his hand, not wishing to feel the cold reality of death taking hold. Grief immeasurable washed over his being. The tears ran down his face and fell upon the naked head of his daughter.

Soft, feathered wings reached around his neck. Hasselpatch and Seivar shed their tears onto the floor, offering the only comfort they could: their silent presence.

For a time Ilfedo remained kneeling. Then he saw shadows creep around him, blocking the sunlight. He looked up.

Five female figures of remarkable likeness stepped forward, robed in purple. Their dark hair tinged red when the sunlight struck it. Their heads hung with sorrow, their dark eyes were reddened from crying.

Wiping the tears from his face, Ilfedo stood. There was no mistaking the women's resemblance and no question in his mind of who they were.

One of the sisters stepped forward, the others wept behind her. All except for one sister however, with her arms crossed and head bowed. She did not look at the body.

"I am sorry we did not show ourselves sooner," the sister said, looking at the infant with tender gaze. "I am Caritha—Dantress's sister—as are they." She swept her hand in the direction of her siblings. "We beg your forgiveness—*I* beg your forgiveness. Our sister was right about you; you are a good man and we failed to see it until too late.

"But we are here now and, with your permission, we are here to stay." She swallowed hard.

Ilfedo laid one hand on her shoulder. "You are family. What I have is yours. I know of nothing to forgive you for, but if you came to seek forgiveness then I grant it."

Caritha smiled sadly, bit her lower lip. "May I . . . hold her?"

One of the other sisters pulled a bottle out of her dress. "We took the liberty of borrowing your neighbor's goat."

Handing the infant to her, Ilfedo turned to the bed and gently wrapped the body of his beloved in the sheets. The sisters sobbed as he covered Dantress's face. "Please, come with me." He lifted the wrapped body and headed down the stairs. Caritha followed, rocking the newborn in her arms.

"Where . . . where are you taking her?" The shortest of the sisters stepped up beside him.

"To the Western Wood where we met. It"—he paused as more tears ran from his eyes—"it seems appropriate."

"It is a beautiful idea," the sister replied. She laid her hand on his arm. "I am Evela."

He loudly cleared his throat and headed into the forest, the sword that had been a gift from his parents clanged against his leg. "Come, I will not be stopping to rest so you'll all have to keep up with me."

"Do not fear." Evela held her chin high and kept pace with him. "We are able."

The trek was a long one. True to his word Ilfedo did not stop even to rest. He led the way into the Western Wood. By the waterfall, at the edge of the pool where he first met Dantress, he set down the body.

"Here." The tallest sister grunted, handed him a spade. "Found this at your house . . . thought you might want it."

Without a word he took the tool and dug into the rich brown soil. Scoop by scoop he carved a rectangular hole. In this he laid a bed of stones and around the base he built walls of stone.

The sisters gathered around as he laid the body in the ground. For an hour or more they stayed silent. Ilfedo knelt and prayed to the Creator. Then he wept beside the grave as he shoveled dirt over the body. When he had filled it in, he gathered stones from the forest and laid them over the top.

Taking the crying child from Caritha, he kissed the infant's forehead. "You will be like your mother. I know you will. And I . . . I will strive to be the best father that ever a man was."

THE SWORD OF
THE DRAGON

Daylight faded into a sky redder than Ilfedo had ever seen, as though the sky was aflame. There was not a single cloud, but the air felt moist, as if in preparation for rain. A stiff wind brushed through the trees. The birds, which had twittered from the safety of the treetops, fell silent.

A sound, like thunder, echoed in the distance. He gazed west toward the sound. A boom deafened him and a ball of white fire shot from the west. He closed his eyes against the brightness.

The infant in his arms started crying and he soothed her with a kiss. The ground shook violently at that instant, as if Subterran split in two. A blast of wind smote him from behind. He clutched his child to his chest, sheltering her in his arms as he fell forward.

Spitting dirt out of his mouth, he got to his feet. The five sisters knelt in front of him, and he furrowed his brow, wondering what motivated their action. Yet suddenly a chill ran down his spine for over and surrounding him he saw the shadow of something monstrous. He could hear deep, easy breaths from some creature behind him.

In one swift motion, he shifted his child to one arm, drew his sword, and spun around, pointing the blade into harm's way.

Courage did not prepare him for the sight that met his eyes. Towering above him in raw power and majesty was a creature of legend . . . a dragon of greater size than he would have imagined possible. The dragon's scales were joined close together and laid thick over its body. Its broad chest heaved with effortless breathing, and its bone-armored face looked down at him with clear, pink eyes.

He drew back his sword, ready to protect his child. But a gentle woman's hand grasped his shoulder. He turned. Caritha stood there, the wind throwing her hair back, away from her face. "Do not hasten to attack, for it is he that made us *and* the one that you loved so dearly."

Looking over Ilfedo's head, the dragon addressed the sisters with a rumbling voice that made them tremble. "My children, you who survive, you have failed me in the highest degree." His claws ripped into the ground, balled into a fist, and pounded it. The repercussions almost toppled Ilfedo again.

"I made you, my daughters, to bring peace and justice into this world. I created you to be the hope of humankind. But when your sister followed the path of unconditional love, you attempted to sway her from it. And when you failed to turn her . . . you attempted to destroy the life she created."

The dragon's eyes glinted as he pointed it at the infant with a razor-sharp claw. "You allowed yourselves to be blinded, my daughters! This life—this *child*—is the offspring of my blood just as surely as you are. Dantress has given the world a child of hope and a child of prophecy."

His nostrils flared and smoke rose from them. "I am ashamed of you this day."

The sisters wept and begged him to forgive them.

Reaching past Ilfedo, the dragon raised the sisters to their feet. "If you have truly repented, then hear the command that I now give you: stay with this man and the child and watch over them. You shall be her guardians and guides to raise her in the love and fear of her Creator, as I have raised you."

With slow nods and their eyes looking at the ground, the sisters agreed.

The dragon rumbled his satisfaction. "A lesson you have learned, one you will not soon forget. See to it that your vows are kept."

Shifting its great body, the dragon angled its head to look upon Ilfedo. "You, Sir, are strong of heart and courageous. I have seen your selfless defense of your people. In the midst of a multitude of men there are few to be found who follow their conscience. Yet you have.

"The Creator has chosen you and your child, Ilfedo, to protect the innocent and execute justice among your people. Do not try to understand all that I am now telling you, but know this: your people will soon be ready to give up hope.

"It will seem to them that the world is falling into darkness around them. But you will lead them from death to hope. Even as I speak, the Sea Serpents emerge from the sea in greater numbers to kill all who dwell in the Hemmed Land. You alone have the power to stop them."

Ilfedo lowered his sword, slipped it into its sheath. "You speak as if I am an acknowledged leader in the Hemmed Land.

But I am not. We have no lord, and it is best that it remains that way." He glanced over his shoulder at the sisters. "And how is it possible for you to know that the Sea Serpents have returned? You are as far from the sea as I am."

Emboldened by the dragon's silence, he took a step forward. "Besides, I barely survived my last encounter with those beasts. I was lucky. How am I to stop a multitude of them? I am a hunter and, now, a widower with a child who needs me. There is nothing to set me apart from my fellow men."

"These five women will be your companions, Ilfedo," the dragon rumbled. "And as to setting you apart from other men . . . I would contest that your actions have already set you apart. As to *luck* . . . luck is for fools and cunning is for the worthy.

"Because of the strength of your heart and the purity of your soul, I have chosen you to protect your people."

"But surely you don't think that *I* can protect a multitude from ruin? There are things out there that are far deadlier than a Sea Serpent, things against which my sword will seem as nothing more than a child's plaything."

The dragon raised its hand and growled. "Do not put such weight on your own strength, Ilfedo. *I* will give you the power necessary to complete your task—indeed, I will give you a gift such as has never before been bestowed on any creature in all of Subterran."

Claws groping, the dragon reached into the pool. The water rippled around the dragon's fingers and mud clouded the current. The dragon's claws ripped into the pool's floor. Slowly he pulled a sword from the water. "Behold your sword, Ilfedo! It has the living fire upon its blade from the ends of the world and the hardiness of diamond in its handle."

Long and elegant, the double-edged blade of the sword mirrored everything. Flames burned within the blade and without, entwining themselves around the metal, wreathing it in red and yellow fire. He could almost see through the sword's semi-transparent guard. A gold vine wound around it, then entwined around the handle, reinforcing the leather gripping underneath.

The dragon beckoned to him, holding the sword by its blade, pommel extended. Before reaching for it, Ilfedo handed his child to Caritha. She stood back while he approached the mighty creature.

Stretching out his fingers, he closed them around the weapon's handle. Immediately flames sprang from the sword's blade with greater intensity. Tongues of fire snaked toward his hands. He let go before the fire touched him.

But the dragon held out the sword again. "You need not fear the power of this weapon, Ilfedo." It rumbled deep in its throat. "Take it!"

Inhaling a deep breath, Ilfedo reached out and closed his fingers over the sword's handle. Again the flames within the blade leaped forth with great ferocity. This time he pulled it from the dragon's claws and held it before him.

The flames snaked up his arms, spreading over his body. Braiding thickly, they covered him from his head to the soles of his feet. Yet they did not burn him. In fact he felt energy pour into his muscles as he'd never felt before.

As suddenly as the fire had covered him, it receded into the sword. Leaving him decked in an armor that glowed with fire and white light of such magnificence that he hardly believed his eyes. On his head he found a helmet, its surface was smooth as glass. He rapped it with his knuckles and, satisfied that it felt thick, he marveled that it weighed like a feather rather than heavy metal.

He twisted his body this way and that, trying to discover a flaw in the design. But he found none. Whichever way he moved he found the armor as flexible as cloth, as breathable as cotton, and as comfortable as silk. The breastplate also proved to be solid. Fire danced within the armor as if it were a window to another realm.

The armor's glow presented a dazzling sight indeed. He felt that the armor was not a mere garment. No, it had become an extension of him—even of his being. He could feel it as though it were his skin

The five sisters stumbled away from him, eyes wide, mouths agape.

Flexing his sword arm, he swung the weapon in a long arc. The blade sang through the air. A strange new strength surged into his body. He felt capable of doing almost anything.

The dragon smote the ground, and his elegant, horned head dipped in Ilfedo's direction. When he spoke, his words rumbled as a solemn prophecy. "Use this weapon for good, Ilfedo, and it will aid you. If you ever use it for evil then it will, of its own accord, turn against you." He heaved a breath, lifted his head, and blew flames into the air. "I must leave you now with one final piece of advice. Mark well what I say because the time will come when you will need these words:

"When your land can no longer sustain you and your people, when the beasts and the birds become scarce, you will look to find another. On that day you must seek out the dragon Venom-fier, for he will be your strong arm and you will be his mighty shield."

Ilfedo lowered the sword and gazed up into the dragon's honest face.

Flexing his wings, the dragon spoke in a low voice.

> "Dragon great, dragon fool
> One wise, the other cruel
> Venom-fier, to man a friend
> The other may be his end."

Spreading his leathery white wings, the dragon launched himself into the sky and flew out of sight.

Ilfedo stood in silent awe. Everything had occurred so quickly that he worried he'd not taken it all in. He looked down at the magnificent sword in his hand. "Return to your former state," he commanded.

Immediately the armor of living fire disappeared and the sword diminished to flames simmering within its blade. A sheath had appeared beside his other one and he slid the sword into it.

The cries of his child reminded him of why he'd come to this place. He turned to the grave, wishing to mark it. But he found that the topmost stone had already been chiseled—by a dragon's claw. The name of 'Dantress Mathaliah, beloved wife and daughter' brought tears to his eyes again.

Darkness covered the landscape. Ilfedo redrew the sword given him by the dragon. "Light the way," he said. The weapon blazed, then covered him in the armor, and by that light he led the way home.

THE END

ACKNOWLEDGMENTS

This project required years of patient toil. Many people have made this book possible:

To Dad and Mom for educating me at home, raising me to love God, and making it possible for me to pursue my dreams.

To Kelley, the love of my life, whose energy, love, encouragement, and belief in this novel made the first book tour possible. To my sister Laura, for laughing and loving even though I made a dragon kidnap her character. To Grandma Gordon: thank you for giving me a copy of *Self-editing for the Fiction Writer.* Thanks to Grandpa and Grandma Appleton. Your love has been a pillar of strength in my life, more than you will ever know, and I love you for that. To my mother-in-law for being one of my very first readers. Thank you for encouraging me to press forward with **The Sword of the Dragon** series.

Special thanks to Bryan Davis for critiquing my writing, for his friendship, and the endorsement. I have learned a lot from him. Louise DuMont for giving me the first professional critique. It was bluntly honest; exactly what I needed. Also, for her friendship and the endorsement of this novel. Thank you, Wayne Thomas Batson, for giving me feedback on my novel and for the endorsement. Mr. Bunn, you made editing a lot more fun than it's ever been, and your suggestions were great. Thanks also to Jennifer Miller for an awesome cover illustration.

I would like to recognize the contribution of Dan Penwell, former editor at AMG Publishers. He first believed in this project and in the short time I knew him I came to regard him as a friend and good counselor. He is sorely missed.

Finally, thank you to all the wonderful people at AMG who made this possible. Especially to Rick Steele for putting up with my phone calls, and for valuing my input.